BLOOD
AND
SAND

BLOOD AND SAND

C. V. WYK

TOR
TEEN

A Tom Doherty Associates Book
New York

BLOOD AND SAND

Copyright © 2017 by Isabel Van Wyk

A Tor Teen Book
Published by Tom Doherty Associates
175 Fifth Avenue
New York, NY 10010

www.tor-forge.com

Tor® is a registered trademark of Macmillan Publishing Group, LLC.

The Library of Congress Cataloging-in-Publication Data is available upon request.

ISBN 978-0-7653-8009-8 (hardcover)
ISBN 978-1-4668-7191-5 (ebook)

Our books may be purchased in bulk for promotional, educational, or business use. Please contact your local bookseller or the Macmillan Corporate and Premium Sales Department at 1-800-221-7945, extension 5442, or by email at MacmillanSpecialMarkets@macmillan.com.

First Edition: January 2018

Printed in the United States of America

0 9 8 7 6 5 4 3 2 1

For the wandering and the wild,
the new heroes gazing fearlessly into the dark.

For the young ones rising.

AUTHOR'S NOTE

Many of the events and individuals in *Blood and Sand* are based on actual historical record, though, for the sake of the narrative, the author has taken creative liberties with dates, titles, places, and characters. All historical discrepancies are intentional.

O, pardon me, thou bleeding piece of earth,
That I am meek and gentle with these butchers!
Thou art the ruins of the noblest man
That ever lived in the tide of times.
Woe to the hand that shed this costly blood!
Over thy wounds now do I prophesy—
Which, like dumb mouths, do ope their ruby lips
To beg the voice and utterance of my tongue—
A curse shall light upon the limbs of men.

Julius Caesar, 3.1.269–277

✦ ✦ ✦

Spartacus was a Thracian from the nomadic tribes
and not only had a great spirit and great physical
strength, but was much more than one would
expect . . .

Plutarch of Chaeronea, A.D. 100

BLOOD
AND
SAND

CHAPTER 1

They called them slaves.

In the shadow of the Coliseum, through the paved streets of Rome, armed guards dragged them by the neck. Rusted iron shackles cut at their wrists and ankles. Each labored breath was fouled by the bitter stench of the city. Old and new blood darkened the rope that bound them together. Clumps of hair, torn fingernails, and other bits were trapped in the heavy, twisted strands. It was a rope that had been used many times before.

A crowd of dusty citizenry parted to let them pass, urged along by the guards and watchmen flanking the slaves on their walk to the auction block.

Twenty-one women in total, and they all averted their eyes, trembled with terror. All but one.

At the very end of the line, a slight figure lifted her head and stared around her, her gaze steady, penetrating. The dirt and mud that streaked her face wasn't enough to hide her disgust.

She knew what was going to happen to her and the others. She knew the warped rules by which the Romans played. Patricians and plebeians. Masters and slaves. They all filled their roles without exception. It didn't matter who she was sold to, just that she would be *sold*. She would be bought, and she would be paid for, and she would be a slave.

She tried to summon calming pictures of her home—the salty air that drummed against the walls of her father's tent, the alternating calm and fury of the Aegean, the stormy gray of her mother's eyes. But the pictures quickly turned to images of carnage and violence.

She'd been a warrior once, and free. Now she was the only one left, the last Thracian the world would never know. She wondered if history would remember the genocide of the Maedi, the annihilation of her people.

Doubtful, she thought. History only serves the winner.

Roma victrix.

She knew she didn't have the luxury of denial—not if she was going to survive. So when the bloodstained rope pulled her forward with a sharp jerk, she focused instead on her training and her discipline and managed to remain steady.

"Keep moving," the guard behind her grumbled.

Gripping her rope with bleeding fingers, she spat into the sand and walked on.

When she was young, her father, Sparro—swordlord of the legendary Maedi and war-king of Thrace—shot a barbed arrow into the heavens. The lives of his wife and unborn son had been claimed in childbirth, and brimming with grief, he forswore his people's gods. In a single night, he'd lost everything. Everything except for his young daughter, and in spite of his sorrow and resentment, he called her to his side.

It was the first time in her memory that all of their people were gathered together. Though their villages were separated by miles of mountain and field, all of Thrace stood as one that day—a proud mass of thousands upon thousands, stretching along the unforgiving coastline of the Aegean. They waited to see if their king would defy the gods one more time. To the east, the sea waited, too, silent and still. Not a single white wave crashed against the rocks below.

The crowning sun glinted off a pendant cradled in King Sparro's palm: finely wrought silver molded into the shape of a falcon in flight. The bird's bright wings spread wide, every feather carved in stunning detail. Its talons clutched undulating waves, and in place of its heart sat a large, clear stone that blazed in the dawn light.

Thracians of old called the pendant *zhimanteia*—"fire of the immortals"—a jewel meant for the swordlord's heir, the crown prince.

A serving woman brought forward a needle and a length of thread, and King Sparro himself made quick, neat stitches, fastening the pendant onto a new cloak. Then he draped the wool across his daughter's thin shoulders so that the pendant rested heavily against her heart.

Even heavier were the words he spoke next.

"I name Attia, my daughter."

Only a moment of silence passed before Crius, Sparro's first captain, raised his sword into the air and cried out the child's name. "*Attia!*"

It was a testament to their loyalty and their love that, without hesitation, all of the people took up the cry. And then as one, ten thousand honored soldiers of Thrace—Maedi warriors all—fell to their knees before the girl. The red of their cloaks spread out like a sea of blood.

Attia became her father's heir that day, the first future queen and swordmaiden of Thrace, destined to rule the greatest warrior kingdom the world had seen since ancient Sparta.

She was seven years old.

Now, ten years later, the once–crown princess found herself bound at the end of the line of new slaves. A fresh piece of meat up for auction, paraded onto a rotting wood platform in the middle of a small plaza. The twenty-one bound women were strangers to each other, all dressed in various shades of filth. At the opposite end of the line from Attia, one woman began to sob. Her shoulders shook with despair as the merchant gripped the back of her neck, shoved her forward, and began the bidding.

The Republic had conquered nearly half of the known world, its rule reaching from the western coast of Germanica to the eastern jungles of Siam. Even the dialects of Thrace shared much with the Latin Vulgate—the common tongue of the Republic. But at that moment, Attia wished it didn't because she understood the merchant's words all too well. "Who will give one denarius for this one? She is strong yet. Look." He slapped the woman's hip. "Pair her with your largest field worker, and she could breed two or three more, easily."

Bile rose in Attia's throat.

The woman he was talking about became rigid with terror. Her eyes flicked back and forth like those of a wounded animal, never once settling as the voices around her rose.

There were at least four dozen people in the crowd, all waving their hands and shouting their bids with enthusiasm. It wasn't often that an auction of foreign women like this took place, and the bidding didn't last for very long. Silver changed hands, the rope was cut, and the woman at the end of the line was dragged away by a middle-aged man in a blue tunic.

Attia was so tired, so full of rage for her own circumstances that she couldn't find the energy to pity the woman. She just stared at the soft line of her bared shoulder until she disappeared, barely even recognizing the fact that the other woman was real.

The nature of the sale became clear soon enough. The women who wept and showed fear were bought by the sadists in the crowd—the ones who enjoyed broken things. The women who looked dry-eyed and defiant were claimed for the brothels. The oldest women were bought by the few female patricians present, probably to clean floors or serve food.

Then, at the very end, Attia's turn came. She stood alone on the planks. There was still a large crowd gathered, despite the other women having already been sold. Attia tried to school her face to look as benign and uninteresting as possible though her blood boiled with contempt.

"And finally," the merchant said, "we come to the prize of the day—a true Thracian beauty. She—"

Before the merchant could say another word, the shouting began, echoing up against the clay walls surrounding the alley. Most of the bidders offered increasing amounts of money, while others tried to sweeten the deal with promises of horses or trades of other slaves. It seemed that everyone wanted the exotic girl from across the Aegean, the first Thracian woman to be captured in nearly a decade.

Only one man stayed silent as he watched from a shadowy corner of the alley. His white hair was cropped short, his mouth pinched into a thin line. His clothing was simple and unadorned but obviously expensive; the silk of his robe shimmered even in the shade. Beside him stood another man, this one dark and hard-muscled. He wore a loose blue tunic with wide sleeves that didn't reach his elbows. His eyes swept over and around the crowd, ever watchful.

"Eighty denarii!" a fat patrician shouted, licking his lips.

It was the highest bid yet, but the merchant waved his hands wildly over the crowd. "Is there a counteroffer?"

The old man in the corner carefully regarded Attia with cold blue eyes before speaking. "Five hundred denarii," he said, keeping his gaze on Attia's face.

The fat patrician sputtered. "Five hundred—you can't be serious!"

"Five hundred denarii," the man repeated, "and let that be the end of it."

The merchant beamed and sent a prayer of thanks to all the gods he could name. "Sold! Well bought, Timeus. Well bought!"

The fat patrician tried to argue again, but the auction was over. The other bidders reluctantly dispersed, grumbling as they went. The merchant waited for Timeus and his bodyguard to approach before saying, "I was almost certain Marius was going to challenge you."

Timeus looked unfazed. "He's too cheap to challenge me."

"She is well worth it," the merchant continued. "Young, spirited, in perfect health, and—as I wrote to you—I have it on excellent authority that she was not defiled after her capture. She is absolutely pure."

Timeus smiled, the calm expression nearly transforming his pinched face. He looked almost kind, until the smile tightened into a cold, harsh line. He tossed a heavy pouch at the merchant, a dismissal as much as a payment. Then to his bodyguard, he said, "Take her, Ennius. She has a job to do."

The merchant could barely contain his glee. He was glad to be rid of the stubborn whelp and thrilled with the small fortune he'd made off her sale. She hadn't stopped struggling since the moment of her capture, so he had kept her tightly shackled and bound for the journey to the city. The merchant sneered as he removed the iron that bound Attia's wrists and ankles. "Good luck, little Thracian."

For the first time in two weeks, Attia flexed her tightened limbs, pain and relief surging together.

The bodyguard reached out a dark, scarred hand to take hold of the rope still hanging loosely around her neck. "Steady, girl," he said. "Relax."

Relax? Attia would have laughed if her throat didn't feel like it had been stuffed with sand. Instead, she looked away from the bodyguard and took in her surroundings.

The little plaza was nearly empty by then. The windows and doors were covered and closed. The alley was narrow, and the vigiles—the watchmen charged with keeping law and order within the city limits—were hardly being vigilant. The nearest one was more than a hundred yards away and preoccupied with a prostitute flashing her wares. Attia saw it all in a single breath. The distance. The positioning.

The opportunity.

The bodyguard was speaking again, and his hand was closing around the rope. "Don't try to fight."

Attia met his eyes with a sudden, unexpected smile.

Challenge accepted.

She snatched the end of the rope from the man's grasp and looped it around his neck, the wiry strands of the cord digging into her bloody hands in the process. With a quick jump, she wedged her feet against the bodyguard's knee and pulled down, hard and fast. There was a wet pop—like pulling apart a roasted chicken thigh—right before they both fell to the ground in a pile of dust and limbs.

Attia gritted her teeth as the pain in her arm flared up toward her shoulder. But just like that, Ennius the bodyguard became damaged goods, crying out and clutching a broken leg that bent at a disturbingly sharp angle. There was not even any blood.

Crius would be proud.

Timeus's pale face turned an impressive shade of burgundy as Attia struggled to her feet again. White spots crowded her vision, and she tried to ignore the rocks and debris that cut into her skin.

"Foolish bitch," Timeus growled before rushing at her.

It was a wholehearted effort, but silly, really. Attia extended her leg and kicked him full in the face with the heel of her foot. With a distinct crunch, his nose shattered, and Timeus fell heavily on top of his bodyguard, eliciting pained screams from the both of them.

Shock and fear were written all over the merchant's face. He clutched his bulging purse before turning and hurrying as fast as he could down the street.

Attia had lifted the rope from around her neck and was beginning to wrap it around her bleeding hand. There was just enough length at the end of it to fit twice around Timeus's neck. She took a step toward him as he shouted through a mouthful of blood.

"*Stop* her!"

The distracted vigil finally took notice of what was happening at the end of the alley and moved to confront her.

Attia actually smiled through the pain.

Her people were a peculiar tribe. Direct descendants of the Spartans of old, Maedi soldiers were hardened by physical labor, honed and bent and reshaped so that the resulting body and psyche reacted like coiled springs. Pain could be tolerated or even ignored. A sword or bow or staff or even a rock was simply an extension of the self. Fighting was instinctual, natural, effortless. Sparro carried—*had* carried—a sword that weighed almost as much as Attia did, and Crius could pin a man to the wall with his spear.

Attia wasn't particularly strong. She certainly wasn't big. But she was a Thracian—a warrior of the Maedi. And this poor, stupid vigil was not.

Attia continued to wrap the filthy rope around her hand as she turned to face the watchman. Timeus and his bodyguard—still immobile on the ground—could only stare as the vigil unsheathed his sword and swung pathetically at Attia, missing by more than a few inches. She dodged the weapon with ease before smashing her rope-hardened fist into the center of the watchman's chest, putting all of her weight behind the concentrated blow. It knocked him back only a little, and pain exploded across Attia's wounded arm and wrist. But a soft snapping sound told her she'd hit her mark. The vigil managed to take just two steps before he fell face-first to the ground, the triangular piece of bone at the apex of his ribs having punctured his heart.

There was no one around who could stop her now. Ennius writhed on the ground, trying and failing to stand on his shattered leg. Timeus barely managed to push himself up to his knees before falling down again with a groan. Still, it took Attia a moment to clear out the dense fog in her head.

Move, she told herself through the pain, the dizziness, the loss of blood and breath. *Move.*

With the rope still wrapped around her fist, she turned on her heel and ran.

The warm air whipped against her face, stinging the little cuts and welts she'd acquired on the journey to Rome. The walls of the city were a brown blur. Everything seemed coated in dust, even though the late afternoon sun lent a slight golden haze to the air. Attia moved so quickly that her feet barely seemed to touch the ground, and for a single brief moment, she relished her victory. *I've escaped. I've made it.* Two young vigiles turned into the alley just then, their eyes widening at the sight of her running with the rope still dangling from her hand. They reached for their weapons. *Or not.*

Attia cut to the left and into another alley so narrow that she could brush the walls on either side with her fingertips. Just as the vigiles appeared around the corner behind her, she leaped up and braced her right foot against the wall. There was enough momentum in the motion that she was able to bounce off and plant her left foot on the opposite wall. She did it over and over, back and forth, climbing like a mountain goat with her cracked and bleeding feet. She didn't stop until she reached the fourth-floor window on the northeast corner of a crumbling insula—one of the multilevel apartments built to house the poor.

Attia hooked an arm through the small opening of the window and tumbled into a stark room. A woman screamed and shrank back against the door, trying to hide a little boy behind her. The shouts of vigiles echoed up from the street below. Attia briefly considered climbing back out the window when she saw light shifting near the base of the wall. The cheap clay insulas were already caving in on themselves. The wall separating this room from the next had begun to collapse and tilt away from the outer wall. The shift had created a narrow crawl space at its base, and Attia dove in.

The makeshift tunnel was so tight and jagged that she had to wriggle through on her belly, and for a moment, she wondered if she'd been too hasty. But she could still move—just barely—and it was better than capture. She could hear someone pounding on the door of the apartment she'd just left. She crawled forward, trying to keep her breath even as she made her way through the passage, not knowing what waited on the other side. Her hands left bloody prints in the dirt. She crawled for another thirty yards before she finally saw another shifting light ahead. At last, the little tunnel curved upward, and she emerged onto a rooftop. The setting sun had already cast the road below in shadow. This sunset marked nearly four days without proper sleep, two without food. But she couldn't afford to stop.

Attia climbed down to the darkened road, turned north, and forced herself to start running again. For a few minutes, she began to think she might actually escape. But her luck ran out. Three vigiles rounded the corner with swords drawn.

"There she is!" one of them shouted.

Attia slowed her pace and considered her opponents. Perhaps, in years past, the old vigil leading the group had been a vigorous young soldier, fighting for the glory of Rome. But time had turned him gray and made him very, very slow.

Still holding the rope in her hand, Attia made two wide loops at each end of its dirty length. Darting forward, she threw one looped end around the neck of the closest vigil. The knot tightened and she dragged him to the ground, rolling out of the way as the other two tried to attack her. She caught the second one with the other loop of rope, then used her captives to knock over the old vigil. Within moments, all three were sprawled on the ground. Dazed, humiliated, and sore, but alive.

Footsteps. Marching. More vigiles.

Attia picked up one of the watchmen's swords from the dust and, with a quick glance around her, ran and cut into an alley.

Left. Right. Left again. Backtrack to avoid two more vigiles who'd joined the chase. Then up a rough-hewn wall onto a flat rooftop.

To the east, she saw darkening clouds. A sharp rock formation on the side of a hill reached up like a fingertip to brush against the evening sky. Attia knew that beyond that hill was a valley, and beyond that valley was a mountain pass, and beyond that was the Adriatic. Then, across the salty sea—the border of Thrace. *Home.*

The streets below her began to fill with an unexpected audience. The spectacle of a female slave escaping with sword in hand was met with both heckling and cheers.

"Someone catch her! She's getting away!"

"Keep running! Don't stop!"

Some even looked as though they were trying their damnedest to hinder the vigiles who gave chase. All Attia knew was that she had to keep moving. Fighting through waves of nausea and dizziness, she took off across the rooftops, using them like stepping stones as she leapt across alleys and narrow streets, always going east.

She didn't stop until she'd come to the outskirts of the city. Behind her, the crowded clay insulas of the poor loomed in growing shadow, while up ahead were the open farmlands, grazing pastures, and sleek estates of the patricians. The dirt beneath her bare feet changed from dust and rock to soil and grass. Her breathing was even, and her muscles sang with the thrill of a chase. Attia paused to watch the sun set over the lip of the horizon, staining the sky red as the moon rose. There wouldn't be any darkness. She'd have to move fast. The long finger of the hill was still to the northeast, but shrouded in clouds.

Then she heard it—boots thundering against the earth. They moved in formation between a march and a run. And there were more of them. Dozens more. *All this for a single runaway slave?*

Attia was certain they didn't know who she was. If they did, she would surely have been executed long before reaching Rome. But there was no time to think about it. She adjusted her grip on her stolen sword—ready for whatever might come—and started to run again.

The estates gave way to wide, empty fields. The nearly

barren land was like a memorial to the thousands of trees and roots and animals destroyed in the making of the city. There was nowhere to hide, no sanctuary or haven. The boots of the vigiles were nearly upon her.

Attia wanted to go home. She wanted to see her father's warrior frame bent in concentration over his beloved letters and scrolls. She wanted to see the familiar bloodred wool of the Maedi cloaks. She wanted to run and run until her breath was spent, until the ashes of her bones mingled with those of her people.

But they're dead.

Above her, the moon rose, the sky blazed, the mountains themselves seemed to sink into the deep, and her people—every single person she had ever known—were dead.

I am dead.

And suddenly, she realized there was nothing left to run to.

She stopped running in the middle of a flat field, and within moments, the vigiles surrounded her in a wide circle of black and iron.

I am nothing. Attia is nothing. Not a name or a sound. There is no me. There is only a ghost of Thrace.

She felt herself going numb as one of the vigiles approached with chains in his extended hands. Moonlight glinted off a silver ring on his middle finger—a tiny, snarling wolf's head. His hand and that ring seemed to move in slow motion. Closer and closer.

It was instinct more than a conscious choice. Attia was just as surprised as the vigil when she deftly grabbed the man's wrist and pulled him *toward* her, right onto her stolen blade. She looked coldly into his eyes as his expression changed from one of shock to agony. Blood oozed from his belly and his mouth, staining the front of his uniform. Attia pushed him off her sword and let him fall to the ground with a dull thud.

Dead. Dead. Dead.

A startled laugh burst from her throat, and she didn't try to hold it back.

The vigiles shuffled uneasily around her like a pack of anxious wolves, wary now, confused, perhaps even frightened.

Attia's maniacal laughter warped into a scream, and then the scream became a keening that echoed against the bare trees, up to the swollen moon above. It was wordless, sharp, and high, a bone-deep lament that silenced the Roman beasts that surrounded her.

Perhaps it was almost over. Perhaps now, the darkness would bring some kind of peace.

"Stop!" The word shattered the tension in the field.

Out of the corner of her eye, Attia saw a mounted centurion, the plumes of his helmet rustling in the wind. His presence only made the vigiles more confused, and Attia understood. A centurion was a Roman officer, not one to involve himself in the simple business of city watchmen.

"She has been bought and paid for by the House of Timeus," the centurion said. "Seize and disarm her, but do not kill her."

The order finally brought the vigiles to their senses. They raised their swords, and more out of habit than anything else, Attia raised hers, too. Relying on reflex and muscle memory, she managed to strike down more than a few before their numbers and her exhaustion got the better of her.

They descended like a swarm.

CHAPTER 2

At first, Attia wasn't sure where she was. The hard pallet beneath her was so unlike the mound of blankets and furs she'd used in her tent. When she reached out, she felt only cool stone, not the hard-packed earth of the Maedi camps. The smell of roses rather than horses filled the air. She realized she was in a small, rectangular room with marble walls and floors—a typical Roman bath. Attia turned her gaze to the freshwater pool built into the middle of the floor. All she wanted to do was close her eyes and melt into that water. But then she realized she wasn't alone. A middle-aged woman hovered over her.

Attia recoiled. Through a fog of sleep and pain, she barely managed to whisper three words. "Who are you?"

"My name is Sabina," the woman said, taking Attia's hand gently in hers. "You've been unconscious for two days." Her gray-streaked brown hair was pulled back in a tight knot. She evaluated Attia's injuries with a penetrating gaze, her dark gray eyes

27

slowly moving over the gash at Attia's temple, her swollen eye, her bruised cheeks. She gently turned Attia's head to examine the most serious injury—the hard, throbbing spot where the hilt of a sword had collided with the base of Attia's skull.

With every breath, Attia's chest ached, likely from several cracked ribs. She was certain that her left wrist was sprained, and at least two of her fingers were broken. She glanced down to see her olive-gold skin splattered with dried blood and grime. But she'd suffered worse in training and on the battlefield. Her body was a proud patchwork of scars, and she knew she would heal in time.

"What is your name?" Sabina asked.

"A—" The coarseness in Attia's throat made her sputter. "Attia."

Sabina tried to give her some water, but Attia choked and coughed, and only a few drops made it down her sore throat. "Try again, Attia. Drink." Sabina held the cup to Attia's lips and made her drink it all. With swift, confident movements, Sabina began to change the bandages on Attia's wounds. She looked grim but determined as she applied pressure to the places that still bled, cleaned the gashes and cuts, and examined the line of stitches she'd sewn along Attia's side. Attia didn't make a sound.

"You're strong," Sabina said, her voice soft with approval. "That's good. You'll need to be."

A man walked into the room, drawn by the sound of their voices. His leather breastplate and greaves meant he was a guard of some sort. The black cape he wore over his tunic nearly concealed the long dagger in his belt. "Is she awake?" he asked brusquely.

Sabina pursed her lips. "Barely," she said over her shoulder.

"Good enough. Bring her. I'll inform the dominus." He left the room, his black cape fluttering in his wake.

"Dominus?" Attia repeated.

"It is the Romans' word for master, and our master's name is Josias Neleus Timeus. He—"

"He isn't *my* master," Attia said.

Sabina put a sturdy hand against Attia's cheek and looked her in the eye. "*Never* say that again."

Attia was too fatigued to argue. It took all of her strength just to get to her feet, and even then, she leaned heavily against Sabina. Standing upright sent a wave of dizziness washing over her, and pale light blinked in her eyes.

Master. A Thracian would never abide the word. It filled her with white-hot anger, a raw hatred that was enough to make her take her first step. Injured as she was, her legs still worked.

"It's not far," Sabina said.

They turned down a long hallway, and Sabina guided Attia into the tablinum—a square, windowless room just beyond the atrium. Two guards flanked the entrance, and a curtain fell behind them as Sabina and Attia entered. The stone walls of the tablinum were almost entirely covered with tapestries that stretched from the floor to the ceiling. The heavy fabric, dark with age, seemed to swallow light and sound, disorienting Attia even further.

Five more guards stood at intervals around the room. Near the back, Timeus sat in a curved cushioned seat. To Attia, it looked more like a Thracian cradle than a proper chair. In the dim light, she could see green-edged bruises spread from the bridge of Timeus's nose to his eyes and even down toward his mouth. The sickly color made the whites of his eyes look whiter and the blue of his irises look menacing.

A fire pit burned in the center of the room. It was barely autumn and a warm, clear night at that. Were the Romans so soft and self-indulgent that they needed the warmth of a fire right now?

"Good evening," Timeus said in an unnervingly gracious tone.

Hearing his voice again—that intonation and cadence that implied wealth if not nobility—made Attia's eyes blaze with contempt. Timeus leaned forward in his chair and cocked his head. Silence descended on the room. Perhaps he expected Attia to say something. Perhaps he expected her to genuflect or apologize or beg for mercy. Perhaps he could jump face-first into the Aegean.

"You do look a bit worse for wear, but whose fault is that now? I paid good money for you to be here, and now look at you— bloody and bruised and covered in filth. If he doesn't want to keep you, it will be no one's fault but your own. It was foolish of you to run."

Attia lifted her chin, but couldn't keep a look of suspicion from her face. *Keep me?*

Timeus almost smiled. "Haven't you accepted it yet? You are a spoil of war, Thracian. You are property. And now, you will be a gift to my champion. I'm sure you'll bring him immense pleasure." He looked her over and sneered. "Once you're clean."

Like hell I will. Digging for her last reserves of strength, Attia straightened her back and pulled away from Sabina to stand on her own. Timeus's eyes bore into hers, and she met his gaze full-on, defiance written all over her.

Timeus's smile faded into a dark, threatening glare. "Understand me, Thracian. There are two ways of doing things in my house: There is the easy way, and there is the hard way."

Oh, how original, Attia scoffed.

"Which way would you prefer?"

Attia would die before she obeyed him, before she was *given* to anyone. And if she was lucky, she'd get the chance to die fighting. She spat on the smooth marble floor—an answer that made her lips crack in new places. The mixture of blood and saliva glistened in the firelight.

"Very well," Timeus said.

The guards arranged themselves around her in a loose circle. They appeared relaxed, but Attia could see how they held themselves ready. Her own heartbeat quickened with anticipation. At some unseen command, the leader reached forward to grab her. She raised her arms instinctively, ready to fight back, when Sabina grasped her from behind.

"Don't," she whispered desperately into Attia's ear. "If you fight again, they'll kill you."

Attia's brief moment of hesitation was her undoing. The guards took hold of her and dragged her to the fire. And Sabina—treacherous Sabina—kept her hand on Attia's shoulder until the last second.

It was only as the guards held her prone beside the fire that Attia suddenly knew. Through the confusion and pain, she knew what the fire was for. Why had it taken her so long?

Timeus walked toward Attia, wrapping a thick length of canvas around his right hand. "I bought and paid for you, girl. If you try to run again, I will hunt you down, and next time, there will be no mercy."

Attia struggled, but the guards held her fast in their firm grip, and she was still broken in so many places.

"Whatever you were before, you belong to me now. I *own* you." He lifted a branding iron from the fire.

Attia's fingers clenched, desperate to reach one of the gleaming daggers in the guards' belts. She could see the handle of one just a few inches away. But all she could reach was the fabric of their black cloaks.

"And if you ever attack me again," Timeus said in a deadly quiet voice, "I will crucify you."

At that, Attia's heart clenched, not from fear, but from memory. All at once, she saw thousands of dying Thracians, all nailed to crosses blanketing the hillsides. She heard the Roman legatus who promised her dying father that all of his people would follow him to the underworld.

A guard ripped a hole in the side of her bloody, tattered war tunic, and Attia turned her head. Her scream seemed to tear through her whole body as Timeus seared his brand onto her hip. Then she saw black.

The brand blistered and burned, the pain insinuating itself into a familiar, relentless nightmare. As she had every night since her capture, Attia dreamed of the Romans invading with the dawn, their legions spilling over the rain-soaked hills like ants. She dreamed of every able-bodied Thracian—men and women—taking up arms to join the Maedi, to defend their families and their freedom. She dreamed of following her father into battle, and the bone-chilling cry he made as he died. The memory of that sound drew her into consciousness.

Attia found herself in a dark room, lying on a pallet on the floor. A tiny window was cut high in the wall. She tried to sit up, but the movement tugged at the tender flesh of her hip. She bit her lip to keep from crying out, swearing she would never again let the Romans hear the sound of her pain. Attia rolled over, trying her best to avoid the new wound, and began to claw her way up the wall. Her movements were painfully slow. She had to fight for every last inch. But finally she managed to prop herself up in a sitting position. Only then did she realize that someone had taken her shredded tunic—the last remnant of her life as a Maedi warrior—and dressed her in what was essentially a shapeless wool sack that fell below her knees. Three holes were cut out for her arms and head. Attia clenched her jaw, bracing herself for what she needed to do next, and pulled up the hem of her pathetic garb.

She saw the brand immediately—a sharp-tipped letter "T," the bottom tail of which tapered down like a knife point. The wound was angry and red, and a shiny blister covered the upper bar of the letter. A simple mark, and yet it cut her in a way the Romans' swords never could.

It was true now. Undeniable.

She was a slave.

CHAPTER 3

A man can get used to any name.

Dog. Barbarian. Savage.

Bastard son of Mars.

Pagan seed.

In the long decade since he'd been taken, the Romans had called him by many names. Now they favored one in particular: Xanthus Maximus Colossus, the Champion of Rome.

The dominus had once told him that the crowd cheered for him more than any other, that in their own twisted, morbid way, they loved him. Funny. And here all Xanthus wanted to do was burn down the Coliseum and every damn Roman in it.

Even though he was a gladiator.

Even though he was very, very good at what he did.

But that would end soon enough. His lips creased in a pained, determined smile as he turned his gaze to the iron gates that opened to the arena.

It would be the last time he walked through those gates, the last time he took his weapons in hand and put on the show these animals wanted. He would go out and lose his first match in ten years, and finally face the long column of broken men who waited for him on the banks of the Styx.

His dominus would undoubtedly rage about his death being a terrible waste, as though Xanthus hadn't been a helpless nine-year-old boy when he was first shoved into an arena.

No, Xanthus wouldn't—couldn't—waver.

After everything, he was just so *tired*.

His heavy sigh broke the uneasy silence of the hypogeum—the massive chamber beneath the arena where gladiators and slaves waited for their turn to fight or die. The hypogeum was a shadowy, damp space with tables and shelves groaning under the weight of weapons and armor. The only light came from flickering torches hung at uneven intervals on the walls. Broad pillars covered in chains and harnesses stretched down the middle of the room, and nearly half a dozen men were bound to them. They weren't gladiators, they were fodder—their sole purpose to entertain by dying in sand and blood.

A man chained to the nearest pillar was sobbing, his tears dripping down to cover the front of his tunic. All morning, he'd been muttering under his breath about the Christians' god and praying for an apocalypse. The Cult of Christ had been causing the Republic problems as of late, and the poor fool was probably in the Coliseum precisely for speaking such blasphemies. Xanthus pitied the man. It didn't matter what god he worshipped. All of them were already in hell.

There were other men, too. Unchained, silent, hulking men. At a glance, they looked massive and muscled, but after so many years, Xanthus recognized a different sort of strength in them. These men were hardened by experience, cloaked in apathy.

They were veteran gladiators, just like him, and they had learned to equate killing with survival. Still, few were willing to meet his eyes, and when they did, they looked quickly away. Xanthus's reputation preceded him.

Of all the men waiting in the hypogeum, only a handful could hold his gaze. They sat apart from the rest because they too had reputations. One by one, they lifted their eyes to look at Xanthus, and their expressions were heavy with unspoken comprehension. Albinus, Gallus, Lebuin, Iduma, and Castor— the men who had been forged beside him in the ludus, who had become his blood-brothers in every way that mattered. He hadn't said anything to them about what he planned to do. But after all these years, he didn't have to. They knew him.

Lebuin tried to smile at Xanthus, but the expression faltered and fell. Gallus and Iduma, usually so quick to laugh, lowered their heads to hide the shadows gathering in their eyes. Castor simply stared, sadness tightening his mouth into a grim line.

Xanthus looked away, closed his eyes, and leaned his head against the wall. He just wanted a moment—one last, single, solitary moment to pretend that he might see Britannia again, that his family might someday be made whole. That he was not the *thing* they'd carved him into.

One last time, he thought. *Just one.*

But as soon as he closed his eyes, the wall against his back began to shake in heavy, pulsing beats. Outside, the trumpets sounded off, high and resonant like the wailing of the Little People who lived in the bogs back home. They were followed by a voice Xanthus had heard for more than half his life.

"Rome's champion needs no introduction," the dominus shouted. "Call his name! Release his fury!"

And the crowd dutifully responded. "Xanthus! Xanthus! XANTHUS!"

After all, no man chooses his own name. Why should he be any different? He wasn't in Britannia; he was in the Coliseum. The trumpets were blaring, and it was time.

The iron of an unsheathed blade hissed in his ear. Opening his eyes, Xanthus looked up to see Albinus standing beside him with two swords—long, straight spathas—held ready in his hands. The man's white-blond hair hung down around his scarred face like a shroud. Albinus didn't speak, but he and the others were all silently pleading the same thing as they looked at Xanthus: *Live.*

Well, life was full of disappointment.

Xanthus put a hand on Albinus's shoulder—the closest he would come to saying goodbye—and accepted the swords. Then the iron bars rose, and bright, shifting beams of sunlight crossed his face. Xanthus sheathed the swords at his back and walked slowly out into the arena, not once looking behind him.

The sand, the shouts, the coppery scent of blood in the air, and the steady drums that followed his progress across the wide-open space were all too familiar. He knew exactly what the Romans wanted.

In one smooth motion, Xanthus drew his swords and struck them together over his head in the shape of an "X." The iron flared briefly in the autumn sun, and he held the position for a long minute, letting the crowd get a good look.

Xanthus was always surprised by how excited they were to see him. Then again, some of these spectators had watched him fight since he was a boy. He wondered if they felt like they knew him, if they considered him one of their own. And he wondered if there would ever be forgiveness for what he'd done to please them.

He would find out soon enough.

Before the cheering faded, Xanthus lowered his swords and

turned to watch his opponent approach from the southern end of the arena.

The Taurus, the Butcher of Capua, had been happily butchering all day long, and Xanthus could see why the crowd was so eager for this fight.

The Taurus was barely a man at all—nearly seven feet tall with the bulk of a bull. His skin was mottled and scarred and looked almost monstrous in the light of the midday sun. Bleached bone horns erupted from the crown of his helmet, and he eyed Xanthus with an eager, hungry expression.

Xanthus recognized his kind—the sort of godforsaken animal that actually relished its enslavement, that saw its chains as adornment and its task of destruction as a giddy pastime. He immediately despised him.

In one hand, the Taurus raised a long spear, and in the other, he gripped an impressive double-sided axe. His fierce, bellowing roar echoed against the walls of the Coliseum.

Sheathing his swords, Xanthus put his hands together in slow, sarcastic applause. "Impressive," he said. "I thought only livestock could make a sound like that."

The Taurus narrowed his eyes. Confusion and irritation warred across his face before settling into scorn. "They call you the Champion of Rome, but you're only a pup," he taunted, loud enough for the crowd to hear. They booed in response, but the Taurus didn't falter. "Have you even been weaned yet, boy?"

"We should salute the Princeps now, even if he's not here," Xanthus said. "Custom, you understand." He turned to the veranda at the end of the arena and inclined his head. The Taurus grudgingly followed suit.

The morituri—that's what they called those who were about to die. After so many years, Xanthus knew the Romans' language as though it were his own. He still had the slight accent of a boy who had grown up speaking a foreign tongue, but these next words had been carved into his very bones.

"We who are about to die salute you." Even the words tasted like blood.

When he faced the Taurus again, he reached for his swords before pausing. "Do you prefer Jupiter or Mars?" he asked.

"What?"

"I'm curious."

"Stop talking to me!" the Taurus growled.

"I only ask so that I know which god to send you to. A courtesy between . . . men." Xanthus followed the significant pause with a taunting, lopsided grin—the kind of cocky expression that had charmed so many drunken patrician ladies and infuriated so many opponents.

The Taurus reacted precisely as he was meant to. He snorted—literally, as though he was the bull he was named for—and charged straight at Xanthus.

Xanthus stood perfectly still, entirely unfazed as he watched three hundred pounds of death hurtle his way. Then, at the last possible moment, he stepped aside and lightly smacked the back of the Taurus's helmet with the broad side of his sword.

The Taurus was so shocked he nearly lost his footing. Humiliation made him turn a bright, blistering red. The crowd's roaring laughter only infuriated him more, and he wasted no time before charging again.

Again, Xanthus used the broad side of his sword to slap him away. He couldn't help it. The Taurus was too foul *not* to play with. Just for a little while. Besides, Xanthus wanted the man to put some effort into the kill.

Their epic battle soon became a violent comedy. The Taurus would lunge, and Xanthus would dance just out of reach until the whole stadium was alive with mockery. The laughter turned to jeers, and the jeers turned to taunts.

"Tame that bull, Xanthus!"

"Charge, Taurus, charge!"

"Lose your horns, you fat calf?"

"Xanthus! Stop playing and kill him!" That last voice caught Xanthus's attention.

A tall, thin man with white hair was leaning over the marble railing of the veranda, one push away from falling straight onto the merciless ground of the arena. His name was Josias Neleus Timeus, but for ten years, Xanthus had known him simply as "dominus."

Timeus's bright blue eyes glared down at Xanthus. "You hear the crowd! Finish him!"

Like well-trained sheep, the people in the stadium took up the cry. "Finish him! Finish him!"

There was no avoiding it now. Timeus and the mob were growing impatient. It would have to happen soon.

The Taurus and the entire stadium went silent with shock as Xanthus dropped to his knees, letting his swords fall to the sand on either side of him. With closed eyes, he tried again to think of home: of the mist that surrounded the Tor, of chalk on the hillsides. Of his mother, his father, his baby sister, his older brother.

And *Decimus.*

The hated name wormed into Xanthus's thoughts, but he pushed it violently away. He couldn't think of him right now or else it would weaken his resolve. He'd rather the faces of his family be the last images in his head before—

"Xanthus! Xanthus, damn you! Get up! Don't leave him to that blubbering heretic!" Timeus shouted.

Heretic? What heretic?

Xanthus grudgingly opened his eyes. The chained Christian from the hypogeum had entered the arena and was already strapped into huge, poorly fitted armor. He held a sword as though he'd never seen one before and gaped up at the crowd in open-mouthed horror.

Xanthus thought they'd send Albinus out next, or one of his other blood-brothers. He had no doubt that any of them would easily defeat the Taurus. But no. They hadn't even sent out a real gladiator. Xanthus realized with a sinking feeling that once the Taurus was done with him, that terrified, untried Christian would be next. Xanthus squeezed his eyes shut and muttered under his breath. "Well, *shit*."

The Taurus's labored breaths and heaving pants grew louder, and Xanthus knew by the sound of the crowd the very second the other man raised his axe.

And his decision was made.

The Taurus launched himself forward with a great lurch and charged.

Xanthus waited until the Taurus was no more than a foot away before his eyes snapped open. Still kneeling, he grabbed his twin swords and thrust the deadly blades outward. The iron reflected the sunlight in a blinding flash.

It was the last thing the Taurus ever saw.

Dark blood sprayed hot and sticky across Xanthus's chest as he buried both of his blades into the man's thick neck. The massive gladiator fell to his knees, and Xanthus forced himself to look straight into his pale eyes until the moment when he pulled his swords free and let the Taurus's head topple to the ground.

Just like that, it was done.

The crowd screamed his name with delight. "Xanthus! Xanthus! Xanthus!"

But Xanthus stayed on his knees afterward. His eyes focused

on the blood drenching his hands and arms and chest. His shoulders bowed beneath an oppressive weight. His ears drowned in the deluge of the crowd's cheers.

No one heard when he finally turned his face upward and whispered a prayer into the swirling dust.

"Please," he said. "Please forgive me."

CHAPTER 4

Even before Xanthus entered the great room of Timeus's house, the gathered throng of lanistae and noblemen were shouting his name. It was like being trapped in the Coliseum all over again. And when the guests finally saw him—completely unharmed from his match with the Butcher of Capua—they broke into raucous cheers, a perfect start to the evening's celebrations.

Xanthus forced a tight smile on his face.

The massive, octagonal room was heavy with incense. The scented smoke curled up in the folds of the silk drapes and curtains before releasing again in intoxicating waves when the breeze blew in from the sea. The westernmost edge of the room had no wall, only a row of evenly spaced pillars separating it from a wide balcony. The floor was a sophisticated pattern of impossibly small and perfectly fitted pieces of white and gray stone. Torchlight flickered off the seven sparkling mosaics on the walls inlaid with gold, brass, silver, and copper. One mosaic showed a man seated on a white throne wearing a tunic fashioned out of deep purple amethysts, his head and fingers lined with rubies. Another depicted Xanthus himself—his eyes made of two large emeralds, his swords inlaid with garnets meant to look like drops of blood, and his feet standing atop a mound of ivory carved into the shapes of hundreds of human bones.

Xanthus turned away, craning his neck to look for his brothers. After the match, they'd waited for him in the hypogeum. One by one, they'd gripped his shoulder hard enough to bruise, their grasps expressing the relief they were careful to keep from their faces. Not one of them said a word.

Now, Iduma was likely somewhere in the room, flirting shamelessly with one of the courtesans Timeus had rented for the evening. Lebuin was probably drinking himself into oblivion in a dark corner. Castor had no doubt remained in his quarters because no one would miss a man who never spoke.

Albinus appeared at Xanthus's side, a cup of wine in hand.

"They look like cattle, don't they? Fat, lazy, angry cattle," Xanthus said.

"Moooooo," Albinus replied before draining his cup.

Xanthus shook his head and chuckled. "Where's Gallus?"

"Probably tending to Ennius's leg."

"I thought so," Xanthus said. Ennius had been the one to train them from the very beginning—to teach six lost, stolen boys how to become gladiators. Watching him try to limp around the household was as painful for Xanthus as an injury to his own body.

"I still can't believe he was taken down by some slave," Albinus said.

"A *Thracian* slave," Xanthus said. "You know how they're trained."

They all knew. When word had reached them of the fall

of Thrace, they could hardly believe it. It seemed that the entire world was crumbling under the heel of Rome, and there was nothing anyone could do to stop it. Not even the legendary Maedi of Thrace.

From across the room, Timeus caught Xanthus's eye and raised a wiry arm, beckoning his champion forward.

"The master calls," Albinus said.

"Where the hell are *you* going?"

Albinus clicked his tongue. "Poor Ennius and his broken leg. I really ought to offer my expertise." Xanthus wasn't surprised. Like Castor, Albinus preferred the solitude and quiet of the gladiators' quarters, especially during Timeus's parties. They grasped each other's arms.

"Watch your back in there," Albinus said, and left.

Xanthus walked across the room, nodding at the men and tolerating the suggestive, fleeting touches of the women. Much as some of the male guests might want to sample his talents outside of the arena, Timeus had never forced such trysts on him. If anything, the old man allowed Xanthus liberties that no one else enjoyed. All he demanded in return were constant victories, and he had yet to be disappointed.

"Good evening, Dominus," Xanthus said. He glanced at the woman at Timeus's side. "Lucretia."

"Champion," she replied. "I believe congratulations are in order." Her dark eyes were already turning away with disinterest while she fiddled with a curl of her smooth black hair.

"You're late," Timeus said. "And the guest of honor must never be late." But his words were softened by the expression on his face—an expression that immediately made Xanthus wary.

"My apologies, Dominus."

Timeus swatted the words away with a flapping hand. "Come.

We need to talk." He dismissed Lucretia with a careless snap of his fingers.

She turned away without sparing a second glance at either of them and went to stand by Timeus's empty chair, where she would wait until he called for her again. She casually rested a hand on the back of the chair, her light brown skin complementing the white and gold cushions. No one spoke to her, but many stared at the dominus's young and beautiful concubine.

"I have another match for you," Timeus said.

Xanthus sighed. Another match, another kill. Or perhaps another chance to do what he couldn't do against the Taurus. "Does this next one have a proper name?"

Timeus's smile darkened. "Decimus."

Xanthus pinned Timeus with a penetrating glare. "What?"

"Do I have your interest now?" Timeus said, his voice laced with just a hint of aggravation. He waved to the crowd and pulled Xanthus out to the balcony. All at once, the drunken, jovial persona that he'd put on for his guests evaporated, and he became the hard, calculating man that Xanthus knew so well.

"When?" Xanthus demanded.

"Two months ago, Decimus killed his old master and was facing execution. He's nearly as good in the arena as you are. His death would have been a terrible waste, don't you think, Xanthus?"

"When?"

"Tycho Flavius seemed to think so, and so he purchased Decimus and took him to his estate in Capua," Timeus continued.

Xanthus clenched his jaw to control his breathing. Red spots blossomed in the corners of his vision and swam before his eyes. "*When?*"

Timeus smiled. "You'll fight him on the first day of spring at the Festival of Lupa."

Nearly six months away. Xanthus stood frozen as a statue, but Timeus could see the rage that clouded his champion's features.

"Decimus has been earning himself a reputation these past few years. Now that a Flavian has purchased him, he'll garner even more attention. A fight this big requires preparation, and Tycho wants to wait until his father can be present for the match," Timeus said. "Imagine the advantage of hosting the fight here in Rome. In *your* arena!"

Xanthus knew he would descend to hell itself to take that dog's life.

"The entire city is talking about your victory over the Taurus," Timeus continued. "Think of the rewards of defeating a gladiator from the House of Flavius. The Republic will remember your name for generations to come. Monuments will be erected in your visage. The House of Timeus will be glorified above all others and you with it."

Xanthus didn't care if the House of Timeus fell into the sea, but he said nothing. His mind was still whirling with the news.

As the silence filled the space between them, Timeus sighed. "Have patience, Xanthus. Besides, I've seen to it that you'll have other things to keep you occupied until then."

Xanthus shrugged the comment away. There was nothing he wanted more than to kill Decimus.

"Patience," Timeus said again. "I promise it will be worth it."

Xanthus nodded and clenched his hands.

Six months.

He could already feel Decimus's neck in his grasp.

CHAPTER 5

I am Attia of Thrace, a Maedi warrior. I am my father's daughter.

Yet for the second time in her life, Attia found herself bound like an animal, waiting in a strange room to be given to a worthless pig of a man—the so-called Champion of Rome. But she kept her face calm and her eyes trained on the door that led out to the gladiators' training yard.

It had taken nearly two weeks before she could walk normally again. Most of her wounds were healing well. The bruises had faded to broad patches of yellow and green, only partially covered by the cheap, sleeveless tunic she'd been ordered to wear. The cuts and gashes would soon add to the tapestry of scars stitched onto her bronze skin. Her head still ached, and she knew from experience that the cracks in her ribs would take at least another three weeks to heal. She'd been captured, beaten, bent. She'd been sold. She'd been branded. But she knew that the deepest cut of all was just beyond that door.

Attia hadn't been surprised when the guards had come for her just after dusk, not after what Timeus had said. She'd been staring out one of the western windows, listening to the gentle roar of the waves beating against the rocks below. Back home, she'd loved to watch the sun sink over the western edge of the Aegean every night—the way its rays pierced through the heavy cloak of mist that sometimes blanketed their shores. Light reflected off of the waves, casting shadows against the mountains. It was a time when the edges of the world blurred, when sea and air and land were nearly indistinguishable, and one could almost believe that the veils between realities existed.

The wild beauty of this foreign sea was enough to keep her still as the guards tied her hands tightly in front of her with a smooth linen rope. She didn't struggle as they pulled her along through the atrium, down the hallway to the main courtyard, and through a broad archway to the champion's quarters. They whispered among themselves, never calling the champion by name, but speaking in low voices about his victories and kills. They called him a god of the arena.

But Attia was more concerned with what Timeus had called her. "You are a spoil of war . . . a gift to my champion," the old man had said. His words, along with his mark, had been seared into her skin.

Now she waited, her eyes trained on the door. The room was surprisingly simple, almost bare. Nothing like what she would have expected for the so-called Champion of Rome. A hard bed was wedged against one corner and draped with a brown blanket. Across from the bed, two short candles burned on a wooden table. Attia saw what looked like a necklace made of feathers and hemp. The moon shone in through a small window in the outer wall.

She may not have struggled when the guards came, but even

before they put the rope on her again, she was ready—ready to spit in the faces of Rome's elite, to scratch and claw and fight. To kill. As for the champion, well. Soon enough, Attia would meet him face-to-face, and she would see for herself whether this god of the arena bled like a man.

The candles on the table had burned to nearly half their length by the time someone pushed the door open. The guards remained outside as Timeus entered, followed moments later by another man, and Attia finally looked into the face of Timeus's monster.

The Champion of Rome towered over her. He was younger than she'd expected, with clear skin tanned by the sun and hard lines of muscle and sinew—tokens of his years spent in the arena. His dark hair was cut short in the Roman fashion and accentuated the strong lines of his face. His eyes were bright and green like new grass. He held himself like a warrior, and his mouth formed a grim line as he frowned at her.

That dark look of his had probably made countless men tremble. Attia nearly expected the walls themselves to move to escape his displeasure. But she held her ground. She had never been cowed by a man. She was not about to start now. Attia lifted her chin and glared back, hating both the gladiator and Timeus with every hot drop of blood in her veins.

Timeus grinned at his champion. "No one else has touched her," he said. "She will be yours to do with as you will—your own little slave, all the way from Thrace."

Attia wanted to spit in the old man's smug, bruised face.

The gladiator didn't seem at all happy with his master's gift. He barely looked at Attia, and when he did, his expression shifted from shock to dismay to curiosity and then to something that almost looked like shame. He quickly looked away again.

"Unless, of course, you don't want her," Timeus continued. "I can't say I'd be surprised. You're too picky, honestly. I can never guess your tastes. But my men will enjoy her well enough, and—"

Only then did the gladiator speak. "No," he said. "Your gift is well received, Dominus. You honor me, and I thank you."

"As I thought." Timeus clapped his back. "The gods and the Republic smile on my house because of your victories, my boy. Now I smile on you. Try and enjoy it."

But the gladiator's expression remained clouded. Despite his words of acceptance, it was obvious to Attia that the man neither celebrated Timeus's offering nor seemed remotely grateful. No, he was . . . resigned. Then Timeus and the guards left, and Attia was alone with the gladiator.

They stood facing each other, both scowling deeply enough to darken the room as a heavy rain began to pelt against the outer walls. Attia clenched her jaw with such force that she felt a dull throbbing start in the base of her skull.

The gladiator looked away first. "I didn't ask for this," he said, speaking almost to himself. When he looked at Attia again, his eyes lowered to the rope binding her hands. "Let me untie you." He reached for a small knife on the shelf behind him.

As the gladiator approached her, Attia had to remind herself again—she had to force the words into being. *I am the war-queen of Thrace. I am my father's daughter.*

With every beat of her heart, she reached for the anger that simmered just below her skin, for the hate that threatened to consume her from the inside out. She forced herself to remember the screams of the women and children, the valiant war cries of her brave Maedi. The jolt of the cart that bore her to Rome. The rough hands of the merchant who sold her as a slave. The brand and the chains and the face of the legatus who murdered her father.

I am Attia. I am a Maedi. And I have killed before. This will be easy.

Just as the gladiator sliced through the rope, Attia neatly twisted the knife out of his hands, whipped around, and kicked him hard in the hip. She followed the strike with quick blows from her elbows aimed at his head and neck. Using the wall behind her for leverage, Attia leapt forward and drove her knee into his side. The gladiator gasped softly and bent at the waist, cradling a newly cracked rib.

Attia adjusted her grip on the knife and pressed the blade against his throat. "You will never touch me," she said. "No man will. And you're not even a man. You're nothing but Timeus's monster."

The gladiator took a deep breath before slowly straightening. "You're right. So what are you waiting for? Kill me."

"I plan to." Just a quick flick of her wrist. That was all she needed.

"Sometime this century?"

Attia pressed the blade harder against his skin. "Aren't you afraid?"

"Afraid? I would be honored to die at the hands of a Thracian. A daughter of the Maedi. That's what you are, aren't you?"

When she didn't answer, the gladiator slowly fell to his knees before her. Attia froze, her brow creasing in disbelief. Whatever she'd expected from the champion, this was certainly not it. Her small blade pressed against his skin, and a thin trickle of blood ran free.

"I didn't ask for this," the gladiator said again. "I didn't ask for any of it. You can believe me or you can kill me. Whatever Timeus says, I won't touch you."

Attia started to shake her head. Why should she believe him? He was a champion of Timeus's house, of Rome. By everyone's account, he *owned* her. Why should she trust anything that came out of the man's mouth? That was when she saw it—the deep sorrow etched into the gladiator's face, the fatigue that weighed on his strong body. He hadn't tried to fight off her attack, and even now, he kept his arms limp at his sides, resigned to the fact that she was about to slit his throat. *Why?*

They said nothing to each other as the rain continued to beat against the walls. The gladiator spoke of her home, but Thrace suddenly seemed so far away. Another world. Another lifetime. She clenched her teeth to hold down the sob welling in her throat, because the truth was, the gladiator was wrong. She wasn't one of the Maedi anymore. She had already betrayed every legacy, every piece of the heritage that her father had passed on to her. She'd let him die on that hillside. She'd allowed her people to be massacred. She was no warrior. Not anymore. How could she ever again call herself anything more than a slave? For the first time, she thanked the gods that her father was no longer alive to witness her shame.

Attia slowly lowered the blade from the gladiator's neck. She almost couldn't feel the hilt of the knife in her palm.

"If you're not going to kill me tonight, will you tell me your name?"

"My name is Attia." She could hear the defeat in her own voice and was sure the gladiator could, too.

He was silent for a long minute though his gaze held hers. "They call me Xanthus." He gestured half-heartedly toward the bed. "Timeus will want to know he's gotten his way. Let him think it. You can have the bed. I won't touch you." Then he took the rough blanket and spread it out on the floor at the farthest end of the room. Attia watched as he lay down, his back to her and his face to the wall. Within a few minutes, it seemed he was fast asleep.

Attia stood where she was for a while longer, never taking her eyes from the gladiator's back. Only when her legs threatened to give out from sheer exhaustion did she gingerly crawl onto the gladiator's bed, pressing her own back against the wall and bringing her knees to her chest. She kept the little knife clutched tightly in her hand. She didn't make a single sound, though every piece of her felt raw and frayed.

The heavy rain continued outside, and Attia wished the sky would release an ocean onto the house. In the silent depths of her heart, she grieved for her people, for her father, for herself. For the promise of honor and glory and freedom. For the warrior that she was and the queen that she should have been.

Her thoughts turned to the gladiator sleeping just a few feet away, and she wondered if he grieved for something, too. He obviously didn't fear death. No, in some manic, desperate way, he almost seemed to welcome it. Maybe that was why he hadn't tried to stop her attack. Maybe that was why she couldn't bring herself to kill him. Because maybe in this house, in this prison, they both wanted the same impossible thing: to be just a man and just a woman, standing free in the rain.

CHAPTER 6

The house of Timeus was a maze of stone. Doorways hid in the shadows. Corridors branched off to other corridors in wide and narrow angles. Stairways plunged down to cold cellars and dark basements. Arched passages led to rooms lined with marble and granite. And everywhere, there were guards. Dozens of them, maybe more. All armed with swords, daggers, even small mallets that hung from their belts. The guards on the upper floor wielded bows, and their eyes moved constantly over the courtyard and the gates.

Every now and then, Attia glimpsed a dark-haired woman walking listlessly through the halls, often dressed in a black stola that clung to the curves of her body. But Attia could never get close enough to really look at her before the woman disappeared down some corridor.

All of it was so foreign and cold that Attia found herself shivering despite the mild southern climate. As swordlord of the

Maedi, her father moved constantly from camp to camp, village to village with his soldiers—ensuring peace and protecting their borders. Attia's room had been a tent on a hillside or a single pallet in a dense wood. She had been surrounded by hundreds of Maedi nearly every minute of every day, and still, the guards in Timeus's house made it difficult for her to breathe under their oppressive watch.

None of them spoke to her or even met her eyes, but she could feel their gazes boring into her back. Attia ignored them. All she knew was that as soon as she regained her full strength, she would kill Timeus and escape this house. In all likelihood, she would be struck down somewhere in the process, but she couldn't bring herself to care about that little detail. After all, what else was left for her? Another tense night in a gladiator's bed?

Xanthus had told the truth; he never touched her. He was gone by the time she opened her eyes that morning, even before the sun had completely risen. In the half-dark, she slipped out of his room, pausing at the archway of the training yard when she heard something that made her body tense instinctively— the surprising sound of synchronized movements and the un- mistakable clang of swords.

In the shadowy yard, she could see six men paired off and sparring with one another. They wore no armor. Their weap- ons were cheap. And their movements—while brutal and effective—were much too chaotic for the auxilia. Not soldiers, then. Timeus's gladiators. And Xanthus was among them. None of them had seen her, and she didn't stay long to watch.

During the long night, she'd come to a decision. Until she had the strength to fight her way out of the estate, she would stay quiet. She would learn the halls and the corridors. She would count the guards. She would sleep in the gladiator's quarters each night so long as he kept his word and kept his hands to himself.

And she would do what small chores Sabina asked of her, even if she did get off to a rather disastrous start. As the house slaves soon learned, the young Thracian might be the champion's new pet, but she was certainly not a domesticated one.

That morning, Attia followed Sabina to the steaming room where the house slaves cleaned the linens and clothes. It was a single rectangular space with raised vats of hot water standing in rows throughout the room. The strong stench of ammonia brought tears to Attia's eyes, and she covered her nose as Sabina introduced her to the laundress.

"She doesn't know much," Sabina said. "But she's a quick learner."

Attia raised her eyebrow. Sabina had no reason to think she was quick at anything except fighting, and she obviously didn't know that Attia had cleaned her own clothes before, as all Maedi had. Attia knew well enough how to launder tunics and other linens. But she didn't say a word.

The laundress looked her over and sighed. "Fine. Come with me, girl." She led Attia to a vat of hot water near the back of the room. A massive wooden paddle rested against the side, and the laundress handed it to Attia. "Stir," she said. "And don't put anything else in there. This one is for the dark tunics."

So Attia stirred. Every slow movement of the paddle made the stench stronger, and she turned her face away in an effort to take a clear breath. Behind her, rows and rows of clean and folded linens filled wooden shelves. Other slaves came in pairs to take armfuls of the sheets out of the steaming room.

Attia paused and cocked her head, her eyes on the last pile of clean linen just an arm's reach away. In the end, she couldn't help herself. She swept the linens up into her arms before clumsily dropping them into the vat. She stirred with vigor before lifting the cloth up with her wooden paddle. The linen was no longer snowy white but had turned to a muddy gray color.

The laundress saw and nearly screamed. "By the gods!" she shouted, hurrying over to snatch the paddle from Attia's hands. "What have you done?" She pulled the ruined linens from the steaming vat with her bare hands and dropped them on the floor when the heat proved too much. With the long end of the paddle, she raised a corner of the linen to reveal singed, frayed edges.

"Apologies," Attia said, not looking apologetic at all.

The laundress turned a dark glare on her. "Get out! Get out! Get out!"

She ran Attia out of the steaming room with the paddle still in her hands.

It took Sabina nearly half an hour to calm the woman down, and she only succeeded by promising over and over that she would never bring Attia back to the steaming room again.

Attia was just fine with that.

Sabina shook her head at Attia before taking her to the kitchens. The slaves there were already hard at work preparing the midday meal. As she'd done with the laundress, Sabina told the head cook that Attia was new, a quick learner, however ignorant she seemed. She turned an exasperated look at Attia when she said that last part.

"Can you cook?" the man asked.

Of course she could. Maedi had to eat, didn't they? But she simply shrugged and let the cook lead her to the roasting pit in the middle of the kitchen.

"All you have to do is turn this spit," he said, "and make sure the meat doesn't burn. The dominus hates burned pork."

So Attia turned the spit. The smell of the meat made her mouth water, and she fought the urge to pull just a small piece from the spit. Her arms were already tired from stirring the paddle in the washing vat, but she kept a steady pace over the fire pit.

Only when the head cook looked away did Attia loosen her grip. She released her hold on the spit, and deliberately knocked it off its stand, sending a whole rack of pork straight onto the ash and coals below. She used the spit to push the meat off the fire, but only ended up burning and smothering it in more ash.

"You imbecile!" the head cook screamed when he saw what had happened. He ran over and snatched the spit from her hands, but there was nothing to be done. The pork was ruined—not just burnt or overcooked, but completely and thoroughly inedible.

"Apologies," Attia said.

It took Sabina more than an hour to convince the head cook not to run straight to Timeus, saying that it would only get them all punished in the end.

"Never bring her back here!" the head cook shouted.

And Attia was just fine with that, too.

When they were alone, Sabina gripped Attia's arm. "Are you *trying* to get yourself killed?" she demanded, clearly exasperated.

"Would it help if I said I was sorry?" Attia asked with feigned innocence.

Sabina narrowed her eyes before leading Attia to a tiny room down the hall from the kitchen. She pulled out a bucket, a handful of rags, and a stiff brush. "Since you're so talented at making messes, maybe you can learn to clean them up as well."

This time, Sabina led Attia through the house to the great welcoming room of the villa. No doubt Sabina had seen it countless times, but Attia hadn't yet, and as soon as she passed through the doorway, her step faltered.

The room was beautiful and terrifying—a massive octagonal space that echoed with the work of dozens of slaves. The complex mosaics and murals, the marble and stone, the silk and satin drapes that hung from the row of pillars to the west, the jewels sparkling on the walls. It was more than Attia had ever seen, and the sight of so much concentrated wealth made her dizzy.

"All this from training gladiators?" Attia asked. "He only has six."

Sabina frowned. "How do you know that?"

"I saw them this morning in the training yard."

"Yes, well, the dominus needs no more. His gladiators are famous throughout the Republic, and his champion is beloved."

"Timeus must treat them all well, not just his champion," Attia said. "Why else haven't they tried to kill him?"

Sabina's eyes flicked toward Attia then away. With capable hands, she began plucking and pruning an ugly arrangement of sticks and flowers in a tall, painted vase. She trimmed away at the brown stems before adding a handful of rust-colored blooms. "Take care, Attia," she said eventually. "He is our dominus, and you should show respect."

"Respect is earned."

"Not in Rome."

"No, you're right. Here it is bought."

Sabina shot her a warning look. "Hush, now. Go scrub that far pillar; then I need you to clean a few of the rooms on the upper floor. Maybe if I keep you away from too many people, I can keep you out of trouble."

Attia shrugged again as she lifted her bucket. "Yes. Maybe."

The autumn sunlight was blinding, reflecting off the pale sand as two of the gladiators paired off.

When Ennius had first begun teaching them, they'd paused

often for instruction or correction. Now, they sparred until someone fell to the ground, and sometimes even beyond that. Only the two men in the circle were allowed to speak. The others watched in silence and kept their comments to themselves. Not even the guards patrolling the walls and gates said a single word. On pain of death, they never interfered with the gladiators' training—an order that had begun with Timeus's father, Quintus.

Xanthus glanced at Albinus, who stood to his left. The bright sunlight made Albinus's scars more pronounced than ever, and Xanthus's expression turned grim as he looked at his brother.

Thin, deep hash marks covered Albinus's entire body, even his face. Some were layered over others, most of them no more than a few inches long. The worst stretched in a jagged line from his temple to his chin. But they weren't Timeus's doing. Albinus had actually arrived like that, bought at the same auction as Xanthus when he too was only a boy. Only once did Albinus tell Xanthus how he'd gotten those scars. They'd never spoken of it again.

The sunlight wasn't doing Iduma's appearance any favors either. The gladiator already looked like he was made of fire with his red hair, red face, and red skin. His whole body was drenched in the color, not to mention the stench of sweat. He pushed away from Lebuin, and the two began circling each other again while the others watched.

Iduma turned his mischievous blue eyes to Lebuin and winked. Thirty seconds later, he was flat on his back, and Lebuin hovered over him with a blunt sword at his throat.

"You almost had me," Lebuin said with a smirk.

"Who says I wasn't aiming for exactly this position?" Iduma said, twisting his feet between Lebuin's legs and pulling him to the ground. They wrestled in the dirt while the others laughed.

Castor and Gallus paired up next, though the match ended quickly when Castor suddenly rammed his bald head forward and struck a solid blow into Gallus's gut. Xanthus nearly groaned in sympathy, and even a few of the guards winced. It was a running joke that Castor's head was probably made of iron.

Gallus fell to his knees, his own head bent down to touch the dirt. He took a gasping breath, in and out, dust and all. No one offered to help him up, though. He had to stand on his own or not stand at all. It took a few minutes, but finally, he raised his head, planted one foot on the ground, then the other. Only when he was standing again did he shake Castor's hand. "Good hit," he said hoarsely. "But I'll have your ass next time."

Castor grinned, silent as ever.

Xanthus wanted to enjoy his brothers' banter. Their familiar playfulness was typically a balm after a match in the arena. But his thoughts were dark and torn. He knew that Attia hadn't slept much in his room the night before, even after he'd promised not to touch her. Could he blame her? A part of him had truly wanted her to simply slice his throat and be done with it. But then he thought of Decimus and the match at the Festival of Lupa. Ever since Timeus had told him about it, Xanthus had wondered whose death he wished for more—Decimus's or his own.

The gladiators quieted as they looked at him. They knew of Decimus, and they knew what the fight meant.

"Come on, Xanthus," Lebuin said, all trace of laughter gone from his voice. "Your turn."

But it was Albinus who joined Xanthus in the circle. The brothers touched swords before taking their stances. When Albinus raised his weapon and struck, he didn't hold back a single inch. If Decimus was even half as ruthless as the rumors said, Xanthus could very well be facing his strongest opponent yet. He couldn't afford to train lightly anymore.

The other gladiators gave the two a wider and wider berth as the sparring continued. They traded blows, one right after the other, each one so strong that the quivering metal of the practice swords resonated with every impact. Albinus struck and stabbed, forcing Xanthus to slide away or be run through. Even though the training swords were blunted and bent from use, they could still cleave a limb with enough force. And Albinus was putting his body weight's worth of force behind each hit.

"You're not trying," Albinus growled as they circled each other. They'd been sparring for nearly half an hour, and their bodies glistened with sweat and dirt.

"The hell I'm not," Xanthus said.

"Well, not hard *enough*," Albinus shot back. He ran at Xanthus with his sword, and Xanthus deflected it with ease. "See? You're just defending."

Xanthus spit into the sand. Sweat stung his eyes, but he was far from tired. He knew that he and Albinus could keep doing this for hours if they had to. "I'm taking my time."

Before he could finish his last word, Albinus attacked again. This time, he had a wild look in his eye, and his entire stance had changed. Xanthus adjusted his footing, swung his sword, and knocked Albinus's weapon out of his hands. That should have been the end of it, but Albinus dove at him, his head and shoulders colliding with Xanthus's torso.

Pain radiated from Xanthus's cracked rib, and he wondered for a moment if it was actually broken now, but he didn't have time to keep thinking about it. Albinus tackled him to the ground and rained heavy blows down on Xanthus's face and shoulders. Xanthus raised his arms in defense as he twisted his body around, knocking Albinus over onto the sand.

Xanthus had the obvious advantage now. He was taller and a fraction stronger. He could grip Albinus's neck with one hand and his dominant arm with the other. Enough force and energy surged through him that it would be easy to keep him down or even render him unconscious. But he simply released Albinus and leapt lightly to his feet.

"Good match—"

"What the hell are you doing?" Albinus interrupted with a shout, scrambling up from the ground. "Why did you stop?"

Xanthus glanced at the others, who were watching with almost hurt expressions. He frowned in confusion. "What, would you have preferred I killed you?" he shot back.

"I'd prefer it if you took this seriously, Xanthus. The Taurus didn't hold back. None of your opponents have ever held back. Do you think Decimus will?"

"You're not Decimus."

"That's not the point! This isn't going to be like every other match, Xanthus, and you know that. You are so used to taking your time, waiting, letting those bastards in the arena practically kill themselves on your sword. But you know what Decimus is capable of. You know more than anyone."

A deadly silence descended on the gladiators.

"And *we* know," Albinus said. He'd lowered his voice, but Xanthus could still feel the frustration seething from him. "We know how much you hate this, Xanthus." Albinus shook his head and smiled bitterly. "You wanted to let the Taurus kill you, but you stayed alive to save that sobbing heretic. But what now? What about your new Thracian? What do you think will happen to her if you're not around anymore? And what about us? We're your *brothers*, Xanthus. Do you plan to stay alive for us?"

It was then that Xanthus understood the hurt he saw on the

others' faces. He'd seen his willingness to die in the arena as a reprieve, a chance to find some semblance of peace. But to his brothers, it must have seemed like betrayal, abandonment. Guilt swirled in the pit of his stomach.

"You've played with death for a long time, brother," Albinus said. "But that needs to end now. It's about time you decide if you want to join the living, or if the next body that falls in the sand will be yours."

Albinus kicked his training sword aside before walking toward his quarters at the rear of the training yard.

One by one, the others went back to their own rooms, leaving Xanthus standing alone in the dust.

It seemed that Sabina had finally managed to find a chore in the house with which Attia couldn't be *too* destructive.

Armed with rags and a bucket, Attia was sent alone to wander from room to room—dusting, scouring, sweeping, scrubbing. Not even this task was new to her. In her father's camp, every warrior was responsible for his—or her—own gear and weapons. All her life, Attia had kept her own tent tidy and her own horses groomed. She might have been the crown princess, but she was far from pampered.

Attia tried not to think about the fact that everything she was touching now belonged to Timeus. Of course, that fact also made it rather easy for her to be fairly lazy about her task. There were plenty of other cleaning slaves, she reasoned. If she forgot to wipe a table or sweep a room or do anything at all, someone else would do it. Probably.

With that in mind, she left the first six rooms as she found them, wandering around just long enough to get a good look at what was inside each one. In one unfurnished room, she saw the dark-haired woman leaning against the balcony, her back to the half-open door. She was dressed differently, though, wearing a formless beige dress with a neckline up to her jaw and sleeves that reached her wrists.

Not in a particularly social mood, Attia skipped that room and kept going until she reached a heavy, ornate door at the end of the hall. She opened it, and her immediate reaction was resentment tinged with curiosity.

Timeus's study.

The room was circular, set into the southeastern corner of the villa, with a single wall that curled all the way around to meet either side of the doorway. Four windows, each covered with thin linen, let in a good deal of light, and Attia saw that the entire room was lined with shelves brimming with scrolls. In the center was a massive desk covered in maps and letters.

She closed the door behind her, heading straight for the desk.

The map grabbed her attention first. It was made of papyrus and composed of thirteen different sections, all fitted together by silk thread. Yet another measure of Timeus's wealth. By the texture of the papyrus, she could tell it was fairly new—probably made no more than a year or two ago—and it was as detailed a picture as she would ever get of the capital city of Rome.

Her eyes followed the blue meandering lines of the city's aqueducts, which the Republic had been building and improving on for nearly two hundred years. Dark brown lines crisscrossed in every direction, denoting streets and alleyways. And marked by thick black lines were the infamous paved roads that led from the heart of Rome to the far corners of the Republic.

For a long time, she studied the tiny script that covered the map, naming the roads and borders and major households. The estate belonging to the House of Timeus apparently sat on the coastline west of Palatine Hill. The writing was neat and straight, and used proper Latin rather than the Vulgate used by the common folk. It was still easy enough for Attia to read. Her father had spent years tutoring her in Latin and Greek writing, insisting that his heir should be educated in literacy before war.

Using her finger, Attia traced the black line of the road that led most directly east—to the shores of the Adriatic and the borders of Thrace. *My way home . . . if there were a home left to go back to.* She let her hand fall heavily onto the corner of the map, hardly caring if her carelessness tore the delicate papyrus. How ironic to have such information and no way to use it. To want to fight but have a body that could barely run.

Frustrated, Attia turned away from the map and started riffling through the letters and papers stacked along the edges of the desk. Most were short and formal—abundant praise for Timeus's victory in the arena, invitations to dinners and political functions, requests for matches with the champion. Just like the map, the language of the correspondences was all in proper Latin rather than the Vulgate, though the language was embellished and stylized. Likely the work of employed scribes. Only when she'd cleared aside a particularly deep stack did she see a name that grabbed her interest: *Flavius.*

She knew that name. Everyone did. It was the name of the royal house perched on Palatine Hill—the family name of Princeps Titus, ruler of the Republic of Rome. Attia pushed aside a few more open scrolls, trying to get a clearer view of the flat sheet of parchment. It was nearly the size of the map, but not as full. There were lines, too, connecting names, dates, ranks, and places. It was a detailed family history of what was currently the most powerful family in the Republic.

Vespasian's name was known well enough, written at the very top. He'd been a soldier and a senator who eventually came to rule over Rome through a combination of cunning and treachery—namely, killing any man who tried to challenge him. After his death the previous winter, his son, Titus Flavius, had inherited the title of Princeps Civitatis, which literally translated to "first citizen." Titus alone had ruled Rome for nearly a year, and if he'd taken a wife since, it wasn't recorded on the parchment.

Mirroring those were names less familiar to Attia. First, there was Vespasian's brother, Crassus Flavius, who was actually a year older and still alive. Below that was the name of Crassus's son, Tycho, who—at thirty-six years of age—was four years younger than Titus. Spread around them were the names of no more than half a dozen cousins, uncles, and other sons. The sparsity of names allowed room for other details to be recorded—years and places of birth, notable events, even military ranks. Apparently some distant cousin had recently been appointed to the Senate, though he was only fifteen years old.

It didn't surprise Attia that Timeus would keep such information or that he would be so meticulous about adding to it. His gladiators had given him absurd wealth and prominence. But Timeus was no senator, and his status as a patrician was bought, not inherited. He didn't even have a military rank to his name, as far as Attia was aware. When it came down to it, he was nothing more than a lanista, a glorified merchant. And for a man as ambitious as Timeus, social class meant everything. If he ever hoped to improve his family's standing within the Republic, he'd need to form strong ties with the only family in Rome who could raise him up.

The one thing that did surprise Attia was that the House of Flavius seemed smaller than she'd expected. Including the brothers Vespasian and Crassus, there were barely more than two generations of offspring listed. *Male* offspring. She had to scan the papyrus several times to confirm that there were no women listed at all. No wives nor mothers nor daughters. A small house, indeed. Attia's own family were direct descendants of the kings of ancient Sparta, and they had led the tribes of Thrace for over three hundred years. Twelve generations of swordlords had all dedicated their lives to protecting their people. Attia frowned down at the papyrus on the table. The size of it suggested the beginning of a dynasty, but really, the Flavians seemed little more than pretenders to a throne they didn't deserve.

Attia's eyes drifted back up to Crassus's name, and she noticed a title beside it. Written in tiny brown letters was a word that had come to haunt her days and nights: *legatus.* So Vespasian's big brother was a general in the Roman army, and of all the people documented, he appeared to be the most accomplished. Just below his name was a long list of places and dates. Jerusalem, Britannia, Germanica. All military campaigns going back more than twenty years.

Attia scrolled down the list with mild curiosity until she reached the bottom. Then it felt as though her stomach had lurched into her chest.

At the very end, written in new, glistening ink, was Thrace.

And suddenly, the face that had burned itself into her nightmares and her memory had a name.

Legatus Crassus Flavius.

The Roman who had killed her father.

CHAPTER 7

Crassus.

A shiver of cold rage trickled down Attia's spine as she sat on a window ledge on the upper floor, watching the soft purple hues of dusk settle on the edge of the horizon. Soon, she'd have to get up and go to Xanthus's quarters for the night. He hadn't hurt her last time, and he'd promised not to touch her. But what was a Roman's promise worth? How patient could any man be about this sort of thing? She wondered if this would be the night she'd have to kill him. In her current mood, she thought she might just want to kill the first person she saw.

With a sigh, she stood and prepared herself for the inevitable. But she didn't expect the man who waited for her at the foot of the stairs. When she recognized his face, her body froze with suspicion and distrust. It was Timeus's muscled bodyguard from the auction. His right leg—the one she'd broken—was wrapped in a stiff leather brace, and he stood with one hand firmly clasped around a thick staff. The whites of his eyes stared out from his night-dark face. Even injured, he looked stoic and forbidding.

Shit.

Attia stared at him with her jaw clamped shut and her nails digging into her palms. He'd probably come specifically to get her alone, to exact some sort of revenge for what she'd done to him. But then he just nodded his head, turned, and began walking in the direction of the training yard.

Well, limping.

Attia had no choice but to follow. She squirmed as she walked in his wake, watching as he practically dragged his leg across the floor with each step. She was amazed he could even walk at all. She'd used that move countless times, but she'd never stuck around to see what happened to the man afterward. The evidence of it was now right before her eyes, and she had no idea what to think.

He couldn't be here as a guard; what use would he be with his injury? So what did he want? An apology? *Like hell.* He didn't know her, but he should know better. Attia was surprised that he was even willing to turn his back on her. Wasn't he afraid that she'd just attack him again and try to escape a second time? She would only have to—

"Clever trick."

The sudden deepness of his voice disturbed Attia's thoughts. She measured her pace to maintain a short distance between them. "Trick?" she asked warily.

He glanced back and tapped his finger against the leather cast. "Where did you learn how to do that?"

Attia couldn't quite place his accent, but she knew that the Latin he spoke wasn't his native language. There was a surprisingly pleasant lilt to his voice, a musical quality that made it sound like he was humming the words rather than speaking them.

"My father," she said.

"A skilled man. My father was also quite skilled. He taught me everything he knew."

What was she supposed to say to that? Why was the man even talking to her?

"His true love was the sea," he was saying. "The waves, the salt, the depth of it. He would have lived and died on the sea if he was able."

"But he wasn't?"

"No," he said in a quiet voice. "He wasn't."

Attia couldn't help herself any longer. "Aren't you angry after what I did to you?" she said, her voice loud in the dark hall.

He looked at her with a wry smile, and Attia realized that she'd closed the distance between them. They were walking shoulder to shoulder as she matched his painful limp with small steps. "No," he said.

"Why not?"

"A man learns to respect others' abilities, or he falls."

Attia snorted. *Oh, you fell, all right.*

"And I've been injured much worse. I was a gladiator for nearly fifteen years."

"I'm surprised that Timeus trusts a slave to protect him."

"I am a freeman." He laughed lightly at the shocked look on Attia's face. "Years ago, when I became champion of the house, I was given a rudis and set free. Now I serve the dominus outside of the arena." He said it so simply, as though it was a matter of course to be given one's freedom.

Attia sputtered. "But . . . but if you're free, why have you stayed here?"

Ennius came to a stop. "Xanthus," he said with a nod of his head.

"What?"

Ennius cleared his throat. Attia turned to see the red "X" marking the doorway to the champion's quarters. They'd reached the training yard without her realizing it, and Xanthus was leaning against the lintel as though he'd been waiting for them.

"A pleasant evening, Ennius, isn't it?" the gladiator said.

"Quite," Ennius, the freeman, replied.

They both looked at Attia, and still bewildered, she shuffled past Xanthus and into his small room.

Ennius lowered his voice, thinking Attia wouldn't hear. "She's very young."

"Goodnight, Ennius," was the strained reply.

"Goodnight, Xanthus."

Attia could hardly think straight. Ennius with his broken leg and musical voice, an old gladiator and former slave—he'd been freed when he became champion. He's *free* and he *stays*. Serving that old pig. And if he'd been freed as a champion, then that probably meant . . .

She swung around to look at Xanthus. "You're the champion of this house. Of Rome." It wasn't a question.

He considered her for a moment before answering. "Yes . . ."

"And that man was champion before you," she said, pointing in the direction of the villa.

His brow wrinkled in confusion. "Ennius, yes."

"And he is free."

Xanthus's expression went blank as understanding began to dawn.

"Are *you?*"

He looked away, but Attia took a step forward and persisted.

"Answer me. Are you a freeman?" It hurt to get the words out. She'd almost let herself think that they were in a similar situation, but if the champion was free, it changed everything.

Xanthus's eyes were a dark shade of green when he met her

gaze, as though a shadow looked out from deep inside him. He walked slowly toward her and lifted his sleeve. Timeus's brand was seared into the flesh of his muscled arm, just below the shoulder. "No," he said finally. "I am a slave, like you. We are equals."

Attia released a breath she hadn't realized she was holding. "We may both be slaves, but we're hardly equals. In case you don't remember, I was *given* to you. The guards don't even lock your door."

"Yes, my door is unbarred. But just how far do you think I'd get if I tried to walk away from this house right now?"

"You could *try*."

Xanthus turned away to pick up a small basket that sat beside the door. "I did try. A long time ago. And someone else paid for my transgression." His face darkened. "I won't take that risk again."

The finality in his voice told Attia that that particular subject was best left for another time. "Why did Timeus free Ennius?" she asked instead.

"He didn't. Ennius was freed by Timeus's father, Quintus, who was a very different sort of man." Xanthus set the basket on the table and started unpacking it.

"Did you know him?" Attia asked.

Fruit, fresh bread, a wedge of cheese, a hunk of seasoned pork, and a small jug of wine emerged, one by one. "No. By the time I was brought here, Quintus had already passed. But Ennius talked about him often while he was training us."

"And now you're the Champion of Rome. Are you as good as they say?"

The corner of Xanthus's mouth quirked upward. "I'm no Thracian."

No, Attia thought. *You're not.*

A heavy silence followed. Part of Attia liked how the gladiator spoke of her home with such obvious reverence. But thinking of Thrace awakened too many memories, too many regrets. Too many plans and intentions that had died with her enslavement. Just a few months before the invasion, her father had hesitantly brought up the prospect of marriage. A queen needed heirs, after all.

But her father was dead, and Attia would never marry, by choice or by force. She realized that this sordid association with the gladiator might be the closest she would ever be to a man. She knew nothing about him—where he came from or who his people were or what he saw when he closed his eyes—but he was considerate and bright, with a quiet voice and hands that hadn't hurt her. At least, not yet.

All marriages were things of convenience, in one way or another, and Attia had no intention of making any vows to Xanthus. She only had to give him her nights, and if Timeus had his way, her body. Not her *self*. Not her soul. A body was a cheap, temporary thing anyway. She didn't realize Xanthus had been watching her—staring intently at the emotions playing out over her face.

"You still don't trust me, do you?" he asked.

"You shouldn't trust me either. We're strangers."

"That's true," Xanthus conceded. He put down his cup and sat down at the foot of his bed, leaning back to rest against the wall. "So ask me something. What do you want to know?"

Attia wasn't sure she had heard him correctly. "What?"

"I'll tell you anything you want to know about me. But the information isn't free."

Of course not.

Attia clenched her hands around her cup, trying to keep from shaking or striking or both. Hopefully, in the dimness of the candlelight, he didn't notice. She didn't want him to know what her control was costing her. She waited to hear his proposal.

"You have to tell me about yourself, too," he said.

Now she was sure she hadn't heard him properly. "Why?" she said, her voice harsh with suspicion.

"Because I'm curious. And because I'd rather be friends if we're going to have to share this little room from now on." He smiled gently as Attia narrowed her eyes at him. "Look, I'm offering you a deal: a question for a question. The Romans call it quid pro quo. You can go first." He gestured to the half-empty bed. "And you don't have to stand all night."

Attia considered the space between them, a mere four feet of separation. She'd known warriors all her life. Men who were meaner, colder, more bloodthirsty than this gladiator could ever hope to be. The Romans called him a god, but Attia could see in his face a sort of regret, as though it was a curse rather than a gift for him to be so good at what he did. In that moment, she realized something that surprised her: She couldn't quite trust the man, but she didn't want to kill him.

She approached the bed slowly and sat down on the opposite end.

Xanthus didn't give any indication that he minded the distance. In fact, he looked rather pleased that she'd sat down at all. He smiled at her—a bright smile that reminded Attia of spring—and folded his hands on his stomach.

Attia cocked her head, staring at the gladiator with blatant curiosity. "Who *are* you? That is, you're obviously not a Roman."

"Obviously?"

"Your accent—you sound like a northerner, though you speak the Vulgate well enough. And you don't have that *look*. . . . That . . . hunger."

Xanthus frowned thoughtfully. "Well, you're right. I'm not a Roman. I'm from Britannia."

Now *that* was surprising. More than a decade ago, when the Romans first ventured onto that lonely northern island, Attia's father had shaken his head, closed his eyes, and said, "The world is falling." She'd only been a child so she hadn't understood what he meant at the time. She understood now.

"Nearly everything is green in Britannia," Xanthus continued with a wistful smile. "Mist hugs the land, the trees, and the hills. And when the sun rises in the morning, the light pierces through the fog and paints the grass a thousand colors." The smile started to fade when he turned to Attia. "My turn. Who taught you to fight? I saw what you did to Ennius, but I didn't realize the Maedi trained their daughters as well."

Attia chose her words carefully. "Mine was a . . . unique circumstance."

"Was your father a warrior?"

"That's two questions."

"But you didn't really answer my first one. Come on, Attia. Play fair. Tell me something about him."

"He lived with courage," she said. "And he died the same way."

Xanthus's face softened with sympathy. "How?" he asked.

Attia tried to push it away—tried to reject the familiar nightmare, but it found her anyway, as it always did. And again, the memory was just as clear, just as brutal. But she didn't describe any of it for the gladiator. She didn't even want to see it herself. "A Roman named Crassus Flavius murdered him and then took me out of spite," she said. "After the invasion, everyone else was crucified. I am the last of them."

Xanthus's face contorted.

"I don't want your pity," she said quickly.

But he shook his head., "It's not pity."

Understanding dawned. "The same thing happened to your people," Attia said.

Xanthus looked away. "Crassus came. My village burned. And my mother . . ." He swallowed hard. "I lost everything, too."

There was more to his story, she could tell. More that he was holding back, just as she had. But she could see his mind working and saw the instant that his face lit up with a sudden realization.

He sat up quickly. "By the goddess," he whispered. "Sparro? Your father was *Sparro*, the war-king of Thrace?"

Attia was a little shocked that he'd figured it out so quickly. A tiny crack was forming in the wall she'd so diligently built around her, but she met Xanthus's eyes straight on. She tried to suppress her sudden wariness, her need to strike at something. She waited to see what he would do next.

"I never even knew he had a daughter," he said. "Everyone assumed the swordlord's heir was a son."

Attia couldn't help snorting at that. Of course they thought so. It was an ignorant assumption that had undoubtedly saved her life. That day on the hillside, the Romans had only seen one young girl who valiantly tried and failed to protect an old king.

More of her people might have been spared if they had simply surrendered, but that word was nearly unknown to Thracians. There wasn't even a true equivalent in their language. The Romans killed so many because they *had* to, because Thracians would never stop fighting and the only way to defeat them was through annihilation. Still, even *if* Thrace had surrendered, Attia doubted that any of the men would have been allowed to live. As the champion said, they thought the swordlord's heir was a boy.

Xanthus was still looking at her, this time with sad wonder in his eyes. "No wonder you wanted to kill me. No wonder you could have. Gods, we're not equals at all. You're royalty." Coming from him, the word sent chills across her skin. "You're a Maedi princess."

Was, she corrected silently. She *was* one of the Maedi. She *was* a princess.

Xanthus relaxed back against the wall and actually chuckled. "A *princess.*"

Attia pulled her legs up underneath her and rested her head against the wall. "And you, a northern barbarian." There was a light, teasing note in her voice that Xanthus immediately responded to.

"Well, you know what they say about barbarians . . . ," he said with a grin.

Attia couldn't help it. She laughed. For the first time in what felt like a lifetime, she laughed—unrestrained and genuine, as though the tragedy of her existence had been erased, just for that one moment.

When she finally got her breath back, she and Xanthus were leaning together against the wall, their shoulders nearly touching. "Your turn again," he said.

Wanting to push away the memories of war and loss, Attia asked an entirely different question. "What kind of animals do you have in Britannia?"

Xanthus watched her sleep as pale gray light filled the room. It was nearly dawn, but he didn't want to wake her. Not yet.

She looked different in sleep. Younger. Softer. Her lips were slightly parted. Her hand rested by her temple. Her neat braid had come partially undone in the night, and strands of dark hair curled around her face. Every now and then, her eyelashes fluttered. What—or who—was she dreaming about?

They'd talked long into the night, until their voices became hoarse. Until their memories hung like bright lights all around them. Xanthus saw sparks of silver in her dark gray eyes every time she laughed, and he found he couldn't look away from her. And when she fell asleep, her head drifted down to his pillow, and her hand—her hand fell perfectly into his. It was so unlike that first night when she couldn't kill him and he couldn't watch her grieve. He didn't want to move an inch, not even when his arm tingled with numbness and his lids became heavy. After a while, she turned over with a sigh. But he still felt the warmth of her skin against his for hours after.

Xanthus had known strong women in his life, but not like her. Even if she hadn't been one of the legendary Maedi, there was a brightness inside her, a core of fire that burned steadily beneath her scarred bronze skin.

Now, there she was. In his bed. Because of Timeus.

Seeing her nearly break the first night had been almost painful, and the memory of it made him shrug his shoulders as though he could throw off that heavy mantle of guilt he'd worn for so long. Attia grieved for her people, as he did. Now who was to blame for her condition? The Romans, yes. Crassus and Timeus, certainly. But what about Xanthus? What did you call a slave who agreed to enslave another?

Self-disgust boiled in his stomach. The gods were taunting him. Wasn't this the nightmare that resurrected itself every Samhain? He'd saved his mother by taking her life when the Romans came. Was he saving the Thracian by taking her freedom? Maybe a man's crimes could be placed on the scales, weighed and measured for wickedness. So, he asked himself again—what did that make him? The possibilities made him shudder.

Xanthus leaned his head back against the wall and shut his eyes. At least there was one other thing he could give her—his silence. No one else knew who she really was, and as Xanthus watched her sleep, he swore an oath to the goddess that he would never reveal her true identity. He would die before that happened.

A soft knock at the door grabbed his attention. He wondered if it was Sabina come to save Attia from his vicious ways. He ignored it, wanting just a few more quiet moments.

The knock came again, louder, more insistent. Then someone slammed a closed fist against the door.

There were stumbling footsteps, and Iduma shouted, "You ass!"

Lebuin laughed loudly. "Well you shouldn't have had your ear to the door!"

"Step aside, ladies," Albinus said.

Xanthus jumped to his feet just as Albinus pushed the door open.

Attia was still fast asleep. Her slender figure was partially covered by the blanket, and her hair was spread out like a fan. She mumbled a word before turning over to face the wall. Xanthus thought it was probably the first deep sleep she'd had since she arrived.

The gladiators were staring wide-eyed, completely still. And Xanthus had had enough.

He positioned himself in the doorway, blocking their view and pushing them out the door.

Albinus lost his balance and grabbed Iduma's tunic. Iduma fell back onto Lebuin, who stepped on Gallus's foot. Then they all tumbled to the ground. Only Castor remained standing, and he took a deliberate step back to separate himself from the heap.

"What the hell are you doing?" Xanthus demanded in a harsh

whisper, holding the door partially closed behind him. He didn't want to wake Attia just yet.

Albinus grunted and struggled to his feet. He pushed off Iduma's face before standing and rubbing awkwardly at the back of his neck. "Time for training," he grumbled.

Gallus stood next but didn't say anything.

Iduma took his time getting up and thoughtfully scratched his cheek. "I didn't realize the Thracian was so pretty. Fair as a princess," he said, raising his eyebrows and giving an appreciative chuckle.

Xanthus extended one arm and shoved Iduma back to the ground. He landed with a thud and a puff of dust while Xanthus turned back into the room and closed the door behind him.

Iduma looked up at the others. "What did I say?"

Inside, Attia opened one eye and glanced around. "What's going on?" she mumbled.

"Just some pests," Xanthus told her. "Go back to sleep."

"Is it morning?" she asked.

"Not yet."

But within minutes the training yard rang with the sounds of sparring gladiators, iron meeting wood, and blows striking their targets. Soft sunlight streamed in through the open window.

Attia opened her eyes. "It's morning."

They didn't speak as she rose from his bed. Even after the previous night, the air between them still felt strange and new.

Then Xanthus remembered something he'd meant to give her. He touched her arm as she passed, and she looked up with surprise but no fear. That was something, he figured.

He reached onto the nearby shelf for the little knife she'd once threatened him with and laid it gently in her open palm. "Keep it hidden," he said.

She nodded once, turned, and left the room.

CHAPTER 8

Two days later, a small party arrived at the villa—Timeus's sister Valeria and her children, apparently returning from an extended holiday in Naples. A holiday from what, Attia couldn't imagine. But they carted along enough baggage to fill half of the main courtyard.

Attia was sitting again on a window ledge on the upper floor, her bucket and rags at her feet. She had the little knife in her hand and was absently spinning it around and around, her fingers already familiar with the blade's shape and weight.

Even from this distance, the family resemblance was clear. Like her brother, the domina had vivid blue eyes that stared out from a pale face. She was nearly as tall as Timeus and thin as a sapling, with narrow fingers that reminded Attia of twigs. Only when the siblings stood together did the differences between them become apparent. Valeria was probably more than ten years her brother's junior, and while Timeus's hair had turned white and silver with age, Valeria's was still as curly and blond as a young girl's. Her face was warmer, too. She looked like she was quick to laugh, with all the little lines around her eyes and mouth.

A young man who was undoubtedly Valeria's son dismounted from his horse. Attia's immediate impression of him was of a boy playing at being a soldier. His light brown hair shone in the sun, and his face was soft in ways that were unlike either Valeria or Timeus. He was taller than his mother and uncle, slender but not thin. He wore a jeweled dagger at his belt that looked more like an ornament than a weapon. He quickly greeted his uncle before hurrying to a closed cart.

Attia watched as he entered it, only to emerge a few minutes later with a large bundle of linen in his arms. She frowned. *What the hell?* Then she remembered what Sabina had said—that Valeria had *children*. Was that bundle of cloth one of them? Valeria's son disappeared into the villa before Attia could get a better look.

Bored again, she grabbed her bucket and went to another room and another window, one from which she could watch the gladiators in the training yard.

Since her arrival, she'd focused all of her energy on surviving, on healing, on reclaiming her old self just enough to kill Timeus and, if need be, follow her family into the underworld. But now that she knew of Crassus, everything seemed to shift. She had so little left to live for except revenge. She hated Timeus, yes, and she consoled herself with the thought of killing him before she made her escape. Still, if anyone deserved to taste her blade, it was the bastard who'd murdered her father. She'd just have to find him first.

She spun the knife around once more before hiding it in the folds of her tunic.

In the training yard below, the blond, scarred gladiator was fighting. Attia knew that violence and ruthlessness simmered just below the surface of most men, but it was particularly plain in that one. She could see the anger etched into his soul as permanently as the scars on his skin. She didn't fault him for it. She had been raised by violent, ruthless men. She had been trained to be one of them, to lead them. If anything, she was more like the gladiators than the rest of the slaves.

When her mother died, Attia had felt like the world had broken in half, like she was straddling the abyss. She was the last of her mother, with a face so similar that it broke her father's heart, and yet she was also her father's daughter and heir. It fell on her to fulfill the destiny of the brother she would never have, and while her people gave their love without question, some still had reservations about following a woman into battle someday. Attia had relieved them of that doubt on her eleventh birthday.

By then, she had been training for almost five straight years, memorizing the curves of blades and the weight of a full quiver. Calluses covered her hands, and her knees were constantly skinned from tumbling around in the sparring yard. For a while, even her hair was cut short for convenience and uniformity. She'd always been smaller, shorter than most. But her training made her strong enough, and a stranger might easily have mistaken her for just another Thracian boy if it weren't for the names.

They'd started out mildly—silly transformations like *A-tik-tok* or the *Girl Prince*—and eventually became completely new renditions, the favorite being *Spattia, Spawn of Sparro*. Attia still remembered the high tenor of their taunts, the sounds of growing boys learning to be men.

And then, one day, she snapped.

One of the older boys had shoved her from behind, and she fell forward onto rough ground.

"Spattia! Spattia!" he chanted. "Spattia! Spa—"

Still on the ground, her hands buried in the dirt, she'd kicked back and up with all her strength, the heel of her foot colliding hard with the boy's face. Everyone heard the sickening crunch of his broken nose right before he fell.

The whole yard was silent as she twisted her skinny body about and leapt to her feet in a technique she'd made up on her own. She stood over the boy with clenched fists and fought the urge to kick him again. "My name is *Attia*," she said to the boys and soldiers gathered around watching.

Groaning, the boy covered his nose with his hands. His eyes stared at her with a mixture of fear and admiration. Only after he nodded did she step back and let him stand. He was almost a foot taller than she.

No one called her names again after that. Jezrael—the boy she'd fought—became her closest friend, nearly a brother. From that day on, Attia had often caught her father watching her with pride. He finally believed she would make a fine Maedi after all.

That future was dead. But below the scars and the wounds that would never heal, there was still the spirit of a swordlord's heir.

Whatever it took, Attia knew she had to find Crassus. She had to make him pay.

The gladiators paused in their training to drink from the barrel of fresh water at the wall of the training yard. Gone were the jests and laughter from the days before. After what Albinus had said, their training had changed. It had to.

Xanthus was sipping from his cup when he noticed his

brothers go still around him. Their faces went blank and their hands tightened their holds on their cups. Even their eyes turned down to the ground, as though they couldn't see or hear a thing.

Turning to the archway of the training yard, Xanthus saw the reason why. He put down his cup and extended his right hand. "Welcome home, Master Lucius."

Lucius, Timeus's nephew, glanced awkwardly at the others as he grasped Xanthus's hand. Xanthus thought he was still too slender for a man of nearly eighteen. He turned Lucius's hand over in his, examining the smooth texture of his palms.

"No calluses," Xanthus said. "You haven't been practicing."

Lucius blushed. "Something I hope to remedy. How are you, Xanthus?"

"The same," Xanthus said, mostly for lack of anything better to say. "How's your arm?"

Lucius grimaced before tugging on his sleeve. A short scar ran along the inner part of his forearm from the time Xanthus had accidentally snapped the bone clean in half with the blunt end of a training sword. Timeus's physicians had been forced to cut into Lucius's arm to repair it.

"I think it's an improvement, actually. Women are always impressed by scars," Lucius said.

Someone snorted behind Xanthus—probably Albinus—but he ignored it. "You're welcome to join us in training, Master Lucius," Xanthus said loudly enough for the others to hear.

His brothers had never been particularly fond of Lucius, though it wasn't anything personal. It was simply too difficult for them to separate the boy from the family, to see him as anything but the heir to the House of Timeus. But Xanthus sympathized with Lucius. He'd been young once, too—untrained and green around the edges until Ennius taught him.

Lucius looked at the gladiators, who'd moved farther down the training yard. "They really don't like me."

"They're gladiators, Master Lucius. They don't really like anyone or anything, except perhaps fighting."

Lucius nodded. "Oh, that actually reminds me. My uncle asked me to extend a message. He says he hopes you're enjoying your gift. What did he get you?"

Xanthus turned away so Lucius wouldn't see him grit his teeth. "Your uncle is generous with me," he said simply. He led Lucius into the training yard and tossed him a staff. "Since you haven't been practicing, we'll start with the basics."

Looking slightly abashed, Lucius caught the staff and tried to ignore the glowers of the other gladiators.

It was midafternoon and warm. A weighty quiet had descended on the estate as the household took its brief daily rest. Attia cut through the western dining room to avoid the guards, thinking she could get to the upper levels and back to Timeus's study unnoticed. But as soon as she entered the dining room, she found a young man struggling to lift a cup of wine to his lips.

She watched him silently for a few seconds before speaking. "Problems?" she asked.

His head jerked up, and his grip involuntarily tightened on the cup. He sucked air through his teeth, trying not to look like he was in such obvious pain.

"I'm fine," he said.

Attia cocked her head at him as recognition dawned. "You're Timeus's nephew."

"Unfortunately," he grumbled, frowning as he tried to get a better grip on the cup.

That one response made Attia smile, and she decided that

nephew or not, maybe she could spare him the benefit of the doubt.

As she slowly approached him, she saw the blisters raging across both palms. She'd had her share of aches and pains from her own training. Really, he should have known better. He could have at least wrapped his hands to protect himself from the rough leather binding on the practice swords. His injuries—if she could even call them that—were his own fault.

When he caught her staring, he put his cup down and tried to hide his hands behind his back. Attia tried not to laugh.

He grumbled again. "It's not funny."

"Forgive me for *not* laughing, Timeus's nephew."

"My name is Lucius, and these are serious wounds, you know. I could have died in the practice yard."

Attia nodded seriously. "Many warriors have succumbed to such hurts."

"I sparred with the *Champion of Rome*. That's not nothing."

"It's rather heroic, in fact."

"Perhaps you could make yourself useful then and help me bind these up." He lifted his hands into the air. The blisters really did look angry. They'd already started to seep.

Attia shook her head with feigned pity, and a short while later, she and Lucius were sitting side by side on a bench just outside of the dining room, Sabina's basket of linen and salves between them.

"You really should have asked Sabina to do this," Attia said, sniffing cautiously at one of the jars. "I'm not a healer. You'll be lucky if you don't lose your hands entirely." She took a generous scoop of the salve that Sabina had instructed her to use and began rubbing it vigorously into Lucius's palms.

He flinched and pulled away. "Gods, you might just take my hands off after all. Aren't women supposed to be gentle?"

"Aren't men supposed to be fearless? Hold still. I can't do this if you keep squirming."

He held his hands up and out of her reach. "You don't need to rub so hard."

Attia raised an eyebrow and tried not to smirk.

A deep blush worked its way up from beneath the collar of Lucius's tunic. Lacking a decent response, he held out his hands again and only hissed a little when she touched the ointment to them.

"You probably shouldn't have practiced for so long," she told him.

"The gladiators train all day every day."

"Their survival depends on their training. Anyway, you're not a gladiator."

"A man should still know how to handle a sword."

"Why? Your uncle has guards posted all over the estate."

"You wouldn't understand. You're only a—" He paused.

"I'm only a what? A slave?"

He shook his head. "I was going to say that you're only a woman."

A harsh laugh broke out of Attia. "Well, that's *much* better."

He shook his head again, fighting another blush, and his shoulders seemed to sink just a little. "I mean no offense. It's just that no one ever expects anything of women. You only have to look pretty and marry someone and give him children. But my father was the Legatus Lucius Bassus. He led an army through Herodium and sacked the mountain fortress in less than three weeks. He and Crassus nearly conquered Jerusalem. Vespasian became Princeps because of my father. I am the only son of one of the greatest generals Rome has ever seen. I am the last to carry on his name, to bring greatness to the house that he built. And . . ." he looked down and away. "And I'm nothing compared to him."

Attia had to swallow hard past the lump in her throat. She had no idea why he was telling her this, but she had to acknowledge the irony in the fact that she probably understood the weight of a father's legacy better than anyone. She carried it with her every second of every day. No one but Xanthus knew who she was, and that was a blessing but also a curse. Her anonymity ensured her survival. But her father's name would die with her.

Lucius's voice softened as he stared out over the wall. "Xanthus reminds me of him sometimes. Not in look or manner, exactly, but in other ways. I've never said this out loud, but I think my father would have liked to have Xanthus for a son. He's intelligent and brave. Men would follow him straight into the underworld. Slave or no."

Attia pursed her lips and paused before asking, "Where is your father now?"

"He died in Machaerus when I was twelve—the year my sister was born. It wasn't in battle. He contracted some sickness. No one knows exactly what, only that one day he had a fever and the next day he was dead. Titus himself delivered the news to my mother."

"Is that when you came to live here? With your uncle?"

Lucius nodded. "It's been nearly six years, but this house still doesn't feel like home."

They sat in silence as Attia finished wrapping his hands in the linen and tied it off with a neat knot.

Lucius flexed his fingers. "Well, you managed to save my hands. Thank you."

"Not half bad for a woman, wouldn't you say?"

He sighed. "You're irritated with me."

"What would you do if I said I was?"

"Apologize again?"

"Is that a question?"

"This coming from the person who likes to answer all of my questions with more questions?"

"Oh, so I'm a *person* now?"

He raised his bandaged hands in front of him. "Truce, please, truce. This is exhausting."

"Well, now you've had your first real lesson on women—never argue with one."

"Perhaps I should practice sparring with you instead of the gladiators," he said with a sudden grin. "Then again, I might lose more than my hands."

"Yes. You might."

"I don't know anything about children," Attia said for the third time.

"Then you'll have to learn. Mistress Aurora's nursemaid took sick in Naples and couldn't return with the household. The child needs someone to watch over her during the day. And we both know you haven't exactly been doing any of the other chores I've assigned you."

Attia frowned and looked away. "What am I supposed to do with a little girl?"

"You were a little girl once, too, Attia," Sabina said.

Attia nearly snorted. She'd been a little girl in a Maedi camp. She couldn't very well teach Timeus's niece to wield a sword now, could she?

"Just figure it out and take care of her. She's not allowed outside anyway. How difficult can it possibly be?" Sabina said.

Attia sighed. They both knew that Sabina couldn't force her to do anything, but they also both knew that Attia would never willingly hurt a child. Oh, she'd ruin linens and burn pork and leave rooms dirtier than they were when she first went in. But a little girl? It seemed Sabina had finally found a responsibility that Attia couldn't completely shrug off.

Attia was still grumbling to herself about children and nurse-maids as she climbed the steps to the upper floor. She paused when she reached the landing, her eyes looking to the east wing, where Timeus's study was located. With a heavy sigh, she turned in the opposite direction and made her way down the hall. She'd passed through these rooms numerous times on her half-hearted rounds of cleaning. Now she ignored them and walked straight to a small door with a ringed handle. Attia glowered at the thing for a long moment before finally pushing the door open.

The only light in the room came from a few candles on the window ledges. The shutters had been pulled closed, prevent-ing sunlight from entering the room. A small bed with patterned blankets was nestled in one corner. And the young mistress Aurora Bassus sat alone in front of a low-burning fire, tracing symbols in the ash that coated the floor there.

The child was small and very thin. She reminded Attia of a baby bird who hadn't yet left the nest. In the dim light, Attia could see that the girl's skin was incredibly pale, but deep au-burn curls framed her heart-shaped face.

Attia took another step into the room. "Mistress Aurora?"

The child smiled up at her. "Please don't call me that. Any-way, my proper name is very long. Do you want to hear it? It's Aurora Morgana Alexandria Bassus. But my brother calls me Rory because when I was a baby, I couldn't say my name, so he shortened it up for me. You're Attia. I know because they told me. It's a pretty name. What does it mean? Are you named after someone? Lucius is named after our father, but I'm not named after anyone. I never even knew Father. He died in battle somewhere a long, long, long time ago just before I was born, so I wouldn't remember him anyway. I only remember Mother and Lucius. He sings for me, you know."

Attia stood staring at the girl, unsure what to say. For a sickly child, little Rory could certainly talk. Probably because she didn't have many people to talk to. Attia glanced at the closed windows.

"I can't be in the sun," Rory explained. "There's something wrong with my skin. If the sunlight touches me, I'll burn up and die." She said it all quite matter-of-factly, as though she was reciting the words from a well-rehearsed lesson.

"Oh," Attia said.

Rory smiled. "It's all right. You don't have to feel sorry for me. How old are you?"

"Almost eighteen."

"That makes you . . ."—Rory counted quickly on her fingers— "almost twelve years older than me—just like Lucius! There are lots of years between us because Mother didn't want another child. I was an accident. But Lucius says that he and father *both* wanted me, so that evens out, right? Lucius is my best friend." She frowned and wrinkled her little nose. "Well, I don't have any other friends, but he's the best one. Maybe now, *we* can be friends!"

Attia looked around uncomfortably. "I don't think your family would find that . . . appropriate."

"Mother doesn't like anything that other people do. Lucius calls her a hippo." Rory bit her lip. "No, that's not right. A hiccup?"

"A hypocrite?"

"That's it! Lucius would like you. You're pretty and smart and the girls he usually courts are only just pretty. I never get to talk to them either, but sometimes I sneak out of my room—just to see. You can't tell anyone though," she said. Her voice suddenly became so soft that Attia could barely hear her. "Lucius is my best friend, but he doesn't know what it's like."

"What what's like?"

"Being alone," Rory said.

Attia swallowed past a lump in her throat. "No, he wouldn't know about that, would he?"

Rory was quiet for a moment. "Would you like to draw with me?"

So Attia sat beside the girl near the fire, drawing random symbols in the ash for what felt like hours. Rory kept glancing back at the closed windows with a hopeful look on her face, and when the sun finally set, she jumped to her feet, pushed the candles aside, and swung the shutters open.

From the northern window, there was a clear view of the coastline and even a bit of the gladiators' training yard. If Attia craned her neck just a bit, she could see the red "X" that marked the lintel over Xanthus's door.

"You have to go now, don't you?" Rory asked.

"Yes, but I'll come back tomorrow."

"Promise?"

Attia knelt beside the little girl and found herself smiling. "I promise."

A light breeze rustled through the trees and plants that bordered the estate walls. The promise of winter lingered in the evening air, though she doubted the weather would be too harsh so far south. It wouldn't be anything like a winter on the Aegean—gray and angry, with salty winds and waves strong enough to drown a ship.

As Attia passed through the main courtyard on her way to

Xanthus's quarters, a beam of light caught her attention. It bounced along the ground, following the uneven line of the shrubbery and drawing random circles on the wall. If the guards at the gate noticed, they didn't seem to care.

Attia's step didn't falter, but she looked back to the upper window of the villa, where Rory held a small mirror in her hand. Her chin rested along one folded arm, and her head lolled from side to side in apparent boredom. As soon as she saw Attia watching, she ducked down to hide beneath the window. She wasn't very good at it; her little fingers still clutched the windowsill.

Attia turned away from the window, but after a few more steps, she glanced back with a grin and caught Rory peeking at her through her fingers. The child smiled, and Attia heard a faint giggle before the girl ducked down again to hide below the window. Attia looked back once more before she reached the training courtyard, and this time the girl didn't hide. Attia could only make out a few of her features in the moonlight— namely the fierce auburn curls that surrounded the girl's face like a halo.

Growing up in her father's camp, Attia had only had boys to keep her company, and training had always taken precedence over child's play. So she was surprised by how charming she found the strange little girl in the window. She'd never thought of herself as someone who cared much about children.

Attia raised her hand in a little wave just as Xanthus's door opened a few feet away. She smiled faintly and shook her head as she entered his quarters.

"What's so funny?" Xanthus asked, his face open and curi- ous, ready to laugh along at whatever joke she might share.

Again, he looked different to Attia. Not the stoic champion or the contrite killer or even the playful barbarian. No, he looked calm. Still. A bit tired. Attia wondered what version of Xanthus she was seeing now.

"I'm to play nursemaid to Timeus's niece," Attia said in a mocking tone before her voice softened. "But she's actually a sweet girl. I didn't expect that."

"I've never really seen her. They say she's quite ill—not allowed outside. Even when the household travels, she's shielded in drapes and curtains."

"I know. The windows in her room were shut tight for most of the day. What kind of sickness doesn't let you go outside?"

Xanthus shrugged. "A very bad one?"

Attia rolled her eyes. "Romans are strange."

"Not at all. They're simple, really."

"Are they? Enlighten me, oh championed one," Attia teased, bowing forward with a smile.

But Xanthus's face had gone cold. "They're wolves torn between pack mentality and inflated ambition. They'll kill and betray as it suits them with little regard for anyone else."

The smile faded from Attia's face.

"Don't tell me you disagree, Thracian."

"I don't," Attia said softly.

They stood in awkward silence until Xanthus grabbed a blanket and spread it out on the floor. His movements seemed more rigid, and his face looked strained as he blew out the candles.

"I'll sleep on the floor tonight," Attia offered. "I'm more used to it, and you can't keep giving me your bed."

Xanthus shook his head. "No, you take it."

"No, it's *your* bed." She tried to move past him to the blanket on the floor.

"No, Attia. Take the bed," he said, his voice hardening as he tried to usher her away.

"No, you!"

She pushed back against him as his hand brushed lightly against her breast. They both pulled away so quickly that they lost their balance and tumbled to the floor. Xanthus managed to break his fall with an outstretched arm and caught Attia as she literally fell into his lap.

They froze. Two hardened, experienced fighters with countless kills and victories, and all either of them could do in that moment was stare stupidly at the other.

A fierce blush began working its way from Attia's neck to her scalp. The only time she'd ever been so close to a man was, well, to kill him. Or maim him. But she didn't think those experiences were particularly relevant at the moment. She bit her lip.

Xanthus's hand rested against Attia's waist, holding her to him. His eyes grazed over her face, and he slowly raised his hand to touch her cheek.

Attia inhaled sharply. Somehow this touch felt a thousand times more intimate than her head on his shoulder or falling asleep in his bed. Still, she didn't resist when his fingers moved to her jaw then down to her neck. The slow movement, the warmth, the solidness of him against her—it almost made her ignore the constant undercurrent of bitterness that hummed through her core. It almost made her forget where she was. *What* she was.

Almost.

Xanthus hadn't hurt her. He'd never even said an unkind word to her. But he was a prize in Timeus's house and a champion of the Republic she despised. To everyone around them, he rightfully *owned* her, and that was something she could never forget.

He said nothing as she pulled away from him and crawled into his bed, turning her face to the wall. After a few moments, he lay down on his blanket and turned the opposite way.

✦ ✦ ✦

Attia walked through the villa, trying not to think about the previous night. Every time she imagined the hurt look on Xanthus's face when she pulled away, she wanted to cringe. It was better to focus on more important things, like getting back into Timeus's study.

She'd managed to memorize the Flavian family tree, and she had a clear idea of the route she could take through the city. But she needed more information: Where was Crassus? Was he on a campaign? If not, where did he live? Was his residence on Palatine Hill? Breaking into the Princeps's palace would be difficult, but not necessarily impossible.

Attia's mind was whirling with plans when she turned a corner and walked right into a lithe figure dressed in black—the woman she'd seen only in glimpses throughout the villa. All she could do was stare.

The woman's thick dark hair was pulled back in the Roman style, all curls and elaborate twists. The neckline of her tight-fitting gown plunged low between her breasts, but Attia guessed that was the point. She was beautiful in an almost inhuman sort of way. Her body curved in all the right places, but her solemn expression made her face seem angular and harsh. She looked more like a statue than flesh and blood. Maybe because of that, Attia couldn't quite determine the woman's age. She was older than Attia, though not by much. Her light brown skin was still smooth and free of wrinkles, but her eyes—Attia could see the shadows lurking in their dark depths.

The woman considered Attia for a moment. "You must be the Thracian," she said. Her voice was deeper than Attia expected. "I've heard about you. You belong to the champion."

Attia huffed in irritation. *I don't belong to anyone.* She nearly said as much when the woman spoke again.

"I belong to the dominus," she said, and something flashed in her eyes but was gone too quickly for Attia to interpret. "What are you doing up here?"

"Cleaning."

The woman glanced at Attia's empty bucket and dry rags. "I see," she said. "Well, the domina has called for us both to attend her. Come with me."

Attia stayed where was. She'd be damned if she let Timeus's concubine boss her around.

The woman raised her eyebrow. "Unless, of course, you'd like to explain to the dominus why you didn't come when called."

Attia narrowed her eyes. She had no choice. She'd just have to get back to the study later.

The woman led Attia to Valeria's quarters on the other side of the villa. Attia hadn't explored that part of the house yet. In stark contrast to the grandiosity of Timeus's formal rooms, a playful whimsy embellished the décor of Valeria's quarters. Pale silk drapes hung everywhere, sweeping along the walls and pillars, covering open doorways and archways. There were statues as well—graceful nymphs lined the hallway, watching Attia with their enigmatic smiles frozen in marble.

In an open, airy room, Valeria sat at an elaborate vanity by an arched window. Her blond hair was curled and piled up on her head with copper pins. A mirror perched atop the vanity—easily the largest Attia had ever seen—and reflected more of the furniture within the room, including a massive bed covered with tunics, shawls, ribbons, and gowns.

"What do you think of this one, Lucretia?" Valeria asked, looking at her reflection but clearly addressing the concubine.

She held an elaborate gold-and-emerald necklace against her pale throat, angling it one way, then another.

"Quite bold, Domina," Lucretia said as she walked up behind Valeria. "But perhaps the sapphires will best complement your coloring."

Valeria frowned but kept still as Lucretia picked up the sapphire necklace and clasped it around her neck.

"Yes, I suppose you're right," Valeria said. "I always did favor blue."

Attia's gaze slowly shifted from the mirror down to the massive tray that held Valeria's jewels. There were so many stones— so many pieces of gold, silver, and bronze—that she couldn't even distinguish them all. It was like Valeria's personal version of Timeus's jeweled mosaics: a dazzling, sickening display of wealth.

"With that, perhaps the cream-colored stola with the sash," Lucretia said.

But Valeria ignored her, training her eyes on Attia. "So you are my daughter's new nursemaid. I am told she is fond of you." She looked Attia up and down, much the same way Lucretia had just a few minutes ago in the hallway. "I am told the champion is fond of you as well. You must be a girl of many talents."

Attia felt her face flush. She turned her eyes to the floor so Valeria wouldn't see the anger beginning to simmer there.

"Hmm," Valeria said. "Lucretia, not the cream stola. Pick something else. The girl can start on my paints."

It took Attia a moment to realize that Valeria was referring to *her*, and when she did, she turned to stare wide-eyed at Lucretia. The woman didn't even look at her. Instead, she turned and busied herself with the domina's many gowns.

"Well, what are you waiting for?" Valeria demanded.

Attia gingerly approached the vanity, looking helplessly at

the dozens of assorted jars, tubes, cups, and bowls scattered among Valeria's jewels. All of them were filled with contents that she couldn't even identify, let alone know how to apply. The colors were just as varied, ranging from deep reds and bright oranges to light pinks and black pastes.

Valeria shifted in her seat, turning her back to the mirror, closing her eyes, and raising her face to Attia. Behind them, Lucretia carefully collected the domina's discarded gowns and began folding them up again.

Attia hesitantly reached for the bowl of pale cream, cradling it in one hand as she dipped a single finger in. It was cool to the touch and thicker than she expected. Biting her lip, she started to spread it on Valeria's cheeks and forehead. Valeria sighed with contentment.

"I purchased this lavender cream in Naples, you know," she said. "It's the best I've ever found for filling wrinkles."

Attia released a small breath. At least she was using that one correctly.

"You don't have wrinkles, Domina," Lucretia said.

Valeria scoffed, but a pleased smile crossed her lips. "I don't look my age, do I? Not even two children could rob me of my figure. Let Flavius choke on that."

The name made Attia stiffen with interest. She dipped her fingers into the cream again and mindlessly added another layer to Valeria's face, her attention focused on the woman's continued chattering.

"Titus could barely hold that wife of his for a year. What does he know about women? His cousin Tycho is a toad, and if Crassus weren't a father, I'd wonder if he'd ever bedded a woman at all."

Lucretia muttered in agreement, though Attia wasn't sure if she was even listening.

"Married three times and only one son. What does that tell

you?" Valeria said with a smirk. The expression quickly turned bitter. "And if he sired any daughters, well, I wouldn't be surprised if those girls were plucked from their mothers' breasts and thrown into the Tyrrhenian. We all know how Flavians treat their women." Her mouth curved in a grimace.

Attia wore a ferocious frown as she listened to Valeria. Was all that true or was Valeria simply repeating some cruel rumor? But Attia thought of the complete lack of women on the Flavian family tree in Timeus's study, and chills blossomed across her back.

"Of course, my brother hopes the Princeps will be at the next match," Valeria was saying. "As long as Crassus and the Toad stay at Palatine Hill, I'll be fine."

So that's where Crassus was staying. It made sense. Where did a soldier go when he returned from war or a massacre? Home, of course.

The irony of the situation wasn't lost on Attia. She'd wanted to go to Timeus's study to look for information on Crassus. Who knew that she could simply have visited Timeus's sister and listened to the latest gossip?

The corner of Attia's mouth lifted in a muted smile, and she focused her gaze on Valeria's face. The woman's already pale skin was practically white now—thickly layered with the special lavender cream from Naples. Attia quickly put the bowl down and searched for another color to put some life back into the older woman's skin. She found a jar of something red, and when she removed the cork lid, the scent of wax wafted out.

The stuff inside was stiffer than the cream, more solid. Attia vigorously rubbed the surface with the pad of her finger to pick up the color, and then tried to apply it to Valeria's cheeks. But the pigment was just as unyielding on skin as it was in the jar. Two bright red spots stood out on Valeria's high cheekbones, and no matter how Attia rubbed at them, the color refused to fade or blend away.

Attia quickly grabbed a shallow plate of bronze powder from the vanity. With a piece of linen, she spread the powder all over Valeria's face, focusing mostly on the red spots. She stood back to consider her handiwork.

Well, the red spots *had* diminished, and Valeria no longer looked pale. No, now she just looked as though she'd been burnt too strongly by the sun. Or acquired some foul infection in Naples.

Attia glanced over her shoulder at Lucretia, who was still busying herself with Valeria's gowns. There'd be no help from her, apparently. Attia scowled with irritation and snatched the jar of black paste from the vanity. It wasn't as thick as the red stuff, nor as soft as the cream, but it stuck to her finger like tar. Not wanting to get the black paste all over her hands, she selected a thin brush and swirled its stiff bristles around in the pot. She bit her lip in concentration as she slowly drew thick lines along Valeria's blonde lashes—a look that Timeus's concubine seemed to favor. Attia allowed herself a satisfied smile before drawing matching strokes along Valeria's bottom lashes.

Only when Valeria opened her eyes again did Attia get a good look at the horror she'd wrought.

Oh. Gods.

"Don't forget the lips, girl," Valeria said—oblivious—and closed her eyes again.

Lucretia chose that moment to approach. She took one look at Valeria, and her blank expression changed to one of shock. Her jaw dropped, her eyes widened, and she clapped her hands to her mouth in an obvious effort to keep from laughing.

Attia aimed a furious scowl at her as she reached once more for the bowl of red goo. That seemed to knock Lucretia back to reality, because the neutral mask fell into place again, and she took the bowl from Attia's hand.

"I'll finish this up for you, Domina," she said, lightly pushing Attia aside. She didn't meet Attia's eyes, only nudged her head toward the door.

Attia didn't need to be told twice. She hurried out the door, fighting the urge to run and stifling her own laughter as she went.

CHAPTER 9

It was all Valeria's idea.

As Attia returned to the villa from Xanthus's room the next morning, Valeria called to her from the eastern sunroom where she, Lucius, and Timeus were breaking their fast.

"I want to bring her with us, Josias. Rory likes her so much already, and you know, she and Lucretia helped pick my outfit just the other day. Let me bring her," Valeria said in a cloying voice. "She can stay up on the veranda with us. I'm sure she won't bother anyone."

Timeus said nothing at first, though the line of his mouth tightened as his sister chattered on. But after a few minutes, a thought seemed to occur to him and he frowned. "She could watch," he said quietly, almost to himself.

"Yes! Yes, exactly!" Valeria said in her animated voice. "She can attend to me and watch. Wouldn't that be wonderful?"

"And he'll know," Timeus murmured. "He'll know she's there."

"Yes, of course!" Valeria laughed, though she clearly didn't know what Timeus was talking about. "So we'll bring her?"

Timeus turned to glare at Attia. "Yes," he said. "We'll bring her."

The look on his face sent chills racing along Attia's skin.

That afternoon, Attia again found herself being led through the streets of Rome. A slender bronze chain wrapped around her waist and tied her to Valeria's litter as befitting the domina's handmaiden. The chain was more for decoration than anything else—proof to anyone looking that she was property. Four strong slaves carried the litter down the street.

Up ahead, Timeus and Lucius rode in a large draped lectica, a more opulent version of Valeria's stupid basket, with tall gold posts and the backs of over a dozen slaves to carry it. The gladiators followed in the rear, with Xanthus at the front of the group. Attia tried to catch a glimpse of him, but her line of sight was obscured by the other slaves and the crowd.

Turning her face up to the light, Attia tried—for a moment— to forget where she was. But even without looking, she could count the footsteps of Timeus's private guard and distinguish the vigiles from ordinary citizens. She could smell the odor of crowded bodies. She could sense the nearly empty space in the plaza just to the west.

Attia scrutinized the façades of the buildings and measured the distance between the main road and the tiny alleys that branched off in every direction. She could run there, then there. She could use that window and that ledge. That fat vigil wouldn't be much bother, though the young one next to him was fit and athletic.

But this time, the impulse to escape was tamped down by another darker urge. Timeus had to die. She trained her eyes on the back of the old man's head and let her hand brush against the fold in her tunic where she'd hidden the little knife. She knew she couldn't—wouldn't—run while Timeus still drew breath. Besides, if she tried to escape now, it would be like the day of the auction all over again—she'd be hunted through the streets by every vigil in the vicinity, witnessed by hundreds. The only way she could safely run from Timeus's household was if she killed the man first. With no one to chase after her, she could then focus her rage on Crassus.

Consoled by her plans, Attia forced her thoughts back to the present, looked up, and got her first clear look at their destination.

The Coliseum was a massive circular structure, freestanding and made of a neutral-colored stone. The top of it pushed at the clouds, and flocks of birds dipped and dove around its edges. Hundreds, thousands of miniature arches marked the face of it like so many eyes, and a muted roar echoed from its center.

"Gods," Attia whispered.

Valeria sat up in her litter and drew her veil aside. "Construction was completed just last summer. It is a true wonder."

Attia couldn't disagree. Before she came to Rome, she never would have believed that men could build something like this. What a shame that such a magnificent achievement was done for such a bloody purpose.

The caravan reached a high archway at the base of the Coliseum, where a round man greeted Timeus with open arms. He wobbled as he walked and looked like he hadn't been sober in years.

"Timeus, Lucius! And lovely Valeria," he said in what he probably thought was a deep voice but only reminded Attia of a cow passing gas. He took Valeria's hand to kiss it.

"Sisera Trevana, a pleasure," Valeria said, smiling graciously even as she pulled her hand away and wiped it subtly on Attia's sleeve.

They passed through a short tunnel before the group began to split off. A few guards and house slaves accompanied Timeus, Lucius, Valeria, and Sisera to a set of stairs. The rest of the guards, the gladiators, and the slaves who carried the litters turned toward a descending ramp that seemed to lead deep into the bowels of the Coliseum.

Attia turned to Xanthus, hesitant and awkward. Sunlight reflected off a pendant that hung on a leather cord around his neck—a silver crescent moon—and Attia stared at it, not quite willing to meet Xanthus's eyes. She had no idea what to say to him. And she certainly didn't know what to do when Xanthus leaned toward her and kissed her temple. The light caress was so tender and so wildly unexpected that Attia felt a fluttering sensation deep in her belly. Then he turned away and followed the other gladiators down the ramp.

Attia stared at his retreating back until Ennius called her name. Together, they slowly climbed up several flights of shallow stairs to the shaded upper level of the arena.

"I don't know how many times I've had to climb up to some veranda or balcony to watch my boys fight," Ennius said.

"Too many?" Attia suggested.

Ennius smiled bitterly. "Yes. Too many."

A dozen armed guards lined the last few steps, and even more arranged themselves in strategic spots around the veranda. Timeus, Lucius, and Sisera reclined in gilded seats behind a man whose face Attia couldn't see. Valeria and a few women sat behind the men, and Lucretia stood just a few feet away, still as a statue. The rest of the slaves lined the back wall. Attia positioned herself near the edge of the balcony and looked down into the heart of the Coliseum.

It was magnificent. Three stone levels rose up around the arena with smaller rows of seats that doubled as steps. The veranda occupied prime position at one end, not too high nor too low, with heavy awnings to shield its occupants from the sun. The marble railings were ornately carved, and the whole space smelled of incense, probably to mask the copper tang of blood.

The sections closest to the veranda were populated by men in immaculate white robes. Attia guessed they were members of the Senate. Another section was filled with patricians in brightly colored clothing and sparkling jewels. The largest section—the rows farthest from the arena floor—jostled with dirty, hungry people who reached over their neighbors to catch the bread being thrown upward by a row of armed guards.

Panem et circenses, as the Roman poet said. Bread and circuses. Attia had never realized how literal the phrase was.

A short blond-haired woman nudged Attia's arm. "Don't fall over," she said. "I almost fainted the first time my dominus brought me up here to the primum. But perhaps you are made of sterner stuff."

"Your dominus?"

"I belong to Sisera," the woman said. "And I'm guessing you belong to Timeus."

Attia wanted to hit something. "I don't belong to anyone." She felt like she'd said the words a hundred times since she arrived in Rome.

The woman gave her a sad smile. "But you do."

Attia turned her face away.

"They call me Aggie," the woman said. "What do they call you?"

Her choice of phrase struck Attia, who tried to remember where she'd heard it before. "What do you mean by that?" she asked.

"Well, I wasn't born with that name," Aggie said. "I come from Gaul."

And then Attia remembered. Xanthus had said something like that to her. *They call me Xanthus.* It had sounded odd at the time, but Attia hadn't thought of it again. Not until now.

Attia looked back at Aggie. "Then what was your name before?"

"It was Galena. I've always liked it for all that my mother wasn't particularly original. You?"

"I am Attia." But she frowned as she said it. Had Sabina been renamed? What about the other slaves in the household? Her eyes drifted to Timeus's concubine. Had she been given a new name as well?

The man sitting in the first row of the veranda threw something over the rail—a piece of fabric—and motioned to Timeus.

"Start it already," he said. "I'm getting bored."

Attia still couldn't see his face, but she saw the gold circlet nestled in his auburn hair and the massive ruby ring on the smallest finger of his left hand.

"Who is who?" the man asked.

Timeus looked at Sisera. "We hadn't decided that yet." He produced a gold coin from a pocket in his robes and looked at Sisera. "You choose."

"Heads," Sisera said.

Timeus flipped the coin into the air, caught it, and slapped it onto the back of his hand. "Tails," he said. "Better luck next time, Sisera. Your men can play the Trojans."

Sisera groaned. "Every damn time," he muttered. He stood and introduced his gladiators as six men rode into the arena. They carried lances at their sides and wore plumed helmets on their heads. One gladiator, who was apparently playing Hector of Troy, wore a bright blue sash across his chest. Sisera seemed to go on for a long time, nearly shouting about the honor of the

Trojans, their skills in battle. When he finally finished, he collapsed into his chair, mopping his brow with a piece of linen.

"Finally," Timeus muttered. He turned to Lucius. "How about it, boy? You'll have to do it someday."

Lucius shook his head. "You are much better at it, Uncle."

"You can't say no forever," Timeus replied, but he got to his feet all the same, walked to the edge of the veranda, and raised his hands for silence. "Romans," he began, and although he didn't shout as Sisera had, his voice carried across the entire arena. "The great poet Homer once told us of the epic battle between the Greeks and the Trojans . . ."

Attia's focus shifted as Timeus went on. Her father had told her about the Trojan War, how a spoiled prince and an arrogant king battled over a woman so beautiful that her face launched a thousand ships. Attia remembered laughing at that.

"How can a *face* do that? You need two dozen strong men, at least, if it's a long ship," she'd said.

Sparro hadn't so much as smiled at her naïveté. "I don't mean it literally, Attia. Helen was famous for her beauty, and her husband Menelaus was angry to lose her. But she was not really the reason for the war. She was an excuse."

"But you said that the king and the prince fought over her."

"Yes, but . . ." Sparro had put his hands together and tapped his long fingers against his chin. "Agamemnon—the brother of Menelaus—used his brother's anger as an excuse to attack Troy. It was a very wealthy city."

"So . . . they fought for gold?"

"And power, yes."

Attia shook her head. "That makes even less sense than fighting for love."

At that, her father did laugh, but she hardly minded. She was only a child, after all.

Timeus's version of events was markedly different. He spoke not of love or even ambition, but of ruthlessness and cunning, of strategy and superiority. And then when he introduced his gladiators, he called them something else—neither Greeks nor Trojans. He called them Myrmidons.

Attia sighed with recognition, finally seeing his game. If the gladiators were Myrmidons, then Xanthus could only be Achilles, and even the illiterate of Rome knew that Achilles slew Hector. Timeus obviously believed his gladiators' victory was inevitable. If it had been any other men down in the arena, Attia would have paid the boatman herself to see them all on a one-way trip to the underworld. But Xanthus was down there, or soon would be, and she found herself hoping that Timeus's confidence was warranted.

The old man raised his hands again. His next words were spoken in such a distinct cadence that Attia thought he'd probably spoken them hundreds of times before. "Our champion needs no introduction. Call his name! Release his fury!"

And instead of calling for Achilles, the entire Coliseum shook with the force of another name. "Xanthus! Xanthus! XANTHUS!"

A loud creaking echoed from somewhere far below as the gate to the hypogeum opened. The crowd became nearly hysterical with excitement when they saw Xanthus walk out onto the sand.

Even from a distance, he looked intimidating—all muscle and bone and pure, deadly force. His black armor wasn't armor at all, but a leather breastplate and greaves that were meant to show off his body rather than actually protect him. He had no shield, only two straight swords strapped to his back. He didn't even have a helmet, and the tips of his dark hair seemed to turn gold in the sun.

The five other gladiators who fought with him were also dressed in black, but they carried round shields, and their armor covered everything but their arms and knees. They raised their swords to Xanthus as if he were truly Achilles—he their commander and they his loyal soldiers.

At the very center of the arena, Xanthus turned to look up at the veranda. With a single fluid motion, he unsheathed his swords and struck them together over his head with enough force to send sparks flaring along the bright metal.

The people screamed with delight.

The man with the ruby raised his fist, trumpets blared across the Coliseum, and the battle began.

Galena turned her face away and closed her eyes. She couldn't watch.

Attia couldn't look away. She stared as Sisera's men charged forward on horseback. Xanthus and his companions stood side by side in a straight line that never faltered, not even as clouds of dust kicked up behind the horses and distorted the sunlight.

The horsemen, on the other hand, had already broken ranks. Hector fell behind while another gladiator charged straight for Xanthus, intent on cutting the champion down. But Xanthus leaned away, just barely avoiding the edge of the horseman's blade. The miss was so close that the crowd gasped in unison.

Iduma used the distraction to launch himself off another's back and mount the horse. He didn't waste any time in burying a dagger into the horseman's chest before letting him fall to the ground. Attia imagined his neck breaking with a jarring crack.

Instead of keeping the horse, Iduma jumped down, landing agilely on two feet before joining his companions with an easy smile.

One down. Five more to go.

The remaining Trojans turned back in a line and charged again.

Attia shook her head in disapproval. That kind of brutal, forward attack was primitive at best. It required no strategy, no planning, no real thought beyond the will to move. She'd heard some call it a brave way of fighting. She called it stupid, and Xanthus and his men seemed to agree.

Albinus scoffed and swung his sword as soon as the first horse reached them. The poorly trained animal reared up, dropping its rider to the ground before running away. A second horse tried to leap to the left, lost its footing, and fell, crushing the legs of the gladiator on its back. Xanthus's men wasted no time dealing the final blows to the fallen.

Timeus smiled at Sisera. "Three of your men gone already, Sisera. Good Trojans, the lot of them."

Sisera grumbled under his breath.

Xanthus and his men now took the offensive and began to advance on the last two gladiators. They walked slowly, each man perfectly spaced from the next. Their heads tilted down, and the sun on their helmets cast blinding reflections onto the crowd. Xanthus led them like a spear point.

One of Sisera's gladiators lost his wits then and threw his sword at Xanthus with a wild scream. Xanthus dodged it with a casual twist of his torso, his muscles flexing. But his arm—and even Attia barely saw this—swung out and caught the sword by the tip before flinging it back with impossible speed. It found its mark in the armored chest of the opposing gladiator who fell to the ground, his eyes wide with shock.

The crowd was silent for a brief moment before stomps, screams, and sworn oaths drowned the arena in sound.

Chills spilled across Attia's skin, and she finally saw what the people saw—not gladiators, not even men, but immortal warriors from legend, perfect and invincible. The whole thing suddenly seemed incredibly unbalanced. Who could ever defeat such a force? Who could ever face Xanthus, the Champion of Rome, in combat and live?

It looked like the fight would be over all too quickly. Only one of Sisera's men remained.

Attia could see the lone gladiator clearly from where she stood on the veranda. The blue sash across his chest billowed in the wind, and the plumes on his helmet trembled. He and Xanthus looked straight at each other for a long moment. Then the other gladiators began taking slow, deliberate steps back, sheathing their weapons as they went. It became clear that they wouldn't take part in this last fight. It was, after all, a duel between Achilles and Hector.

When the lone gladiator realized that, he looked down at his hands. His chest rose and fell as he took a deep breath before dismounting and removing his helmet. Black hair curled tightly against his scalp. He was younger than Attia expected. Perhaps no older than fourteen, a boy who was more Paris than Hector. And Xanthus was about to kill him.

Her stomach turned. She'd never shied away from combat, but this was no fight. It was a slaughter. Against her will, she remembered Xanthus's unguarded laughter, the steadiness of his voice, the soft touch of his hand on her face. She'd seen a gentler man, but the one who stood in the arena now—his name ringing out through the city—was little more than a murderer.

She closed her eyes just as iron clashed against iron.

Suddenly, the entire arena was silent.

Looking down, Attia prepared herself for the worst.

Xanthus and the young gladiator were locked against each other, swords crossed. With a lurch, Hector pushed away, and for a single breath, their weapons lowered. Then a few moments later, he raised his sword to strike.

The pattern went on for several minutes. One attacked, the other deflected. Then one lunged forward and the other dodged neatly aside. Thrust, parry, dodge, attack. Xanthus aimed to punch the young man in the gut with his left hand, but managed to miss even that as Hector twisted himself out of the way.

It dawned on Attia that Xanthus was holding himself back. It was the only explanation for why the boy wasn't dead yet.

Xanthus looked completely unaffected, as though he'd been lounging up on the veranda rather than fighting to the death. The young gladiator was panting and heaving with exhaustion. His sword hand lowered more with every passing minute, and he struggled to his feet after each fall. But still, he stood. He rushed forward over and over. He had courage, at least.

Then Xanthus thrust again, and this time, Hector didn't react quite fast enough. The blade sliced a deep wound in his arm, and he fell to his knees, his hand losing its grip on his sword.

Xanthus rested one sword on the boy's shoulder, and his lips formed whispered words that seemed to make Hector straighten up and lift his chin.

Up on the veranda, the man with the ruby and the circlet stood and approached the stone railing. He extended his right fist outward, and Attia felt the entire arena hold its breath. He made a motion that she couldn't see, though the rabid cheers of the crowd told her exactly what it meant: permission—or an order—to kill.

But Xanthus didn't move for a minute, then two. The seconds trickled by as everyone waited. Confused murmurs began to rush through the crowd, heavy with speculation and wariness, until Timeus stood and leaned over the railing.

He didn't say a word. He hardly made a sound. But Xanthus's

gaze sharpened on him, then drifted to where Attia stood. A look of terrible resignation settled on his face. He took a deep breath and looked down at the young gladiator.

"You fought with courage," he said, his deep voice carrying through the now silent arena. "You might almost be a prince of Troy, our . . . Hector reborn."

Attia wondered if she was the only one to hear the hesitation in his voice.

Xanthus lowered his sword and turned his face away. For a moment, the whole crowd believed he would defy orders and let the boy live. Then he plunged his blade into the boy's heart, killing him instantly.

Galena smiled through teary eyes. "Mercy," she whispered.

Attia swallowed against the tightness in her throat. Yes. It was merciful. As merciful as any death could be.

"I don't think he's ever let a losing gladiator live," Galena said. "Xanthus?"

Galena shook her head and nodded toward the railing, at the man with the ruby. "Princeps Titus."

An escort of Praetorians suddenly filled the veranda and surrounded the man. Together, they left in a frenzy of black cloaks and heavy steps.

Galena looked at Attia's shocked face as they passed. "Didn't you know?"

Attia gaped. The Princeps of Rome—a kinsman to that bastard Crassus—had been sitting just a few feet away from her the entire time, and she'd had no idea.

"Oh, wasn't that delightful!" Valeria said, though her voice shook just a little. "A bit short maybe, but vastly entertaining."

"Length is not always the determining factor in such vigorous exercises," Timeus said before turning away from the railing.

Despite his loss, Sisera burst out laughing.

Xanthus let his brothers carry the boy's body away. There was one more thing he had to do.

Raising his swords, he opened his arms in victory. Bile rose in his throat, but the people—and Timeus—expected him to play his part. The crowd was still cheering maniacally when Xanthus finally sheathed his swords and passed back through the gates.

Respect and fear—that was what made the other gladiators and even the guards lower their heads as he passed. They knew better than to talk to him after a kill. They thought he was still hungry, that he was still consumed with bloodlust.

Only a handful knew the truth, and they waited for him deep in the hypogeum.

Castor and Lebuin had cleared off a stone table and gently laid the boy's body down on it. Iduma had found a cloth to cover him, but there was already a red stain seeping through. Sisera's Hector was younger than any of them had expected, and they watched Xanthus warily as he entered the small room.

No one said anything. Xanthus's last words to the boy screamed in his head.

Be brave.

And he had been, in the end. The boy had lifted his chin, straightened his back, and met his death with what courage he could.

Xanthus's mouth tasted like blood, a thousand times worse than the dust of the arena. He realized he'd bitten his tongue when he plunged his sword into the boy's chest.

The others left him without a word.

Alone, Xanthus braced his arms against the stone table, trying not to shake or move or breathe. But his hands curled themselves around the closest thing at hand—a helmet that Castor had left behind. He grabbed it and hurled it at the wall with a feral scream.

The swords on his back followed, iron chipping and sparking as it glanced off the stone.

Then an ancient urn filled with sand.

A heavy, jagged rock on the ground.

Anything he could grab. Anything he could throw. Anything he could break.

And when there was nothing left but his own bloody hands, he fell to his knees before the table. Familiar, painful words crawled past his lips as he tried to make his penance.

Just like before.

Just like always.

"Forgive me. Oh gods, please forgive me."

A few minutes later, he heard the sound of shuffling feet. Timeus had come. Xanthus knew he would. He hardened his features but kept his back turned.

"A fine match," Timeus said, his voice low.

"He was just a boy."

"You were just a boy when you became a champion."

"It's not the same."

"What do you want me to say? I didn't tell Sisera to use someone so young. The man is a fool. You know that."

"I know that he is a man easily fooled." Xanthus practically spit the words over his shoulder.

Timeus bristled. "You are a gladiator," he said, stepping closer. "You are *my* gladiator, and when the Princeps of Rome tells you to kill, you *do not hesitate*."

Xanthus rose to his feet. "I thought it would make for a better show—"

"Don't!" Timeus shouted, a thick purple vein pulsing on his

forehead. "Don't treat me like an idiot, Xanthus. What did you think would happen if you disobeyed? If you let the boy live? Do you think Titus Flavius is so willingly offended? I know you, Xanthus. Much better than you think. Even if you don't care about yourself, you'll die—you'll *kill*—for the others. If you had spared that boy, many more would have suffered, and your new pet would probably have borne most of it. Why do you think I allowed her to come? Why do you think I *bought* her? To keep you in line!"

Gods, Xanthus wanted to kill him in that moment. He'd known since childhood that Timeus was as coldhearted and cruel as they come, whatever indulgences he granted him. But he knew the man was right. If he'd spared the boy, then Attia would have been punished. And Albinus. And Gallus. And Iduma and Castor and Lebuin.

All of them. Anyone he'd ever cared for. Just as Timeus said.

Xanthus closed his eyes, and Timeus put a hand on his shoulder.

"You are a gladiator," he said again. But softly this time. Almost a whisper. "Remember that, and remember who depends on you now."

Xanthus nodded his head slowly, because really—how could he ever forget?

CHAPTER 10

Xanthus looked down at the cold, muddy water filling the court-yard and tickling his calves. The clouds were wringing them-selves out, and rain had been pouring for more than seven days. The waterline climbed steadily while slaves hammered at the outer wall to make an opening. Gaping, uneven chunks of stone fell with heavy splashes.

Some months earlier, when Timeus began his renovations to the estate, the architect had warned him to include a drainage system. The stone walls were too tight, he said. When the rainy season came, they would end up with their own private lake right in the middle of the estate, he said. And of course Timeus, brilliant ass that he was, disagreed. He hadn't wanted to jeo-pardize the perfect design of his wall.

"Damn bloody shit!" Timeus shouted from the protective arch of the house.

Behind him, Ennius sighed heavily and gave Xanthus an exasperated look. Xanthus shrugged.

"Don't say it! Don't either of you say it!" Timeus warned with an outstretched finger wagging at each of them in turn.

Xanthus chewed on the inner part of his cheek to hold back a comment that was sure to make Timeus even angrier.

"It'll take weeks, *months* to fix the damages!" Timeus fumed.

"Yes, Dominus," Xanthus said.

"All that damned money! Wasted!"

"Yes, Dominus," Xanthus said again.

"Oh, I can just see Tycho Flavius *rolling* with amusement at the news of this!"

Xanthus scratched the light stubble on his chin. It was probably time for him to shave again. He wondered idly if the Thracian preferred clean-shaven or bearded men. Did the Maedi grow beards? He'd have to ask her.

Timeus gritted his teeth and ran a hand through his hair. "Don't either of you have anything to say?"

Ennius glanced calmly up at the sky. "It's raining," he said.

Timeus glared at him. "Prepare the household," he said. "We leave for Pompeii."

Xanthus smiled. He looked forward to leaving the city for the duration of the rainy season. But the weather also reminded him of Britannia and its damp, green valleys. Coming on the heels of the dark night of Samhain, the heavy rains almost managed to wash away the shadow and the dust and the blood that always seemed to stain his hands.

Xanthus closed his eyes and turned his face to the sky.

He always did love the rain.

Attia carefully pulled the cap onto Rory's head, stuffing the girl's unruly curls beneath the fabric.

"Is that too tight?" Attia asked.

Rory, standing with her little arms outstretched, shook her

head. "No, but it itches." She fidgeted and squirmed as Attia began to wrap layers and layers of fabric around her body. Eventually, only Rory's pale, heart-shaped face was left exposed.

Valeria stood at the window, arms folded across her chest while her eyes focused on some spot outside. Lucius hovered just behind Rory and winked when she looked back at him.

"Do I still need to cover my face if it's raining?" Rory asked. "There's hardly any sun, and I can't breathe with the mask on."

"Don't argue, Aurora. You will do as you are told," Valeria said without turning.

Lucius knelt in front of his sister. "I know it's difficult, Rory, but it won't be for very long. Once you're in the cart, you can take it off."

Attia watched as Lucius lifted a mask to Rory's face and carefully fit it on. It was a single piece of thin white ceramic with gold edging. Precious stones bordered the eye holes, and blue, green, and purple paint swirled together in whimsical patterns around the temples and forehead. Lucius drew the bright gold ribbons around Rory's head and tied it in a simple bow. Sitting back on his heels, he took his sister's hands. "It will be another grand adventure."

She blinked owlishly at him with her wide blue eyes. "Will you stay with me?" she asked, her small voice muffled by the mask.

Lucius shook his head. "I can't. You know I have to ride with Uncle. But Attia will stay with you."

Attia met Rory's eyes and tried to smile, but it was a painful effort.

When Sabina had told her that the household would be leaving Rome, Attia had nearly gone mad with desperation. She couldn't afford to leave the city, not now. Her body was almost completely healed, and she'd only been waiting for the right moment to kill Timeus and escape the estate. She still needed information to find Crassus, but now all of her plans were drowning in Timeus's damn courtyard. A part of her hoped that maybe, just maybe, she would be left behind. But as Rory's nursemaid and the champion's nighttime companion, there was no chance of that.

It had taken the household three days and three nights to make the preparations to leave, and Attia had needed every second to rein in her frustration. *I'll kill Timeus and find Crassus,* she promised herself. *No matter what it takes.* She'd snuck into Timeus's study one last time and taken one of the maps, which she'd smuggled away among Rory's things.

In the child's small room, Attia watched as Lucius swept Rory up into his arms with a big smile, cradling her against him like a glass doll.

The rain had eased a bit, becoming more a curtain of heavy mist than an actual downpour. But the slaves had still been forced to erect a makeshift bridge to bypass the flooded courtyard. The rest of the household waited by the main gate. Timeus sat astride a reddish brown Iberian stallion, the rain creating rounded droplets in his white hair. Valeria retired to her own closed cart.

Nearly the entire household was journeying to Pompeii—the house slaves, the garden slaves, Timeus's private guard, and of course, his gladiators. Altogether, there were close to a hundred people scattered through the column of wagons and horses that made up the caravan.

Another group of men stood at attention along the road, and Attia frowned at them as she passed. Each man palmed the rounded hilt of a gladius and sported a distinct tattoo on his left shoulder: SPQR, *Senatus Populusque Romanus.* The Senate and the People of Rome. They were soldiers—members of the Roman infantry who still bore the symbols of the Republic even though Princeps Titus had all but called himself emperor. Attia couldn't decide if their presence made the caravan more secure or more dangerous.

Lucius lifted the bundle of linen that was his sister into a closed cart before moving aside so Attia could follow her in.

Attia blinked rapidly while her vision adjusted to the surprising darkness. It took her a minute to realize there was a second door a few feet away from the one she'd just used. It was easy enough to open, and she entered the main compartment. Narrow slits in the sides of the cart let in tiny shafts of light that didn't reach the floor. They were barely enough to see by.

"Here, take my hand," Rory said. Her small form was little more than a shadow. "Don't be afraid. You'll get used to the dark."

Attia smiled, knowing the child couldn't see. There were few things she feared, and the dark had never been one of them.

Xanthus walked unchained at the rear of the caravan, flanked by soldiers in front and behind. Beside him, his brothers were bound together with iron shackles that were already cutting into their wrists. But from the sound of their constant banter, they hardly noticed.

They're used to it now, Xanthus thought bitterly.

"Why are we moving so damn slowly?" Iduma complained. "At this rate, it'll take us a month to reach Pompeii."

"Don't be stupid," Albinus said. "You know the rains always worsen the roads."

"I'd rather walk in the rain than be carted around like an invalid," Lebuin said.

A few yards ahead, Lucretia walked beside one of the carts.

Instead of her usual sheer black gown, she wore an opaque gray dress that clung to her body and a long veil over her hair. Her hips swayed with each step. When she turned her head, Xanthus saw that the light rain had washed away a bit of the kohl she often wore around her eyes. With her face almost bare, she looked much more like her twenty-one years and less like the woman whose soul had withered in Timeus's bed. Xanthus realized suddenly that he had never seen Lucretia smile. He wondered if she still remembered how.

Fingers snapped in front of his face, and he turned to look at his brothers. "Xanthus, have you been listening?" Gallus asked.

"To your whining? No, not really," Xanthus said.

Iduma rolled his eyes. "You never listen. And here I was talking about how you're such a great mentor to us all."

Xanthus smiled. His brothers' teasing rarely failed to lighten his mood, whatever the topic. "I'm your mentor, Iduma? I'm touched, truly."

"Don't be *too* flattered," Albinus said. "We all know how low Iduma's standards are."

Their laughter echoed down the caravan.

They stopped just before dusk, and Attia found the sudden stillness disorienting. Her limbs cried out with the need to stretch, to walk, to move. Trying not to wake Rory, she opened the doors at the back of the cart and jumped out. Her sandaled feet sank a few inches into the cool mud. The rain soaked her hair and tunic within moments.

Attia saw that they had made camp in a clearing surrounded by trees almost a half mile from the main road. Sunset still lingered on the western horizon, but slaves had already begun to hang dozens of lanterns on sturdy poles throughout the camp.

The carts, wagons, and people had been positioned in a sort of three-ring formation. The slaves and servants filled the large outer ring, huddling in tiny, tattered tents that were somehow meant to accommodate as many as five people. The guards' larger tents formed a smaller ring within the first. And in the very center stood Rory's cart and three tents that looked more like pavilions than anything else, each twelve feet high. This inner circle was undoubtedly where Timeus and family would sleep. The Roman soldiers who accompanied the caravan hadn't erected any tents at all. They simply strolled around the edges of the camp, seemingly oblivious to the rain.

Sabina approached with an oilskin cloak held over her head. "I'll stay with Mistress Aurora. You go to the champion."

Attia sighed. She no longer distrusted the gladiator as fiercely as she once had. But their last few nights together had been awkward and stilted. She dreaded finding out what tonight would be like. She turned around and stared out through the rain. "Where exactly am I supposed to go?" she asked as Sabina draped the oilskin cloak over her shoulders.

"There," Sabina said, pointing at a dark gray tent set apart from both the ring of guards and the inner circle. It wasn't as big as the family's tents, but it was at least three times the size of any other.

Less than a minute ago, the rain had felt fresh and cool, but now Attia could feel a chill seeping into her bones. She wrapped her arms around her chest and walked through the encampment that was Timeus's household. Four women huddled together in a tiny tent nearby, holding open the flap to let out the smoke from their small fire. They glanced at Attia and just as quickly dismissed her. Two of Timeus's guards talked under the cover of another larger tent, sharing a cup of some steaming drink and laughing.

Attia quickened her pace until she reached Xanthus's tent and pulled the flap open. A smokeless fire warmed the space, and after so much cold, the sudden heat made chills blossom along her skin.

Xanthus sat shirtless by the fire. When he heard her enter, he looked up with a smile. He already had a sheet and clean tunic set aside for her.

Attia raised her eyebrows in surprise. "What's this?"

"I thought you'd be soaked through in this rain," Xanthus said as he handed her the linens.

"Thank you," Attia said. She waited a moment. "Will you at least turn around?"

Xanthus turned obediently to face the wall of the tent, putting his back to Attia and the fire.

Attia used the sheet to dry her skin and get most of the water out of her hair. Then as quickly as she could, she undressed and pulled the clean tunic over her head. The frayed hem fell below her knees. "I feel like I'm wearing this tent," she said. "But at least it's dry. Thank you."

"Of course," Xanthus said as he turned around.

Attia took a seat beside him and accepted the proffered piece of hard bread and some dried beef.

"There will be more meat when we reach Pompeii."

"This is plenty," Attia said. She'd been worried that the awkwardness between them would continue, but she was surprised to find that they ate in rather comfortable silence.

Every now and then, her shoulder bumped his, or his elbow brushed against her knee. Small, fleeting touches that made Attia's skin prickle. She was acutely aware of just how close they sat, but she didn't move away, and she tried not to feel pleased by the fact that Xanthus didn't either.

The food was long gone by the time either of them said anything again.

"I'm sorry that Timeus made you watch," Xanthus said eventually, his voice hoarse.

It took Attia a few moments to realize he was talking about his match in the Coliseum. Neither of them had spoken of it in the days since, and Attia was surprised he was bringing it up now. She glanced at Xanthus then away.

"I see now why they call you the Champion of Rome. You were good. Incredible, really. But you hate it, don't you? You hate what you do."

Xanthus rubbed at the calluses on his palms. "I never thought death would be my calling." His words were barely audible over the rain and the crackle of the fire.

Funny, Attia thought. *I grew up thinking the exact opposite.*

"I met a woman at the match," Attia said. "Her name was Galena, but she said that the Romans had given her a new name." She paused.

Xanthus's body stiffened as he waited for her to continue.

"And there was something in your voice when you said the name Hector in the arena. I heard it before when you first told me that *they* call you Xanthus."

His profile was illuminated by the glow of the fire, but his eyes were like dark emeralds. Shadowed. Murky. "I am a gladiator, Attia."

"You weren't always."

"That was a long time ago," he said, weariness heavy in his voice. "Does it really matter?"

"It matters to me. What is your real name?"

Xanthus's lips tightened, and he trained his gaze on the far wall of the tent.

Attia waited. She'd never thought of herself as a patient person, but she decided that she could wait for this.

Finally, he said, "In another life, my name was Gareth, and I had a brother named Hector."

Attia pursed her lips. She'd been expecting an answer along those lines, but hearing it still made her heart clench with fury and sorrow. "Do they take everything?" she murmured.

"It's a different sort of branding."

"Then why hasn't Timeus tried to rename *me*?"

A pained expression crossed Xanthus's face, and he hesitated again. "Because . . ." He swallowed hard and stared into the fire. "Because he wanted me to do it," he said, his voice filled with shame.

Attia stared at him. "But you haven't."

Xanthus shook his head. "And I never will."

"Timeus truly favors you."

"He favors winning," Xanthus said bluntly. "When I get old or start to lose my popularity, I'll lose other things as well."

"Like me?" Attia said. She'd meant to tease him, but the words came out sounding harsher than she intended.

An unexpectedly fierce expression transformed Xanthus's features. His jaw clenched, and his brow furrowed into a deep scowl. "That won't happen." His eyes bore into hers, and Attia felt rooted to the earth. "No one will take you from me."

She'd never seen that look on his face before—hot and cold at the same time. She imagined she should feel angry or resentful. He'd just sworn he'd never let her go, no matter what Timeus or anyone else might say. He spoke of death. He spoke of eternal bondage. But there was something else.

Past the furious light in his eyes, Attia saw something she'd been trying hard not to see. It was infinitely more dangerous to her than his hands or his hate, and suddenly, she couldn't ignore it anymore. She couldn't keep turning away. She just had to know one thing.

"Would you force me to be with you? Regardless of what Timeus says—would you try to keep me against my will?"

The hurt that filled Xanthus's eyes made her chest ache.

"No, Attia. I could never let anyone take you, but if you don't want me, you only have to say so."

Attia reached for his hand, and he took it immediately, wrapping his fingers around hers in a tight grasp. The simple touch wasn't so much a show of affection as it was an expression of solidarity, of mutual comfort. For the first time in months, she didn't feel so completely alone. Maybe, in spite of whatever else was forced upon her in this new life, whatever else might become of her, she could choose this one thing. Make this one single choice.

She raised her free hand to his cheek before passing her thumb lightly over his lips. Xanthus drew a shuddering breath. This time, when he reached for her, she didn't pull away. She let the heat of him warm her skin, and she smiled at the expression of wonder on his face. Closing her eyes, she leaned her forehead against his.

They barely moved, just a slight shifting of warm skin on skin. Then their lips touched, and everything beyond them disappeared.

Attia's head felt light, and the tips of her fingers tingled. If Xanthus weren't holding her, she thought she might just float away, lost in the flood of so much feeling. Driven by instinct and need, she parted her lips to deepen the kiss.

Xanthus responded immediately, tightening his arms around her with almost crushing force. A part of Attia realized that this new thing was incredibly fragile. But as heat coursed through her body, she thought it was probably the first time in her life that she'd ever felt something so right. Nothing else mattered but this one touch, this one shared breath.

When Xanthus began to kiss a trail down the side of her neck, Attia leaned her head back and closed her eyes. He moved slowly, so slowly, taking his time not just to touch but to *feel*.

His lips pressed against the hollow of her throat as he whispered her name against her skin. His fingers touched her cheek, her lips, and her lashes in the lightest of caresses before he put his mouth to hers again. His arms fit around her as though they were made to hold her, and he was gentle. So much gentler than Attia could have imagined.

Then, just as he shifted their bodies to lie down, a terrible scream cut through the night.

CHAPTER 11

The scream was followed immediately by the clang of iron.

"We're under attack," Xanthus said. But before he could move, Attia whispered a single word.

"*Rory.*"

Between one blink and the next, she was on her feet and gone. Xanthus didn't even have time to shout her name.

He had no choice. He had to follow her.

All across the clearing, tents were on fire, burning through the fog and rain. Slaves struggled to put out the flames and defend themselves while armed men charged through the encampment.

In the dark, it was hard to tell the difference between Timeus's men and the attackers, but Xanthus was only really looking for Attia. He ran after her and watched her agile frame duck and roll and jump over and under spears and swords and the swinging fist of a man twice her size. When one of the attackers tried to grab her arm, she wrapped her fingers around his wrist, twisted until the bone cracked, then pulled his body toward her raised knee. His cry of pain was quickly silenced as he fell unconscious to the ground. Another attacker came for her, then another. But she dispatched the poor bastards with ruthless efficiency.

She was impressive. And too, too reckless.

Xanthus was only a few feet away when someone finally caught her by surprise. A man grabbed her ankle from beneath one of the carts. She lost her balance for half a second before twisting her body and stopping her fall with two outstretched arms. Then she raised her right foot and smashed it into the man's face. Xanthus actually heard his neck snap.

Xanthus should probably have been watching his own back half as well. He might have noticed the man running straight at him with a sword raised high. As it was, the tip of the blade sliced along his shoulder, but he was able to use the other man's momentum to drive his fist into the man's throat. He grabbed the sword before catching up to Attia just outside of Rory's cart.

"Still in one piece, I see," he said with a tight smile.

"You're a little bit worse for wear," Attia said, nudging her chin at the cut on his shoulder.

"I need to find my brothers. You should stay here." When Attia started to protest, Xanthus lowered his voice. "If you keep fighting, the soldiers might take notice. It's not worth the risk. Besides, someone needs to stay with the child and make sure no one tries to break into the cart." He waited until Attia nodded grudgingly. "I'll come back when it's clear."

"Should I warn you to be careful?"

"Probably wouldn't do any good," he said before winking and shutting the door of the cart. He heard a lock bolt into place from the other side.

At least he knew she'd be safe. At least he could take a proper breath again. He squeezed his eyes shut to block out the scene around him. The concept of fear had become a diluted emotion long ago, but the sounds of men fighting and dying—the sharp ring of their swords, the sickening crunch of bone—all reminded him of the arena. He had to fight the urge to recoil in disgust.

Then again, this was something else entirely, wasn't it? Not death for sport or entertainment. This was survival, and he didn't think he could afford the luxury of detachment.

When he opened his eyes, he tried to find familiar faces.

Lucius was the closest, gripping his sword with both hands. His eyes were intent on one of the bandits—watching and matching the movement of shoulder and torso and skittering gaze. Maybe those training sessions were paying off after all.

Ennius protected Timeus's tent near the tree line. An attacker charged at him swinging a club. Ennius simply ducked his head before punching the man square in the face.

Not far away, Gallus and Lebuin fought back-to-back against six attackers. Neither of them had any weapons save their scarred, scabbed hands. Still, they didn't look like they were having much trouble. Xanthus made his way toward them.

"Should you take a look at that?" Lebuin asked, nodding at Xanthus's bleeding shoulder before jabbing one of his attackers in the stomach.

Gallus scoffed. "It is but a scratch!" he said. "Not like his arm has come off." He caught a bandit's fist in midair and used it to shatter another man's nose. "Besides, I bet his new bedmate is probably much rougher on him."

"Did you *see* her?" Lebuin said, his voice full of admiration. "Gods, she really is a Thracian. I'm surprised she doesn't want to come out and play some more."

"At least she's not off breaking Ennius's *other* leg," Gallus said with a dark chuckle.

"Now that would just be cruel," Albinus said as he joined them. He knocked down the last of the attackers. Xanthus hadn't even bothered to help.

Someone whistled, and they all turned to see Castor incline his bald head toward the northern edge of the camp. Dozens of horses bearing Timeus's mark were being corralled into the forest.

Gallus snorted. "Well, Timeus probably stole them first."

"He might be a tad bit upset," Lebuin said with a grin.

"Good," Albinus said. "They can all rot."

"So bitter, Albinus. So bitter." Gallus slung his arm around Albinus's neck. "Shall I cheer you up, brother?"

Albinus slammed his elbow through the gap between them, knocking down a man as he tried to attack them from behind.

"I am in a perfectly agreeable mood," Albinus said.

Gallus glanced over his shoulder without releasing him. "Yes, I can see that."

"Where's Iduma?" Lebuin asked.

They looked around to see their blood-brother fighting two attackers some twenty yards away. His wet red hair was plastered against his skull. In one hand, he wielded a lit torch that flared in the rain. In the other, he swung . . .

"Is that a *ham bone?*" Gallus said with a snort of laughter.

Iduma swung his torch and his ham bone, taking a bite out of the meat every few seconds. The attackers looked at each other uncertainly but held their ground.

"Stop dawdling, Iduma, and finish already!" Albinus yelled.

"I do believe that is what Layla said to him last night," Lebuin commented with a smirk.

When the attackers noticed the rest of them watching, they

finally seemed convinced of the futility of their mission. They dropped their weapons, their heels kicking mud up into Iduma's face as they raced for the forest.

"How rude," Iduma said, wiping the dirt from his chin.

Lebuin took the opportunity to reach up and snatch the ham bone out of his hand. "Where the hell did you get this?" he said before taking a full bite.

"I was eating that!" Iduma said, and shoved Lebuin's shoulder, causing the ham bone to slip from his hands onto the muddy ground.

"Oh, well done, Iduma," Lebuin said.

"You both eat too much anyway," Albinus said.

Gallus began sorting through the weapons. He handed swords to Iduma and Lebuin, a double-sided axe to Castor, and a spear to Albinus. Xanthus still had his stolen sword. Seconds after they were armed, a new group of bandits charged at them.

It certainly wasn't the arena. There were no cheers, no lewd encouragements from a drunken crowd to urge them on. They had no uniforms, no glossy black armor or heavy shields. But they had their training and their strength.

Xanthus fought with an inner quiet that was almost foreign to him. When had it ever been so easy to kill? When had he ever swung his sword without that gnawing sensation of guilt?

Never.

Because there had never before been a good reason.

Now his reason was crouching in a dark cart protecting a Roman child. Attia didn't need him, but she wanted him. That was more than enough.

So Xanthus raised his fist and his sword. The men who challenged him died for it, and he had no regrets. It was the first time in almost ten years of killing that he didn't ask for forgiveness.

It seemed that close to a hundred bandits were spread out through the camp. That didn't include the ones who'd already gotten away with horses or other loot, nor the others who had retreated into the forest earlier on. Xanthus had no idea what they were doing there. Thieves never travelled in such numbers, not even roaming gangs. What kind of idiot had decided to attack a camp protected by Roman soldiers on a Roman road?

Another high scream cut through the sounds of battle. A bandit dragged a hysterical Valeria out into the middle of the field. She wore only a thin, gold-colored tunic that soaked through almost immediately in the rain. Her face was starkly pale, and her round blue eyes skittered about like those of a trapped animal. She struggled desperately to free her tangled hair from the man's grasp, screaming again and again.

Xanthus didn't care for Valeria. But she had never done anything to directly hurt him, and whatever her sins, she didn't deserve *this*.

"Look," Iduma said suddenly. "The boy!"

From the other side of the clearing, Lucius was fighting as hard as he could to reach his mother, stabbing and slicing through the air as Xanthus had taught him. His nose was bleeding, and his tunic was drenched with water and mud. Xanthus ran to his side, and the gladiators followed. Between them, the guards, and the soldiers, the attackers were struck down or chased off until the only man left was the one who held Valeria hostage.

Lucius's face was contorted with anger when he finally reached the man. "Let her go. *Now*."

"Stay back or she dies!" the man shouted. The tip of his knife pressed into Valeria's belly, and she started to sob quietly.

"Let her go," Lucius said again. "I'll pay you anything. Whatever you want. Let her go, and I'll let you live."

The man was concentrating so hard on the woman he held captive that he didn't hear the gladiator who snuck up behind him. Before he could respond, Xanthus grabbed his arm from behind and snapped it back with a sickening pop. Valeria fell forward into Lucius's embrace.

"Lucius," she sobbed.

"Are you all right?"

She managed a nod. Lucius squeezed her shoulder once before letting two guards escort her back to her tent.

Leaning forward, Lucius addressed the injured bandit with frightening calm. "You picked the wrong camp, and you grabbed the wrong woman. Tell me why I shouldn't kill you here."

"You *should* kill him," Timeus interjected. He was standing just a few yards away with Ennius at his side.

Lucius stared at his uncle, conflicted.

"Send a message, Lucius. No one attacks our house without retribution." Timeus's cold blue eyes bore into his nephew.

Xanthus knew that Lucius had never killed before. But Timeus was ordering him to perform an execution, and Lucius couldn't deny his uncle. Certainly not in front of an audience. The rest of the bandits had been struck down or chased off, and now nearly everyone in the household was watching Lucius. He had no choice. He schooled his features and gave Xanthus a reluctant nod. The bandit fell at their feet, and two of the guards started to drag him away. The man's sobs rang through the sudden silence of the night.

Lucius started to follow when Xanthus stopped him. "Make it quick, if you can," he said in a low voice that only Lucius could hear. "Aim the tip of your sword at the back of his neck."

Lucius nodded. His face was pale, and beads of sweat gathered along his forehead and upper lip. He looked at the bloody sword in his hand with disgust. "Back of the neck," he muttered.

The guards waited with the man sobbing on his knees be-tween them. The bandit's head hung low, chin against his chest as his shoulders shook.

From a distance, Xanthus watched Lucius swallow hard—probably against the urge to retch in the grass—before he positioned himself behind the man. Their eyes met for a sec-ond. Then Lucius raised his sword and plunged it into the back of the man's neck with all his strength.

The silence that followed was deafening. Blood gurgled out of the man's mouth, and the guards let the body fall.

The household began to disperse, focused on the task of try-ing to salvage whatever they could from the destroyed camp.

Lucius stared at the body, his sword still gripped tightly in his hands.

Xanthus's stomach twisted with pity. Iduma had been wrong. Lucius wasn't a boy. Not anymore. Not after this. The sharp, tangy, familiar scent of blood filled Xanthus's nostrils.

Lucius blinked rapidly, as though he couldn't quite get used to the sight of the dead man before him. He ran a hand through his hair, barely aware of the blood coating his hands and now his face. He stood beside the body for several long minutes.

It was past midnight, and the storm clouds had moved to ob-scure the stars and the moon. The massive stone pines that bor-dered the forest in densely packed clusters creaked in the wind and made long, menacing shadows across the clearing. The rain had finally stopped, but cold, fat droplets still fell sporadically from the swaying branches. Even with the light of the lanterns and torches, the night seemed darker than usual. It was almost impossible to see anything anymore.

Xanthus finally approached Lucius, put his hand on the younger man's shoulder, and squeezed. There was nothing for either of them to say.

Lucius looked up. With a nod of appreciation to Xanthus, he wiped his sword on his tunic and sheathed it before forcing his feet to walk straight toward his uncle's tent. Xanthus followed close behind.

Timeus's captain of the guard, a few soldiers, and Ennius were already inside. Timeus was leaning over a map spread out over a table.

"It is done," Lucius said. His voice was different. Heavier. Deeper.

Timeus looked up from the map and scowled at his nephew. "More than half of those bastards got away with some kind of loot, and my horses are missing. Do you really think this is *done?*"

Dozens of tents and wagons were still burning. The food had been raided, and what was left was barely salvageable. Dozens of people were dead, missing, or seriously injured. Guards, soldiers, slaves—they all bled the same.

But Timeus didn't give a shit about any of that. Why would he?

The old man leaned over the map again. "We won't make it straight to Pompeii," he said. "We'll have to stop off here—in Ardea."

"Dominus," the captain of the guards said, "in our current condition—"

"Ardea isn't safe."

"Perhaps we should just turn back to Rome and—"

"No," Timeus said firmly, silencing the men. "I won't go back looking like this. Ardea will have food and supplies, and everyone accepts gold—Roman or not. We'll go there." He turned his cold gaze to Lucius. "Did he say anything useful before you killed him?"

Lucius frowned at his uncle.

"Come on, boy! Did you get any information at all about who was behind this?"

"Aurora is safe," Lucius blurted out.

"What?" Timeus said.

"I said that my sister is safe. And my mother, as well, once I intervened."

"You mean once *Xanthus* intervened."

"I didn't need him to—"

"No?" Timeus laughed coldly. "Tell me, what would you have done if my champion had not incapacitated that man? Would you have tried diplomacy, perhaps? Would you have asked *nicely?*"

"I could have handled it," Lucius spat out. "I *did* handle it. What more do you want from me?"

Timeus slowly approached his nephew. "I want you to *think,* for once in your goddamn life. I want you to have the spine to punish anyone who dares raise a single finger against this house. I want you to be decisive and firm. I want you to act without me having to tell you what to do. I want you to be a man. *That's* what I want!"

Lucius's breathing stuttered then stopped altogether.

No one spoke, and no one looked at uncle or nephew.

Timeus turned back to the table, his hands rustling the map. "We stop at Ardea," he said again with finality.

A murmured chorus responded, "Yes, Dominus."

Xanthus couldn't listen anymore. He walked out of the tent, closely followed by Ennius.

"Who do you think they were?" Ennius asked quietly.

"Thieves? But common thieves would never have attacked a camp this size."

Ennius nodded. "And certainly not with soldiers present." He paused. "Did the man say anything to Lucius?"

Xanthus shook his head. "Not that I heard." He glanced back into the tent.

"That is what it must be like to be raised by wolves," Ennius said, his face drawn with pity.

Xanthus touched his hand to the man's shoulder and walked away.

A soft knock sounded on the door to the cart, and Sabina and Rory huddled closer together on the back cushion. Attia went alone to unlock the outer door and found Xanthus standing just outside. Laying down a sword she'd taken from one of her attackers, she jumped from the cart and ran her hands over his body. Her touch was hurried and not particularly gentle. She wasn't trying to be affectionate; she was looking for wounds.

"I'm fine," Xanthus said.

She ignored him, frowning with concentration as she continued to look him over. The only injury she could see was the shallow slice at his shoulder. Satisfied, she stepped back and nodded. "Good. I would have been rather irritated if you'd gotten yourself maimed."

Xanthus smiled at her teasing tone but quickly sobered. "We won't make it to Pompeii like this. Too much was taken or destroyed."

"And Timeus? Is he dead?" She couldn't decide if she hoped the old man had been killed or if she'd be disappointed that she didn't get the chance to do it herself.

But Xanthus shook his head. "He hid in his tent."

Attia's mouth quirked in bitter amusement. "Of course he did. So what happens now? Do we turn back to Rome?" Hope flared in Attia's breast at the thought of going back to Rome, back to where Crassus was apparently staying.

But Xanthus shook his head. "Ardea—it's a province about two days away. Timeus is too embarrassed to go back to the capital like this."

"What's in Ardea?"

"No one is sure. The people there don't consider themselves a part of the Republic. The soldiers and Lucius are against it, but Timeus is adamant. Some of his men will stay behind to see to the bodies. The rest of us will leave at first light."

Several armed guards approached.

"Master Lucius has requested that his sister and her nursemaid be housed in his personal tent." They glanced at Xanthus. "Please bring the child and come with us."

Attia wondered if they would have been so polite if Timeus's champion weren't present. "All right," Attia said.

The guards waited patiently while Sabina wrapped Rory up in a thick blanket, moving to surround them as they walked across the wrecked camp to Lucius's tent. Xanthus walked with them, stopping short several feet from the tent's entrance. He gave Attia a small smile before walking away.

Attia kept her face impassive, but she could feel her pulse racing as she and Sabina readied Rory for bed. Like the rest of the household, she had no idea what kind of welcome they'd find in Ardea. All she cared about was that she'd soon find herself outside of the Republic's authority. She bit her lip, contemplating what to do, when Rory's voice broke through her thoughts.

"Attia?" Rory's small voice trembled. She'd been terrified in the cart, listening to the screams and the fighting. The only thing that could console her was Attia clutching her tight. "Will you tell me a story?"

Attia went to the girl's bedside. "A story? About what?"

"I don't know. Anything. Please?" she begged.

Attia slid onto the bed next to the little girl. "All right. Well.

Let's see. I'll tell you the story of . . . of a young girl who was a princess and a warrior, and whose people loved her."

Rory laughed, though her body was still shaking with fear. "Princesses can't be warriors," she said. "Can they?"

"Of course they can. Sometimes. Sometimes a princess must be strong and learn to fight so that . . ." Attia paused, her throat tightening.

"So that what?" Rory prodded.

Sabina busied herself by the fire, but her eyes kept flicking back toward Attia.

"So that she can protect her people," Attia finally said, swallowing hard. "This princess—well, her father taught her that the most important thing in her life was protecting her people. He taught her honor and glory and pride. But most of all, he taught her duty. It was her job to remember all of those lessons, no matter what."

Attia paused again, this time blinking against the moisture that gathered in her eyes. It was probably from the perfumes in the air. The night was cool, but the tent was stifling in its finery. Attia cleared her throat and opened her arms so that Rory could climb onto her lap.

"Was she a good princess?" Rory asked.

"She tried to be."

"Was she a great warrior?"

"She tried to be."

"Did you know her?"

Attia closed her eyes and rested her head against the little girl's hair. "Yes," she whispered. "I knew her once. A very long time ago."

As Rory fell asleep in her arms, Attia focused her thoughts on the days ahead.

Ardea. That's when she'd get her chance. Outside of Rome's authority, she would finally be able to make her move, and she promised herself that she wouldn't fail. As soon as they reached the province, she would escape. She would kill Timeus, take what supplies she could, and finally go after the man who had ruined her life. *Even if it means leaving* him. *Xanthus.*

No. *Gareth.*

Attia fell asleep with his name on her lips.

CHAPTER 12

After a full day and a night of travelling with little rest and even less food, Xanthus expected more. But all that greeted them when they finally reached the outskirts of Ardea were ghosts and dust. The city looked entirely deserted sitting atop its gentle slope—all stone outcroppings and high, crumbling walls. No men. No flags. No movement. The paved Roman road leading to Ardea's rusted gates had been hammered away, leaving behind an uneven dirt path littered with discarded stone. It was as clear a confirmation as any of Ardea's rumored secession.

Timeus and Lucius exchanged heated words at the head of the caravan as they argued over what to do. They could backtrack to the fork in the road that led on to Pompeii, but they would lose a full day in the process. They had no more food, no supplies, and now they were more than three days away from Rome. But they couldn't stay where they were. Even an idiot knew better than to camp on an open road, and the soldiers and guards were already paranoid after the attack in the clearing. Their eyes continually scanned the hills and woods to the east. With daylight waning, anxiety began to seep through the caravan.

The setting sun sparked like fire on the flat expanse of the sea. Deep reds and flowering oranges flickered and flashed, though they couldn't quite compensate for the gray stillness of the city above. The glare of the water made Xanthus squint as he watched Timeus and Lucius argue. But all too soon, night fell, and with it came a gloomy darkness that blanketed the road in shadow.

Then Xanthus saw it—movement. Too much movement. He hurried toward the front of the caravan, his eyes trained on the rise of the hill and the seemingly abandoned walls of the city.

Except they weren't abandoned anymore. Men—and women, too—had appeared like wraiths, all strapped with blades and bows and clubs. The people of Ardea looked more like a colony of outlaws, and within minutes, more had appeared from the forest to surround Timeus's caravan.

They were trapped.

Lucius glared at his uncle even as he rested a hand on his sword. When he saw Xanthus, he spoke in a low voice. "Do you think these are the thieves from the clearing?"

Xanthus shook his head. "No. I doubt these would have run."

Timeus scowled. He looked more irritated than frightened. "They're rabble in need of a bath. Nothing more." The man was too proud for his own good.

Xanthus tried not to look back down the road, at the cart where Attia rode with the child. If he'd learned anything these past few days, it was that the Thracian could take care of herself. At any rate, he knew he'd have other things to worry about soon enough.

The Ardeans' leader emerged from a break in the city's wall.

He was a blob of a man with black hair that hung in strings around his face. His rounded belly bulged against his tunic as he shuffled toward the caravan.

"At least they don't seem to be short on food," Lucius quipped.

Xanthus actually smiled.

The man walked right up to Timeus, who was still atop his horse. "Well. Who in Pluto's name are you?"

"I am Josias Neleus Timeus. And who"—he looked over the man's body with barely concealed disgust—"are *you?*"

"Fido. I am master of this city, and you are uninvited. But since you've already walked down my road, you'll have to pay the toll."

Xanthus glanced back at his brothers, who'd come to stand a few feet behind him. The gladiators weren't restrained this time. But they didn't have weapons, and they could all count.

"Five to one," Lebuin murmured. "At least."

Albinus's hands twitched at his waist.

"The Princeps has not instituted a toll to use his road," Timeus said.

The Ardeans laughed.

"Neither your Princeps nor any Roman has standing here," Fido said. "And we are a simple people. You pay the toll, or you die."

Everyone in the caravan knew they had little to offer. The whole point of coming to Ardea was to seek shelter and try to resupply. Whatever debts they incurred would have to be paid at a later date. At least, that was Timeus's plan, and he said as much.

"I can give you whatever price you wish. *After* we reach Pompeii," he said.

Fido shook his head. "I don't want gold," he said. His eyes turned to Xanthus. "I want him."

Timeus didn't even blink. "A single slave?" he said, infusing his voice with skepticism.

Fido shook his head and clicked his tongue. "I am not stupid, and we are not so removed from the Republic that I can't recognize the Champion of Rome when I see him. His reputation precedes you all, and he'll be worth more than any price *you* can pay once I put him up for auction. Give him to me, and in exchange I'll offer shelter and whatever else you need."

Timeus narrowed his eyes. "No."

"You're hardly in a position to deny me," Fido said. "But if you insist, then *you* can leave. Without your property. Without your horses. Without your women or your guards or your slaves. Just you—walking off into the sunset on your way to . . . Pompeii, was it? Do you think an old man like you can survive a week on the road alone? Choose carefully, Josias Neleus Timeus. If you want to keep your household intact, the champion is the price."

Timeus looked ready to tear Fido apart with his bare hands.

But then Lucius spoke up. "I have a better idea," he said. "Let Xanthus fight."

Fido cocked his head, considering.

The vein in Timeus's forehead was bulging again. "Lucius . . ." he said in a dangerously low voice.

"Xanthus is the Champion of Rome," Lucius said. His voice hardened and his expression became unreadable. "Let him fight, and if he lives, you give us what we want. If he dies . . ." Lucius shrugged. "You keep whatever we have left. Simple. But I think we can all agree that Xanthus is the best fighter in Rome. He'll beat any man you have and then some."

"Really?" Fido said with a slow grin. "Any man?"

"Any," Lucius said again.

"And *then* some?"

"That's right."

Fido looked at Timeus.

The old man glared back. "That's our offer."

Fido's grin widened, and he spread his arms to the Ardeans gathered around. "Do I have any volunteers?"

Every single Ardean man let out a loud shout. The sound reverberated against the darkened sky.

Fido clapped his hands. "He fights until dawn. If he survives, so do you."

The cart lurched and rocked on the uneven road. Rory still had her arms wrapped around Attia's waist, and Attia could feel her tiny body trembling. At least an hour passed before the cart stopped, and then it took yet another hour before someone opened the outer door. Attia leaned out to take in their new surroundings.

Timeus's guards paced warily around the cart. Tall, bright torches lined the road on both sides. Empty insulas rose up around them, the windows dark and the doors thrown carelessly open. A row of silk awnings had been erected from the back of the cart to a pitted wooden door on ground level.

It seemed that Rory's cart had been driven down a street that curved through the city of Ardea, right up to the door of a small, windowless room that had been allotted to the Mistress Aurora Bassus and her nursemaid.

Biting back her questions, Attia carried Rory inside. A fur rug covered the hard-packed earth floor, and old tapestries hung crookedly on the walls. Against the far wall, a bed of blankets, pillows, furs, and other soft things had already been prepared. Water steamed from a copper tub in the middle of the room, filling the space with the scent of lavender.

"Do I *have* to take a bath?" Rory asked, her head resting on Attia's shoulder. "I'm not the least bit dirty."

"Then it shouldn't take very long, should it?" Attia said.

She tried to make a game of it—frothing up the soap and water so that a thin layer of bubbles coated Rory's pale skin. The poor thing must have lived quite a boring life; she was so easily amused. She laughed and giggled and made little splashes in the water until Attia declared she was quite finished.

"You're going to look like a prune if you stay in the water much longer."

"Mother loves prunes," Rory said.

Attia hid a smile before pulling a sleeping tunic over the girl's head and tucking her into the blankets and pillows. Within moments, the girl was asleep, and Attia knew from experience that nothing but the falling sky could wake her now.

Sabina entered the room a few minutes later. Her face was damp with sweat. She walked to the copper tub and splashed water onto her forehead.

"There are people everywhere," she said. "The Ardeans were hiding—waiting for nightfall."

"Clever of them."

"Timeus has arranged for us to stay a while, but the soldiers have to wait at the gates. They aren't allowed into the city."

"So Ardea has seceded after all."

"It certainly looks like it," Sabina said. She looked toward the bed, and seeing Rory already asleep, she smiled sadly. "You're good with her. You'll make a fine mother."

Attia shrugged, suddenly uncomfortable. She felt more affection for the child than she thought she could ever feel for any Roman. But Attia wasn't the tender kind, and she only had a few memories of her own mother. How could she ever be one? Especially now?

"You kept her safe, too," Sabina said, almost to herself. "Who knows what might have happened otherwise?"

"Timeus's men would have intervened."

"If you thought so, then why did you bother?"

Attia didn't respond, and neither of them said anything for a while.

Somehow, despite the fire, the room had gotten colder. Attia could even see her breath. The burning coals shot little sparks of red up the shaft in the wall that served as a vent. An unexpected funnel of cold air swirled through the room.

Attia turned, and her eyes settled on the door before she even realized why. It was only a dark, ugly thing separating them from the guards who paced in the street. Heavy and pitted, it blocked out all of the light from the lanterns outside, except for one bright, narrow crevice along one vertical edge. Attia stood and began walking toward it.

"There's something I should tell you," Sabina said, though her voice sounded far away. Attia's gaze was focused solely on the door. "The dominus, he's agreed to . . . Attia, what are you doing?"

Attia stood before the door, reached out, and pushed gently.

The unlocked door swung open.

Xanthus stood alone in the middle of a pathetic excuse for an arena. Fewer than thirty yards across at its widest point and bordered all around by rotting wooden boards, it held over five hundred spectators. The ground was nothing but dirt and excrement, and squeaking critters raced along the edges.

It had taken less than an hour for the news to spread throughout the city: The Champion of Rome was among them and ready to fight. Borrowed swords in hand, Xanthus waited in the center of the arena as Timeus introduced him.

The old man's long face had calmed, but there was an edge to his voice as he forced the familiar words out of his mouth. "Rome's champion needs no introduction," the dominus shouted. "Call his name! Release his fury!"

The crowd screamed.

Finished, Timeus met Xanthus's eyes, and for a split second, an emotion that Xanthus had never seen crossed the old man's face. If Xanthus didn't know better, he would have thought it was regret. Then it was gone, and the first of his opponents entered the arena.

The Ardean seemed to think he was some kind of dancer. His feet moved in ridiculous, circular movements, and he bobbed his head to music Xanthus couldn't hear. He made a big show of edging around Xanthus but staying just out of reach. His comrades cheered him on.

Even if Xanthus wanted to look that stupid, he couldn't afford the luxury. According to the terms of Timeus's agreement with Fido, Xanthus had to fight until dawn. To do that, he needed to conserve his energy as much as possible. So when the man finally charged at him with a shout and a lazy swing of his sword, Xanthus simply ducked. He smacked the broadside of his weapon against the man's thigh before moving calmly to the other end of the arena.

The Ardeans weren't expecting that. They began laughing and pointing in delight while Xanthus's opponent reddened with embarrassment.

From the balcony above, Timeus muttered, "I hate when he does this."

Ennius smiled. "But the crowds always love it."

The man was too easy to play with. Xanthus managed to

draw the fight out for ten minutes. Then twenty. If circumstances had been different, he might have seriously considered simply falling to his knees and letting his opponent's sword drive home. But his mind swirled with images of Attia—the olive gold of her skin in the moonlight, the way she unconsciously scrunched her nose when she was annoyed, the curve of her mouth when she granted him one of her rare smiles.

"Damn it all, Xanthus. Finish him!" Timeus shouted.

Xanthus blinked, flexing his callused hands around the grips of his swords. A second later, he ducked his opponent's blade, came up on one knee, and struck the other man in the back. The man fell with a hollow thud.

The Ardeans clearly didn't consider themselves Romans, but to Xanthus, their cheers sounded exactly the same.

Cold air streamed in, raising goosebumps all along Attia's arms. The hanging lanterns glowed against the sky. The guards outside were asleep, having succumbed to fatigue and hunger.

This was her chance. With the soldiers shut outside the city gates, the guards asleep, and nearly everyone else preoccupied with the match, she could run. Better yet, she could find Timeus's chambers. Once she had him alone, she'd kill him. Then nothing would stand in the way of her hunt for Crassus.

Attia hurried to one of the chests in the room and started rummaging through it for proper shoes and clothing. She knew she wouldn't get anywhere in the dress and flimsy sandals she currently wore.

"Attia, stop," Sabina said, grasping her arm. "You're not thinking this through."

Attia shook her arm free. "As you've been so keen to remind me, I am a slave in a Roman household. Escaping is nearly all

I've thought about. Do you really expect me to just sit here now with an open door staring me in the face?" She pulled out a pair of dark trousers, a matching tunic, and soft boots that likely belonged to Lucius. They were too big, but wrapping her feet in fabric helped with the fit and the cold. Attia burrowed through one of Rory's chests, looking for the last thing she needed.

"Timeus will find you. You know that. You're risking your life for nothing! You want to escape? Escape where?"

Attia reached to the bottom of the chest and pulled out the map she'd stolen from Timeus's study.

"You can't go, Attia," she said firmly. "It's not just Timeus's guards you'll have to worry about. If the Ardeans find out someone's escaped the city, everything will have been in vain."

"What are you talking about?"

"It was the price Timeus paid for us to stay here—the toll the Ardeans demanded for accommodating us and for letting us all leave together."

Attia frowned. "What toll?"

"Xanthus has to fight."

His name made Attia pause for an instant as she remembered the feel of his hands, his arms, his lips on hers. Escaping meant leaving him, and her stomach twisted with regret. But she pushed the emotion violently away. "Well, so what? I've seen him in the arena—he's just as good as everyone says. He'll win easily. No Ardean is going to beat him."

"But he's not fighting just *one* Ardean."

"What do you mean?"

Sabina released her wrist. "He has to fight every man who volunteers, and he has to last until dawn. No other gladiators are allowed, and no one in the household can leave the city unless he wins. If you go missing, the entire deal will be forfeit."

"Well, how many Ardeans have volunteered?"

"All of them."

Attia sat back on her heels. The map fell to the floor at her feet. She shut her eyes and turned away from Sabina, swallowing past the lump in her throat. She imagined Xanthus in an arena somewhere in the city. She imagined him fighting at this very moment, forced again to do the one thing he hated most. Alone.

"He's good enough. He's the best. He can do this. He can . . ." Attia clenched her hands as her vision collapsed to a single point, bright as a dying star. Sabina's words echoed in her head, each one sharp, each one cutting into Attia with unforgiving precision. She felt as though she were bleeding from the inside. "I . . ." The choice should have been obvious. In so many ways, it was. She looked down at her closed fists, and words bubbled up from deep inside her. "I have to help him."

Sabina grabbed her arm again. "That's *not* what I'm saying, Attia. I'm telling you that you can't help, and you can't run. You'll only make everything worse. If Timeus tells Xanthus he has to fight the whole world, there is nothing we can do about it. No one defies Rome."

"Rome?" Attia spit on the floor. "Rome has taken everything from me—my family, my home, my freedom. I won't let it have Xanthus."

"It already has him—it *owns* him. He is a gladiator. His life and death belong to the Republic, to Timeus. Just as we do." Attia tried again to pull her arm free, but Sabina's grip tightened. "Attia, *don't*."

"What happened to you?" Attia said, hurling the words like stones. "When did you become such a coward? Or were you a coward to begin with?" She pushed Sabina away. "*I* am not. I am a Thracian."

"So was I."

The breath caught in Attia's chest, and she could do nothing but stare at Sabina as though seeing her for the first time.

"I am a slave in a Roman household, Attia," Sabina said, softly but clearly. "But I and my mother, and her mother, and her mother were born of Thrace. And my father and husband were Maedi warriors."

"That's not possible," she whispered. "That's not . . . it can't . . . no! No! I don't believe you. You're a liar. You never said anything!"

Sabina's expression turned sympathetic, but Attia shook her head.

"If that's true, why wouldn't you tell me? You let me feel like I was alone in the world. I wanted to *die*."

"But you didn't. You couldn't die because you were born for greater things. A warrior princess does not lose hope so easily."

Attia laughed bitterly. "You knew that, too? How? How could you know?"

"I know because ten years ago, the swordlord of Thrace named his daughter as his heir," Sabina said. "And I was there to see it."

Attia stared at her.

"You were so small and so brave. When I heard what happened—" Her voice broke, but she took a breath and went on. "I wondered if it was you. It didn't matter, not really. But as soon as I saw you, I knew."

Attia turned away, wanting to weep and completely unable to. Maybe she'd already spent her share of tears, or maybe there was nothing left to grieve for. Her last hope seemed to be fading right in front of her.

A lifetime ago, she'd wanted nothing but the strength to lead her people. A minute ago, she'd wanted freedom, justice. But now all she could think of was Xanthus fighting alone in the arena.

"I have to help him. I'm *going* to help him," Attia said.

"The moment you step outside that door—to go to his aid or to attempt an escape—the guards and the Ardeans will see you. They will arrest you. You will be crucified."

"They won't catch me."

"Even if you make it to the arena, I already told you, Xanthus has to fight alone."

"I'll find a way."

"I won't help you get yourself killed. Not after everything."

"I don't need your help, Sabina. You know that."

"Attia, *please*," she begged. But she saw the steely resolve in Atta's eyes.

Attia grasped her hands. "I would do it for you."

With a sigh of resignation, Sabina helped Attia secure her hair under a tight black wrap that covered her head, neck, and most of her face. Attia used ash and soot to smudge rings around her eyes and across the bridge of her nose. Rory's darkest linens were employed to fashion wrappings around her hands and wrists, while Lucius's trousers, tunic, and boots clothed the rest of her in layers of black.

By the time they were done, Attia looked a bit bigger, a bit broader, and nothing like a young woman. Funny. This was how Attia had thought to make her escape. Now she was ready to run straight into the wolves' lair.

"How do I look?" she asked.

"If someone stares at you too long, you might still be re-cognized," Sabina said.

"I won't be."

Outside, the moon had disappeared behind heavy clouds. Xanthus must be growing tired, and dawn was still far away.

"Please," Sabina begged, one last time. "Don't go."

Attia leaned forward to kiss the older woman's cheek through the scarf that covered her face. Then she slid out into the night, gripping the lintel of the door and hauling herself up, using the deep pockmarks in the wall face to climb to the roof. She might as well have been a shadow, silent as she was.

She raced along the roofs of insulas and shacks toward the brightly lit arena in the distance. She could see them easily in the darkness—the hundreds of torches glowing from the depression of the stadium. And she could hear them—the excited shouts of men as they watched their brothers fight to the death.

When Attia reached the arena, she climbed to the top of the outer wall just below the balcony where Timeus sat with Fido, crouched down, and listened.

"It's not possible," Fido grumbled. "Seven men in a row? No one is that good."

Timeus spoke through gritted teeth, but his words sounded slurred. "He is Xanthus Maximus Colossus. Of course he's that good."

Attia couldn't disagree, but she still frowned with worry as she looked down onto the arena floor. To any other observer—like Timeus or Lucius or Fido—Xanthus looked resilient as ever. His breathing was slow and even. His green eyes were bright and alert. He fought with a ferocity that left the Ardeans gasping in fear and delight.

But Attia saw how he kept flexing his shoulders and hands. That slow breathing of his was intentionally deep and carefully measured. Only a truly experienced fighter would notice the signs, and Attia saw them all—the fatigue, the exhaustion. She knew he wouldn't last till dawn.

Above her, Timeus stood, sending his chair toppling backward. "I'm tired," he declared.

"The night has just begun," Fido said. "Sit, Timeus. Drink!"

"Ennius, stay with my nephew," Timeus said. "He may need some . . . advice as acting lanista." Then he turned away, surrounded by his guards, and left the arena to the jeers of the crowd and the drunken supplications of Fido.

Ennius and Lucius said nothing, but Attia had a good idea why Timeus refused to stay till the end: He honestly didn't know if Xanthus would survive this, and he couldn't sit there and watch his champion fall.

Coward.

Attia looked out over the grimy, bloodthirsty faces of hundreds of Ardeans before slipping from her perch and working her way through them like a wraith. Between the wine and the excitement, no one paid her much attention. And when the next fight started, she found herself watching as spellbound as anyone else. But she kept silent amidst the cheers and taunts. She felt like she was holding a vigil rather than witnessing a death match.

The skin on the back of her neck prickled, giving her the unnerving sensation that she was being watched. Her eyes drifted back up to the balcony only to look straight into Ennius's curious, penetrating stare. She wasn't sure what had made him look down at her. Perhaps it was her stillness in the midst of the stadium's discord. Perhaps it was the fact that her appearance was almost entirely obscured, though no one else had seemed to notice yet. Whatever the reason, Ennius narrowed his eyes before turning and making his way toward the stairs.

Attia hurried through the crowd to wait for him on the second-floor landing, wondering just how she would explain herself to him and hoping that he would somehow understand.

Ennius paused several steps above her. "Who are you?" His eyes narrowed with suspicion.

Attia didn't answer, only took a step toward him.

"What's your name? Your house?"

Still, she didn't answer, but took another step closer.

Ennius's eyes widened, and she knew she didn't have to say anything at all. He hobbled down the last few steps until he was only inches away from her face. She could tell he was fighting the urge to grab her—probably shake her—but guards patrolled nearby, so he struggled instead to keep his voice even and his composure calm. "Are you insane? If you're caught—"

"Sabina has given me this lecture," Attia said quietly. "You can either waste time repeating it or help me."

"Help you? Help you with what?"

"He's been fighting for hours, Ennius, and he's getting tired. You see it, don't you?"

"You came to help Xanthus?" He couldn't keep the astonishment out of his voice.

"Yes. Will you help *me*?"

He shook his head. "You are not a gladiator. You would get killed in the arena. Besides, even if you could help him, it's not part of the deal. There can only be one gladiator for the House of Timeus, and he has to fight until dawn."

"It's my lucky day, then. I think you should be able to see the obvious loophole in that. You said it yourself, Ennius: I am no gladiator."

"No, Attia," Ennius said, shaking his head. "I can't believe that you made it here unseen, but you have to go back. Leave before the guards catch you!"

"He needs me. I can't leave."

"I know you're quick and apparently talented at moving in darkness, but this is no game," Ennius said.

"You're right. It's not."

"I could have you dragged back to your quarters."

"You could."

"You could be flogged or even crucified for this."

"And Xanthus could die in that arena. Death is inevitable, Ennius. That doesn't mean we should stop fighting."

Ennius stared at her. "You would risk your life for him?"

"I suppose it was only a matter of time before I started to see him the way the rest of you do," Attia said. "If you love him at all, you'll help me."

"Ennius?"

They both looked up to see Lucius and Fido leaning over the third-floor railing.

"What's going on? Who is that?" Lucius asked.

Ennius sighed before turning back to Attia. "A contender."

CHAPTER 13

T

Xanthus would say this much for the Ardeans—they knew how to handle themselves. After ten years in the arena, he could take one look at a man and determine how well he was going to fight. New slaves panicked. Their motions were erratic, and they often died quickly. Former soldiers tried to jab and cut, following too many rules that no longer applied. The best gladiators had a mix of formal training and good instincts. Their eyes took in everything—arm movements, leg movements, the twitch of a brow or quirk of the mouth.

The Ardeans didn't seem to have any training to speak of, but their instincts and ferocity almost made up for it. It was clear to Xanthus from the very first contender that these were men who had fought often and for much of their lives.

His eighth opponent strutted into the arena like a peacock, but he was light on his feet, for all that he looked slightly drunk. Back and forth, they circled each other. He didn't seem to be in any hurry. Xanthus wondered if he could keep this up until dawn.

During one particularly long circuit around the arena, Xanthus's attention drifted, and the peacock chose that moment to take a jab and nick Xanthus's side. Blood spilled from the narrow cut, and the crowd began to scream in earnest. Xanthus reacted instinctually, spinning around and restraining the man's arm. The peacock kicked backward and broke free. With a shout, he raised his sword high and brought it crashing down. It was almost too easy for Xanthus to block the hit and drive his own sword into the man's chest.

The words that followed felt like they'd worn themselves into his soul. "Forgive me," he whispered as the body was dragged away.

Gods, he was tired. It had been days since he'd had a proper night's sleep. He just needed to close his eyes for a moment. He could feel his lids starting to drift shut when the sound of shouting caught his attention.

"He is *not* a gladiator!"

Xanthus looked up in confusion.

"He is barely a man!" Lucius was shouting. "Yet his one true wish is to fight beside his hero, the Champion of Rome! Are you not bored with these cheap wins? What do you have to be frightened of? Look at him!" He swung his arm around to point at the figure standing at the edge of the balcony.

Xanthus had no idea what was going on, but Lucius was right about the stranger—he was barely a man. His short legs were strapped with leather manicas meant for a soldier's arms, and he wore a light, useless piece of leather across his chest. Black clothing covered the rest of his body and most of his face. He was laughably small.

Amusement and curiosity bloomed on the Ardeans' faces.

Xanthus gritted his teeth in exasperation. Lucius wanted to send *that* boy into the arena with him? Was he trying to get them *both* killed?

"And *when* he dies," Lucius continued with a broad, fake smile, "wine for everyone!" He raised his hands, and the crowd conceded with deafening cheers.

Xanthus groaned and pinched the bridge of his nose.

This is going to be a long night.

There was no other way to put it—Fido smelled like literal shit. It was as though a fat hog had eaten a dinner of moldy boots, sour wine, and month-old cheese, and then proceeded to defecate all over the tunic that Fido wore. Standing a few feet away from him made Attia gag as she tried to focus her watering eyes on Xanthus.

She listened as Lucius convinced the crowd to let her join, and smiled when she saw Xanthus pinch the bridge of his nose in exasperation. It was a motion she'd seen a few times already.

Ennius led her to a table that held all manner of macabre toys for her to choose from—curved swords, knives as thin and sharp as razors, double-headed axes, blunt machetes, star-shaped pieces of iron with pointed tips. But she chose the gladius, simple and short. The grip of the sword fit perfectly in her hand. The weight was well balanced.

The weapon was an easy choice. The name was a different matter entirely.

Ennius escorted her to the gate of the arena. "What are we supposed to call you?" he asked.

Attia thought she wouldn't care what they called her now that they'd called her a slave. But she found that she still did care, and the one name that meant the most to her was the one that would most probably end her. She looked into Ennius's night-dark eyes. "They say Spartan blood flows in Thracian veins. And I am a daughter of the Maedi. Call me Sparro."

Ennius showed no outward reaction, though he did stare at her for what felt like a long time. Finally, he said, "I hope you know what you're doing, Thracian."

So Attia waited impatiently at the gate to the arena while Lucius introduced her from the third-floor balcony, sounding so much like his uncle that chills rose along her skin.

"He has appeared like a shade from the underworld. Light as smoke, small as a demon," Lucius said.

Attia rolled her eyes.

"Not quite a man—but not a boy either," he said.

If only he knew how right he is.

"And he has come for one reason—to fight beside a favored son of Rome, like the shadow of death itself! I give you . . . Spartacus!"

Attia looked up at Ennius. She'd given him her father's name, but apparently, he wasn't quite willing to let her be as reckless as she wanted. He shrugged one shoulder in non-apology as Attia was pushed forward into the arena.

No one made a sound.

The silence was uncomfortable, to say the least. A part of Attia had expected at least a few cheers. Maybe the idea of her had seemed more appealing from a distance. But now that the crowd was actually looking at her, their expressions were a mixture of disinterest, disappointment, and boredom. Someone dropped a cup of wine, and Attia actually heard it clatter down the steps.

Attia scowled. Really? Not a single shout of welcome? Not even a little bit of polite applause? She knew it shouldn't bother her, but it did. Her irritation only grew when the next Ardean contender approached, and the stadium practically vibrated with screams for the man. She crossed her arms over her chest as the man stepped forward.

He was easily twice her width and at least a head taller. If she stood close, she'd probably have to crane her neck to look him in the eye. None of that was particularly important. She focused instead on his body language as he chose a long weapon with three sharp points. Like Xanthus's last opponent, this man was cocky. He sauntered into the arena, kicking out his legs with each step, jutting his chest forward, and throwing his shoulders back.

Attia lowered her arms and flexed her hand around the hilt of her sword, letting her body adjust to the weight of the weapon.

For his part, Xanthus seemed totally unimpressed with both of them. "Just stay out of my way," he said to Attia without even looking at her. "I have plenty to feel guilty about without adding your death to the scales."

Then he moved away, leaving her cross and alone as he and the new fighter started to circle each other.

Attia had the incredible urge to throw her sword at someone. Ennius was probably pleased. Maybe he thought if she didn't have the chance to take part—if she saw that she wasn't needed—then she'd just go back to her little rock-walled cell and stay quiet.

We'll see about that.

The Ardean's trident met the angle between Xanthus's crossed swords, sending sparks raining down onto the sand. The man pulled free before striking again. Xanthus blocked with ease. They continued their striking and dodging while Attia stood uselessly off to the side. She needed to find a way to join the fight without interfering with Xanthus's concentration, but she couldn't see an opening.

Maybe she *had* made a mistake. Maybe her presence would only put Xanthus at even greater risk. For now, she couldn't do anything but wait and watch.

The Ardean contender swung his trident at Xanthus's legs. Xanthus jumped to dodge it, but he wasn't quite fast enough. The heel of his right boot caught on one of the prongs, and he tumbled to the sand, rolling to a stop just a few feet away from Attia.

The Ardean charged.

No.

Attia took a running step and used Xanthus's shoulder as leverage to launch herself into the air, twisting her body so that she landed on her feet just behind the Ardean. She drove her sword into his back, and the tip emerged through the front of his chest. When she pulled the gladius free, the Ardean fell to the ground with a thud.

The entire arena went deadly silent again, but this time it was with shock. They all stared at Attia as though she'd spontaneously grown a new limb. Then someone in the crowd started to cheer—finally—and soon everyone joined in.

Attia's satisfaction faded when Xanthus stood, sheathed his swords, and grabbed her arm. He peered into her eyes, and the same expression that Attia had seen on Ennius's face dawned on Xanthus's—shocked, terrified recognition.

"Attia?" The exhaustion vanished as his face contorted. "What are you doing here?"

Attia grasped his tunic, belatedly realizing that he wore no armor. "I couldn't let you do this alone."

"You need to leave—"

"No, I can help," Attia said. "I . . . I don't want to lose you."

"And how do you think I'll feel if you die here? You *have* to leave."

"I won't."

Xanthus's fierce green eyes bore into hers.

"You're stuck with me," Attia said. "And if we die, we die to-gether."

Xanthus released a heavy breath, his eyes never leaving her face. "Together," he said, and raised their clasped hands into the air.

They released two contenders at a time after that, but Attia's presence had sparked a fire in Xanthus. He'd looked close to submitting from sheer exhaustion, but with her at his side, he seemed to find renewed energy to keep fighting, not for himself or for the crowd, but for her.

And, yet again, she had little need of his protection.

Lucius's introduction proved chillingly prophetic. Attia moved like a demon of myth—quick, light, so fast that it looked like she could walk on walls and appear like a phantom behind her target. Her style was a complete contrast to Xanthus, who moved as purposefully as the sun.

They were shadow and light. Death in two forms. Together, they killed ten, twenty, forty men before the sun rose.

At last, when predawn turned the sky a deep gray that mirrored Attia's eyes, they panted beside each other, almost completely spent. They had a short reprieve while Fido and Lucius argued over who the last contestants would be.

"One more," Attia said, breathing hard.

"You mean two."

"So what usually happens when you win?"

"What you'd expect," Xanthus said with a shrug. "Food, gold, jewels, horses. Sometimes new slaves, but not always. In this case, we'll get another night in the city, supplies for the journey, and Timeus will be gifted twelve Iberian stallions."

"Lovely. And the ass isn't even here."

Up on the balcony, Fido grumbled and rubbed his rolling gut.

Lucius raised his hands. "Ardeans!" he cried. "We have witnessed a true spectacle tonight! Xanthus, the Champion of Rome, and Spartacus, the Shadow of Death, have shown us something that we have never seen before—invincibility!"

The crowd jeered. They had gotten their spectacle. They had seen the Champion of Rome in action. But it had come at the price of Ardean lives.

"For their final feat, let them prove that they are truly immortal!" As he spoke, Lucius looked straight at Xanthus and nodded his encouragement.

A rusted gate opened just below the balcony, and wet snarls rippled out from the dark. Little clouds of dust rose into the air as furry paws stomped onto the sand. Flat heads, long snouts, elongated canines attached to gray, matted bodies.

Attia almost laughed as five wolves prowled into the arena. "You know, it's fitting," she said. "I've wanted to gut a true Roman for some time now."

"You're being unfair to the wolves."

"Shall we make this interesting? One kill with one hit. Consider it a challenge."

Xanthus laughed bitterly. "You mean something beyond the challenge to live?"

"Yes, and the prize is that you name what you kill." Attia winked at him before running straight toward the center of the arena.

The crowd took one long, simultaneous gasp.

Attia jumped off the ball of her foot and twisted in the air, narrowly missing the snapping jaws of the first wolf. She landed on its head and stabbed it through before coming to rest with both feet on a narrow ledge protruding from the far wall. She raised her sword with a flourish to the roar of the crowd.

Xanthus couldn't help but glare at her from across the arena, but Attia thought the expression warred with a slight smile.

The four remaining wolves stalked her from below, snarling in frustration. Xanthus gripped his swords and feigned an attack on the wolf nearest to him. When it lunged, he caught its neck between his swords and beheaded it in one smooth motion.

While the wolves were distracted, Attia leapt off her ledge and landed close to Xanthus. "I name the first one Timeus."

"You're mad, you know that?" Xanthus said.

"I'm tired, though at this point there's not much of a difference." She glanced at him with a raised eyebrow. "Well?"

"That one's Sisera," he said, nodding at the other fallen wolf.

Attia laughed and jabbed her sword at the forelegs of one of the animals. It growled ferociously and lunged, baring its belly to Attia's blade. "Fido," she said as it fell. "They actually smell quite similar."

"Again, you're being unfair to the wolves."

They crouched back-to-back as the last two wolves circled them.

"You take that one, and I'll take this one," Attia said.

"How am I supposed to tell which is which?"

"Do I really need to explain the fundamentals of 'right' and 'left'?"

Xanthus sighed and went for the wolf closest to him at the same moment that the second wolf launched itself at Attia's throat.

The animal snapped at Xanthus's legs as he circled, looking for a weak spot. Xanthus stabbed one of his swords at the wolf's rear. It twisted away to defend itself, exposing its neck. Xanthus's sword sliced clean through it. The animal was dead before it hit the ground.

Someone in the crowd shouted, pointing to the other side of

the arena. Attia lay completely still with the last wolf stretched on top of her.

Xanthus ran to her side and slashed at the animal's back. Its body shuddered for a moment before toppling over, Attia's gladius protruding from its belly.

"Crassus," she said breathlessly before pulling her sword free. Blood drenched the front of her clothes, lending a shine to the dark material. Attia got to her feet and clasped Xanthus's hand.

And the Ardeans cheered.

"Xanthus!" Lucius called from the edge of the arena. Fido stood beside him.

Lucius shook Xanthus's hand, dirty and bloody as it was. His face was carefully neutral. "Well done," he said simply, with no small amount of relief in his voice.

Fido glowered. "The horses will be ready for your master on the road. I must admit that I have never seen such an exhibition. I didn't believe you would live past dusk, let alone dawn. What are you? Some gods from legend? Spawns of Mars himself?"

Xanthus glanced down at Attia. Her face was still covered by cloth and grime and blood, her eyes red with exhaustion. "Not gods. Just . . . men."

Behind Fido, Ennius smiled.

Lucius turned to Attia. "Spartacus, the Shadow of Death," he said. "For whom do you fight?"

Attia glanced at Xanthus, then at Ennius, before finally shrugging.

"No one? No lanista or master?" Lucius asked. "What, are you just a freeman looking for thrills?"

Attia nodded.

"Are you mute?"

She nodded again.

"Were you born that way?" Lucius asked.

She shook her head and tried not to glare at Ennius's amused smile.

"Well, anyway, consider yourself our honored guest," Lucius said.

Attia shook her head again.

"I insist," Lucius said. "You fought honorably beside our champion, after all. No doubt my uncle will convince you to make your oath with us before the day is through." He motioned to Ennius. "Will you find him a place?"

"He can share my quarters," Xanthus said.

"It's settled then." Lucius turned to Fido. "The House of Timeus will not soon forget the . . . hospitality you have shown us."

"And Ardea will not forget the House of Timeus," Fido said, turning his eyes to Attia.

The crowd parted to let them pass. Everyone bowed their heads in deference to Lucius and Fido. But the names on their lips did not belong to noblemen or even freemen, but to a slight figure in black and the gladiator behind her.

"Xanthus!" they cried. Then, a chant.

"Spartacus! Spartacus! Spartacus!"

CHAPTER 14

The room smelled like mold. The air was heavy and damp. A lantern flared to life, and Attia could see rock walls glistening with moisture. She wondered if the door to this room would be locked or if even in this strange place, Xanthus had his privileges.

Now that they were finally alone, Attia pulled away the linen that covered her face and took a deep breath. It had been a long, long night, and all she wanted was warm, dreamless sleep. A bath wouldn't hurt either.

Xanthus crouched beside a bucket of water, washing his hands of some of the blood and grime. He hadn't said a word since they'd left the arena.

"Are you injured?" Attia asked softly, breaking the silence.

Xanthus stood but couldn't lift his eyes to meet hers. "You were incredible out there."

Attia frowned. "We're alive. That's the important thing."

"We're alive, yes. But we killed men tonight, Attia." His voice hardened. "Many, *many* men. They may have been good or they may have been bad, but they died for sport."

"It's not our sport," Attia said. "And I'm not sorry for what I had to do to keep you safe."

Xanthus closed his eyes, but not before Attia saw the deep pain there. "You shouldn't have bothered. I'm damaged. Can't you tell? I can't be fixed. There is no forgiveness for what I've done."

"What you've done," she said. "Do you mean like when the camp was attacked? How many did you kill *that* night?"

Xanthus's eyes snapped open. "That was different."

"Was it? How? Tell me, Xanthus—tell me how you weigh each of those men against the other and determine their worth."

"Those men in the camp attacked us first. I only wanted to protect you."

Attia scoffed. "We both know that I can take care of myself. Try to protect me all you want, Xanthus, but you can't change who I am. Fighting is what I know, and I will fight for what matters to me until the day the Romans hang me on their cross."

"Stop!" Xanthus cried. The raw anguish in his voice was startling. "Don't you understand? I *can't* lose you!"

A sudden wave of guilt washed over Attia. She realized she was looking at a man who had never really been a boy, a man who knew death and bondage and little else. His bright green eyes had turned dark with a remorse she couldn't feel. And she had almost disappeared on him without a word. She wished she knew how to comfort him now. But she'd never been taught how to soften her voice or ease hurts with a touch. She knew iron. She knew strength.

"Well, I fought for you, gladiator. I killed because *I* couldn't lose *you*."

His shoulders fell, but his arms were around her in seconds. The embrace felt like an apology, and not just to her. She felt him shake his head. "I see their faces, Attia. I see them in the shadows. I see them when I close my eyes."

Attia rested her forehead against his. "Then keep your eyes on me, champion. And we'll face the shadows together."

They held each other in the dark. Their clothes were stiff with blood, and Xanthus's short hair was even matted down with it. But Attia kept her eyes on his face. His brows were clenched in a scowl that a stranger might call fearsome, his lips flattened in a hard line.

Attia touched the crease between his eyes with the tip of her finger. "If only the fierce gladiator could smile."

Xanthus tilted her chin up and kissed the corner of her mouth with a caress that was more breath than touch. The bond between them was still so new and fragile, and yet Attia found that she survived on that breath. She wondered if she'd ever really lived before.

"What would the Maedi warrior know about smiling?" he said against her lips as he pulled her closer.

"Not enough," she murmured.

Gray-blue light filtered in through the tiny crack that opened high in the rock wall, mocking them with the time they didn't have.

"It'll be daylight soon," Xanthus said. "If they find Spartacus here, there will be more questions. And if they find Aurora's nursemaid, there will be punishment." His hold tightened, and he whispered her name against her hair, soft and earnest as a prayer.

Attia touched the silver crescent moon that hung at his throat. "They don't have to find either of us. I can lead us out of the city. I know the way now. We're right by the sea and there's a great forest to the east. We can disappear." She pulled away to look up at him. "No more matches or arenas. No more chains. We can be free."

But Xanthus shook his head. "There is no freedom in Rome. Not for me. Timeus will hunt me all the way to the underworld." His face settled into a calm, empty mask. Only his eyes betrayed the emotions boiling underneath.

Attia could sense a hurt, a deep anger that he was keeping from her. She knew he wanted freedom just as badly as she did, but he was holding back. She wanted to ask why. But more, she wanted him to tell her.

"You should go," he said. "You can make it, and I told you before that I would never force you to stay with me. There's nothing for you here. You have the chance at a real life again." He gently touched the backs of his fingers to her cheek, staring into her eyes for a long minute before kissing her tenderly. "Run," he whispered against her lips. "Just run."

Attia gripped his tunic in her fists and shut her eyes. There was a terrible sinking feeling in the pit of her stomach. The urge to run was so great she could barely contain it. Every fiber in her body was pulling her toward the door, urging her to make her escape. But there was Xanthus—warm and solid and good. Attia wrapped her arms tightly around his neck, feeling the desperation and hope swirling around them like smoke. Even before she opened her eyes again, she knew. They lived amidst ugliness, but between them there was light. *This is real,* she thought. *The only real thing left.* She kissed him again before pulling back just enough to look into his eyes.

"I can't," she said. "Not without you."

Their arms tightened around each other once again, and so the princess of Thrace found herself bound to a gladiator.

Outside, a heavy mist hung over the city of Ardea. The sun had risen but had yet to break through the fog. When they opened the door, they saw two guards sleeping soundly across the road.

Attia pulled the linen over her mouth again and turned to look at Xanthus one more time. Her heart ached when he tried to smile at her.

"You look like a boy, Thracian," he teased.

"You look like a savage, Briton." Her voice was muffled by the fabric over her mouth.

She put a hand against his cheek, her gaze caressing every hard line and curve, the fantastic life in his green eyes, the way a day's growth of stubble darkened his jaw, the soft streaks of gold in his brown hair.

Already, so many other faces had begun to fade from her memory. Her mother's was like a dim reflection in her head, nothing but gray eyes and indistinct features, as though she looked into a rippling pool. How had she smiled? And her father—how had Sparro laughed? The sound of his voice slithered through Attia's mind like smoke, translucent and just as brief.

This is our curse then, she thought. *Xanthus is haunted by his ghosts. I forget them.*

She pressed her mouth to his palm in silent promise before stepping out into the morning.

No torch-lit stadiums guided her this time, and the fog was thick. But once she climbed onto the roof of Xanthus's rock-walled room, she looked out over the city and remembered her way. It wasn't far after all. She could be back with Sabina and Rory before a single Roman—or Ardean—knew that she'd gone missing.

Before the day began, she would become a slave once more.

Attia snuck back into Rory's room just as the sun finally broke through to light the sky.

Hands immediately grabbed her.

"You're alive! Are you hurt? Did they recognize you?" It was

Sabina with red, watery eyes. She ran her hands over Attia's face and arms and stomach, looking for wounds that weren't there.

"I'm fine," Attia said as Sabina pulled her close, wrapping her strong arms around her.

"Don't do that again," Sabina said. "Promise me."

Attia said nothing. She simply let Sabina hold her and let herself believe that it was for the older woman's comfort rather than her own.

After she helped Attia undress, Sabina flung the dark, bloody clothes into the fire. Smoke bloomed out into the room before drifting up through the column that led to the roof. The copper water tub still sat in the center of the room, cold now. But Attia slipped into it and tried to scrub the arena from her skin.

She'd just pulled a clean tunic over her head when there was a knock at the door. She could hear a man muttering something, and the sound of heavy, departing footsteps.

Attia nearly didn't recognize the broken woman who stood just inside the door. Her black hair was knotted and hung in uneven sections around her tear-streaked face. A cut still bled from her swollen lips. Dark bruises covered her arms, shoulders, and neck.

Bile rose in Attia's throat. "Lucretia? What happened? Who did this to you?"

Lucretia didn't answer. She let Sabina guide her through the room to a cushioned chair by the fire. She flinched only a little as she sat down. With pursed lips, Sabina sought out her basket of salves.

Attia approached slowly, trying not to startle the woman. "Lucretia?"

And still the woman didn't speak. She lifted her chin and tried to pull the torn sleeve of her gown over her shoulder.

Attia knelt before Lucretia and waited until she met her eyes. "I am so sorry. You don't deserve this. No one does."

Lucretia managed to keep her composure for a few more seconds before her face crumpled and she started to weep. She fell forward, and Attia caught her in her arms. Lucretia's nearly silent sobs racked her whole body as she shuddered and trembled. The shoulder of Attia's dress dampened with her tears and blood.

At least Rory wasn't awake to see the terrible, bloody thing her uncle had done. Because Attia knew it had to have been Timeus. Who else would touch the dominus's concubine?

Sabina laid out her bandages and salves with such stoicism that Attia knew she'd done it before. No wonder the woman had known how to help Attia heal. She'd been treating Lucretia's injuries for far longer.

If Attia's hate for Timeus had not yet known its reach, it did then. Disgust and loathing flared up like kindling, doused in the toxic fumes of every remembered hurt—the brand on her hip, the sword in her father's chest, the despair in Xanthus's eyes. And now Lucretia.

"Lucretia, drink this," Sabina said. She handed over a small cup that Attia put to Lucretia's sore lips.

"I'm sorry," Attia said again. "No one deserves this."

Eyes closed, Lucretia smiled bitterly. "You are still so young, Thracian."

"I've grown a lot in recent days. And I know that not every man is like Timeus."

Lucretia opened her eyes, and more tears spilled free. "For me, there is no other man."

Attia shook her head. "He has no right to do this to you."

Lucretia turned to Sabina. "Is she really this naïve?" Then to Attia, she said, "Haven't you learned yet? He is our master. He has *every* right. This is my fate, and it is fixed."

"Your fate is what you make it. My father taught me that."

"I'm guessing that was *before* the Romans speared him through." Lucretia pulled down the neck of her gown to expose the horrific bruises forming just above her breasts. "Look closely, Thracian. Look long and hard and *learn*. This is my lot until death, and if you're not careful, it will be yours, too."

Oh, and Attia looked. She saw what Timeus had done to Lucretia—the cuts and bruises and scars that maimed her skin. She couldn't look away.

Lucretia got up from the chair, slowly, and walked to stand in front of the fire. The flames deepened the shadows and lines of her lovely face.

Attia didn't know what to say. She didn't know how to give comfort. She felt so terribly helpless.

"Come, Lucretia," Sabina said softly. "Let me see to your injuries; then you can rest."

"Yes. Rest," Lucretia murmured, still staring into the fire. "So I can do it all over again."

After Attia left, Xanthus leaned his head against the door, shut his eyes, and slammed his fist into the wood so hard that it splintered.

She should have run—she should have escaped without him, damn the consequences. She could be free at that very moment. But she stayed because he stayed.

They both knew that Timeus would hunt them down. The man would tear through every province in the Republic, burn every forest, cross every sea. He was that tenacious and that possessive. But Xanthus had another reason for staying—one that he couldn't yet bring himself to tell Attia. One that involved

C. V. WYK

the arena at the Festival of Lupa and a vendetta that was more than ten years old.

His blood turned cold at the thought of Decimus. Old screams rang in his ears.

In his memory—the worst of his memories—Xanthus saw flames.

He'd been called Gareth then, nine years old and at the end of his last summer in his mother's village. No man was allowed to live in the holy community of priestesses, so at the celebration of Samhain, he was to be given over to his father's clan in the highlands of Alba, just as his beloved half-brother Hector had been given to his own father in one of the southern villages five years earlier.

He'd been running along the crest of the hill they called the Tor, looking over his home spread out below—the misty glass surface of the lake, the rocky crags of the surrounding hillsides, the broad green swath of dense forest, and . . . smoke. Shielding his eyes, he squinted and saw the fires just starting to burn on the far shore. Then he heard a piercing scream.

He did not know it yet, but the Romans had come.

He raced back down the hill as the fires burned away the thatch-and-wood huts. A small group of children ran toward him, and he herded them into the forest, into the hands of the Little People and the goddess. Running back to the village, he watched in horror as a Roman soldier thrust a sword into the old high priestess. Her blue robes turned black with her blood.

The other priestesses wailed and pulled their hair, calling down curses upon the foreign soldiers. But Xanthus heard his mother's keening more than any other. Two soldiers grabbed her, dragging her away from the other women. She struggled mightily and spat in their faces as they forced her down onto the stone altar in the center of the village.

184

The boy found a half-burnt bow in the tall grass. His fingers closed around the wooden shaft of a single arrow as the sound of ripping fabric echoed across the lake. Twenty yards away, his mother was tied down, spread-eagled on the stone altar. The boy raised his bow, aiming his arrow at the soldier who approached her with such obvious lust in his eyes.

Before he could let loose his arrow, he glanced away from the soldier and straight into his mother's brilliant green eyes. The corners of her mouth lifted up slightly, as if she wasn't about to be torn apart in front of her people. Her mouth formed a word that struck Xanthus to the core.

"Run."

The soldier began to part the leather straps of his armor.

That moment had felt like an eternity, one that looped back on itself until the past and present and future became a tangled web of space and time. There was no yesterday, no tomorrow. There was only a young boy watching, furious and terrified, as a nameless army destroyed everything he held dear. The boy saw his mother's face, traced the tears that tracked down her cheeks.

And then the moment was over. With heartbreaking resolve, he inhaled, aimed, and released. Three black raven's feathers guided the arrow to its target—straight to his mother's beating heart. She looked up at the sky as she breathed her final breath.

In the semidarkness of the damp stone room in Ardea, Xanthus choked back a sob. He'd saved her; he knew that. There were fates worse than death. But his mother was still dead, and at the hands of her own son. How could the gods not curse a man who had committed so many unforgivable sins?

He wasn't a boy anymore. He wasn't even Gareth. He was Xanthus, the Champion of Rome. In the long decade since he'd been stolen, he'd been made into something ugly, something monstrous. But he remembered—he remembered everything he'd lost when a legionary named Decimus led Crassus and his Romans into Britannia.

Xanthus knew that fighting Decimus at the Festival of Lupa couldn't change the past. But it would satisfy his hate, and that, he decided, was enough.

Someday, he would tell Attia the truth. But after. When it was done.

Until then, there were rituals he could not abandon and a vigil he would always keep.

Facing east, he dropped to his knees and raised his hands in supplication. "Goddess, guide Attia's steps. Hold my family in your hands. And for all I have done, and for all that I have yet to do—forgive me."

His brothers came at midday, deep in silence as they entered Xanthus's room.

"By the gods . . ." Gallus muttered.

Xanthus looked down at the dried blood that still covered nearly every inch of his arms, legs, chest, and face. He knew the bruises would fade. Water and soap would wash away the blood and dirt. He was barely wounded. At least on the outside.

Lebuin's large hands clenched into fists like hammers. He gritted his teeth so hard that the muscles of his jaw twitched. Gallus's broad, usually smiling face was gloomy and drawn. Iduma was deathly pale, and his breath hitched in his throat. Castor's face was contorted in a painful grimace.

Albinus stepped forward. "Is any of it yours?"

"Maybe a scratch or two."

"Bloody bastard," Albinus replied. He gripped Xanthus's arm and pulled his brother into a tight embrace.

"Literally," Iduma commented. His voice shook with relief.

His brothers didn't ask any other questions. They'd fought side by side for nearly a decade. All that mattered to them was that he'd survived.

Another figure appeared in the doorway, and they all turned to see Ennius.

His dark eyes darted around the room. When he realized that only the gladiators were inside, his face relaxed into a relieved smile. "Tired?" he quipped.

Xanthus and his brothers laughed.

They walked together down the long avenue toward the sea. Guards accompanied them—some at the front, some at the back—though none of the gladiators were bound.

"It's like having an honor guard," Gallus said. "Makes me feel a little special."

"Shut up, Gallus. Do you always have to be such a simple idiot?" Albinus said. He spat on the ground to his right, barely missing the boot of one of the guards. Xanthus smiled to see Albinus being his usual, personable self.

"I wonder at your definition of honor," Lebuin said.

Iduma snorted. "Lebuin is right. First Timeus forces us to sit on our asses while Xanthus fights alone in that damn arena, and *then* he makes us spend half a day rubbing down those damn horses as though we wouldn't be more useful elsewhere. What next? Perhaps he'll cover us in bells and silks and make us dance. Damn ass."

Castor hit him hard in the side before nudging his head toward the nearest guard.

Iduma promptly turned to the young guard beside him. "Do *you* dance?" he asked, plastering a leering smile on his face.

The man palmed the hilt of his sword but averted his eyes.

"I'm actually looking forward to a bath," Gallus mused as though he hadn't heard a word the others had said.

"Are you a man or a woman?" Iduma asked. "Only women enjoy baths."

Gallus snickered. "Not yours." He opened his mouth to make another joke, but then raised a hand to shield his eyes. "Look."

Iduma stuck his head between Gallus and Albinus to see. "The younger Master Lucius," he said with mock formality.

Lucius was standing on the beach some twenty yards away, eyes trained on the horizon. He was still wearing the same clothes from the night before. His hair was sticking up as though he'd been running his hands through it, and even from a distance, Xanthus could see that his face was a patchwork of color—pale skin, purple and blue shadows around his eyes. He almost looked worse than Xanthus. After a minute, Lucius turned and started walking slowly in the opposite direction.

"Why does he always look so sad?" Iduma asked. "Like a puppy that someone's just kicked."

Albinus pushed Iduma back. "I know you think I'm pretty, Iduma, but try not to breathe down my neck so much."

Iduma closed his eyes, puckered his lips, and made a loud, wet kissing sound.

"What is he even doing over there?" Lebuin asked.

Gallus shrugged. "Walking. I think."

"Brooding, more like," Albinus said.

Castor shook his head.

"He fought well the other night, at the camp," Lebuin said quietly. "He has plenty left to learn, but still."

Even Albinus couldn't argue with that.

They finally reached the water. As his feet hit the salty surf, Xanthus sighed. "Gods, I need a bath."

"So do Iduma's women," Gallus said.

His brothers were still laughing as Iduma lifted Gallus up and tossed him into the cold water.

CHAPTER 15

Sleep eluded her.

It seemed like she and Xanthus had spent a lifetime in that arena. She hadn't felt so alive in so long, nor as comfortable as she was with a sword in her hand.

Now all she wanted to do was *stop*—stop seeing, stop hearing, stop thinking, stop remembering. She was exhausted. Her muscles burned. Her joints were sore. Even her bones felt tender. But every time she closed her eyes, all she could see was the broken image of Lucretia.

It was noon before Attia finally conceded the inevitable. She wouldn't sleep. Maybe the next day. After a moment of hesitation, she went to sit beside Lucretia in front of the fire while Sabina played with Rory. Lucretia said nothing as Attia settled beside her.

"I wish there was something more I could—"

"I don't need a savior, Thracian."

"What do you need?"

"Nothing. I need nothing."

"I thought you'd be a better liar than that," Attia said.

A smile teetered on the edge of Lucretia's cut lips. "I'll take that as a compliment." The firelight reflected sparks of orange and red in her dark eyes. The hint of a smile faded. "Don't start thinking we're friends, by the way. I don't have friends."

"I never said I wanted to be your friend. I don't even know if I like you. You're moody and proud."

"You're arrogant and entitled."

"You're bossy."

Lucretia scoffed. "You're stubborn."

"You're too tall."

"You're too short."

Attia shrugged her shoulder. "We can't all be perfect."

Lucretia smiled despite herself but sobered quickly.

"He'll answer for his cruelty," Attia said.

"I wish I could believe that."

Attia hesitated only a moment before taking out the little knife that she'd kept for so long. It was a good knife, solid, reliable. She closed Lucretia's fingers around the hilt.

Attia didn't tell her what it was for, and Lucretia didn't ask. But after a few long moments, Lucretia tucked the knife into a fold of her dress.

There were no spaces between them now.

They finally left Ardea on the third day. Fido had given them two nights to resupply and rest, but Attia still hadn't slept.

The caravan gained twelve horses, fifty pounds of silver, and enough food and necessities to see them to Pompeii. Fido and his Ardeans were undoubtedly bitter over their losses, but that didn't come close to how furious Timeus was over his.

Lucius had recounted Spartacus's feats in the arena with gusto. It was the first time he'd taken any interest in Timeus's business, and now they couldn't find the man anywhere. Timeus insisted that everyone be questioned, but no one could say where Spartacus had gone—not the guards or members of the household, not the slaves or the soldiers who'd been forced to camp outside of the city walls. Even the Ardeans were unable to say whether or not Spartacus was one of them. The only thing everyone could agree on was that the Shadow of Death had vanished with the dawn, and Timeus felt as though he'd been cheated out of a great prize. His anger made him colder than usual, and his blue eyes glared at everyone and no one. He snapped and shouted every order.

The gladiators were able to avoid him by clustering together near the back of the caravan. Lucius avoided him by riding alongside Rory's cart. Right by Attia.

All she'd wanted was a fresh breeze and the sun on her skin. Being joined by Lucius minutes after she'd emerged from Rory's cart made her tense immediately. She hadn't spoken to him since that day when she'd bandaged his hands, but she couldn't be sure that he wouldn't recognize her from the arena. What set her on edge the most was that she could sense a severe change in him, and she didn't yet know what it was.

"I've been meaning to thank you for taking such good care of my sister," he said as he dismounted to walk beside her. "First you save my hands, and now you're my sister's companion. I'm glad you're with us."

"She's a sweet girl, but I'm not her companion."

"What do you mean?"

Attia raised an eyebrow. "Don't you know? Timeus bought me for Xanthus. I'm *his* companion."

Lucius hadn't looked particularly happy to begin with, but

Attia watched the last bit of light fade from his face when she said that. Without his easy smile, he looked like a different man entirely—less himself, more his uncle. A deep frown carved new creases into his face, and he turned his eyes down to look at his boots. "You weren't born a slave, were you?" he said.

Attia turned her face away.

"You were free once. My uncle told me that you're a Thracian. You probably know more about battles and soldiering than I do," he said with a little smile. "You must miss your home. Ever since I was a boy, I've wanted to see Thrace. It's a shame that . . . well . . ." His voice faded off, and he glanced sidelong at Attia. They both knew there was no good way for him to finish that sentence. Eventually, he said, "You know, I met a senator once who was born in Egypt. No one is really from Rome anymore, not even Romans."

Attia couldn't hold back a snort. "Funny how that happens when you try to take over the world."

"Do you oppose the Republic on ideological grounds then? We have law, order, and prosperity here. Many would say we bring civilization to barbarous nations."

"Yes, if by civilization you mean destruction, terror, famine, slavery, death. Even you must see the hypocrisy of it all. You and your kind would like to believe that Rome is the light, but it's not. Rome is the darkness."

Lucius bristled. "You don't know me. Perhaps *I* believe in justice. Perhaps slavery disgusts me."

"Perhaps your inheritance rests on the backs of slaves."

Lucius became very quiet then, and Attia couldn't believe she'd just said all of that to Timeus's nephew. *Stupid. Stupid. Stupid.* What would happen when he told his uncle about all of the clever, perfidious things the little Thracian had said? The punishment could easily cost her—

"You're right." Lucius's soft words interrupted Attia's self-rebuke. He ran a hand through his hair. "Rome isn't what it was meant to be. My father used to tell me stories of how the Republic was founded. There was equality and freedom of thought. No one suffered."

"The founders of Rome may have tried to build something pure. But it seems corruption will always bleed through."

"That doesn't mean we should stop trying," he said earnestly.

"No, but you can't keep doing the same thing and expect different results. Look at Carthage, Antioch, Jerusalem, the Germanic tribes, Britannia—look at what's happened to their people. Conquest is not the same as liberation. Whatever past your father remembered has long been lost. Rome has changed, and I think it will be a very different beast before the end."

Lucius's expression hardened again, and a faraway look came into his eyes, as though he was remembering something he'd rather forget.

A part of him had definitely changed, and though Attia couldn't know for sure, she thought it had something to do with the attack in the clearing. Lucius was colder now. Angrier. The same thing had happened to her the first time she'd killed a man. The difference was, her kill had been for survival, so she'd eventually been able to let go of her anger. She wondered if Lucius ever would.

"Is there no chance for redemption?" Lucius asked in a strangely hollow voice. The words came slowly, as though he had to force them out. "Do you think we're all damned?"

"I wouldn't know about damnation. I don't know what comes after this. But we're here now, and that's all that really matters."

"What about the afterlife? Don't you believe in the gods?"

"Only when I curse at them."

Lucius smiled—a sad contrast to the deep shadows and lines in his face. "Well, I knew there was something different about you."

Oh, Lucius, she thought. *You have no idea.*

"I should get back to Rory," Attia said.

Lucius nodded and raised his hand in a weak wave as Attia tugged on the door and disappeared into the darkness of the cart. She leaned back against the wall to get her bearings.

She shouldn't have spoken to him. She shouldn't have said the things she had. But somehow, her time in the arena with the ghosts and the dust and the specter of Spartacus had resurrected memories that she'd tried to push away. Beneath everything else, buried in rubble and the fires of conquest, she was still her father's daughter. She could still hear the outrage in his voice as he cursed the Romans with his dying breath. And she remembered the day they lost her mother and stillborn brother—how her father had held her in his arms, rocking her gently to the rhythm of a lament so bone-deep that its message echoed through her even though the melody had long been lost. She remembered the strike of her sword as she killed more legionaries than she bothered to count the day of the invasion. And she remembered the face of Crius, her father's first captain.

When she was young, Crius had given her a small wooden practice sword. She'd swung it over her head like a sling until Crius snapped at her. "You are a Maedi, Attia! For the gods' sakes, act like one!"

Incensed, Attia had swung her wooden sword into his side as hard as she could, cracking two of his ribs. She hadn't realized her own strength. She'd immediately dropped the sword and taken a step back.

But Crius had barely flinched. He'd simply picked up the weapon and put it back into her hand. "I'll make a warrior of you yet," he'd said with a grin.

This is who I am.

Those thoughts and memories, jumbled and sharp, comprised her very essence. She couldn't go numb. She couldn't push it away. The best and the worst—she couldn't forget.

The rumble of the cart's wheels made her teeth chatter as she opened the inner door. The road to Pompeii was worn and pitted, causing the cart to rock dangerously. Then she stepped through the door and saw something that nearly made her heart do the same: Rory stood on her toes on the bench with her little face pressed against one of the slits in the side of the cart. Sunlight streamed in through the narrow opening, kissing the pale skin of her nose and cheek. She closed her eyes and inhaled deeply.

"Rory, no!" Attia yanked her away from the side, using her body to shield the girl.

"I did it!" Rory said, gripping Attia's shoulders. "I felt the sun!"

"You're not supposed to!" Attia said in a horrified whisper.

"But I did, and it was warm and soft and not at all like mother said it would be. Look!" She turned her face to the side. "I didn't burn!"

Attia wasn't sure what she'd expected. Blisters maybe, or some kind of terrible rash or swelling or bloody wound. But all she saw was a flushed cheek like berries and cream, and bright blue eyes that shone with delight.

"It didn't hurt! It felt like . . . like fire, only softer and just on this spot," Rory said, pointing at her cheek. "I used to feel the moon. But it was nothing like this."

Attia smiled, though her heart was still racing. "You can feel moonlight?"

"At night, I open the windows in my room and pretend the moon is a sun just for me. But that wasn't like this. Not at all." Her eyes grew round. "I have to show Mother and Lucius," she said, and hurried to the back of the cart to open the door.

"No, Rory, wait!"

The alarm in Attia's voice caught her attention, and Rory turned back to stare at her. "What's wrong?"

Attia probably should have realized it during their time together. Rory was clever and vivacious, and her little limbs were perfectly normal. She lost breath quickly, and she was so incredibly pale, but what else could be expected from a child who'd been shut away in the dark her whole life?

For a reason that no one said out loud, her family had kept her hidden—kept her from friends, from society, even from sunlight. They claimed it was for her health, and the household believed them. Why wouldn't they? But the clear skin on Rory's face was proof enough. She wasn't really ill, and her family knew it. So what were they hiding?

"We can't show them yet," Attia said.

Rory cocked her head as she pulled her hand away from the door. "Why not?"

Because they can't know that I know.

"Because . . . well, because the cart is still moving, and . . ." Attia swallowed hard. "We should keep this our secret."

"Even from Lucius?" Rory asked, her mouth puckering into a frown.

Attia nodded. "Yes. Just for a little while."

"All right, but . . ." She looked up at the little slits in the cart. "Can I look out again?"

She looked so excited, so hopeful, that Attia couldn't bring herself to deny her. With a weak smile, she unwrapped Rory from the yards of cream-colored fabric. She still looked so small, so fragile, but determined, too.

Attia kissed her cheek and held her close for a moment before positioning her hands under her arms. Then she held Rory up to the light.

CHAPTER 16

Timeus's estate in Pompeii sat on the very edge of a cliff that jutted out over the Tyrrhenian Sea. Somehow, it was a different sea from the one that had greeted them in Ardea—no fiery colors, no glittering expanse. Near Pompeii, the sea was calm and deep, its blue a hundred times darker than the evening sky.

Silence and stillness, Attia thought. Much like the gladiator standing beside her.

As soon as she'd entered Xanthus's room, she could see the guilt and sadness written across his face. She could feel it in the hesitant touch of his hand on her cheek before he turned away. He was glad she'd stayed, and yet he wished she hadn't. Attia knew he blamed himself for her bondage now more than ever, and they held themselves on the sharp edge of so many unspoken words. Attia wished he could just understand that freedom wouldn't mean much without him. Not anymore. She wished he knew that, for her, there was no escaping what was between them.

Like statues, they stood together at the single window in his room, where they had a clear view of Mount Vesuvius to the north. It loomed over the city like a storm cloud, angry and brooding. Ash dyed its sloping sides in broad strokes of gray and black. Its mouth frayed at the edges, exhaling gusts of smoky breath that melted into the sky above it. Despite the coolness of the evening, the air around the mountain shimmered with low heat, ominously caressing the houses tucked into its dark folds.

The main road snaked along the edge of the jagged coastline below. Merchants, fishermen, and vendors rushed back and forth like ants, frantic to finish their work before nightfall. As Attia watched, a driver pulled a little too hard on the reins, and his cart's wheel nearly slipped over the edge.

"You'd think they would just build a wider road," Attia muttered as men hurried to right the cart. "Save themselves the trouble." Her eyes drifted back to the mountain. "Then again, you'd think they wouldn't have tried building a city at all next to *that*."

"Attia."

The moment Xanthus said her name in that heavy tone he used when he was upset, her insides clenched.

"There are things I haven't told you yet," Xanthus said.

Attia sighed. "There are things I haven't told you yet either."

He watched her patiently, obviously hesitant to speak his own truths just yet.

"Sabina is a Thracian," Attia said.

Xanthus's brows rose. "What?"

"She told me in Ardea. I still can't believe it."

"Who else knows?"

"No one."

"Attia, I'm not asking out of curiosity. If anyone else heard her say that—"

"No one knows," Attia said. "No one else was even there. Well. Except . . ."

"Except?"

"Rory was in the room—"

"Attia!"

"But she was asleep! She didn't hear anything, and even if she did, what would it matter? Why would anyone care if Sabina is a Thracian?"

"Because you're all supposed to be dead!"

Attia froze.

The statement, in and of itself, was not surprising. Thrace was attacked and defeated, and everyone knew that Thracians didn't surrender. It would follow that there were no other survivors.

But there was something deeply disturbing about Xanthus's tone, about the way his face tightened with frustration and horror. Attia swallowed hard and waited for the next part. Not an apology, no. Comfort? She didn't need that either. An explanation, then.

Xanthus leaned his elbows on the windowsill and rubbed his face with his hands. "You don't know that House."

"The House of Timeus?"

"The House of Flavius."

Attia frowned. "The Princeps?"

Xanthus turned to her with weary eyes and breathed out slowly through his nose. "What do you know about Titus?"

"His father was Vespasian," Attia replied. "When he died last year, Titus inherited and became the leader of Rome."

"And do you know what Vespasian said on his deathbed?"

Attia shook her head.

"He said, 'Oh, I think I am becoming a god!'"

The fine hairs on the back of Attia's neck stood up. "How do you know that?"

"His brother Crassus told his nephew Titus, who told his good friend Timeus." Xanthus scoffed. "The world still believes that Rome is a republic at heart, with elected officials and the Senate to represent the people. Not emperors or godheads. But it was the *Republic*—under Vespasian and Crassus—that forced its way into Britannia, that sacked Herodium, then Cremona, then Jerusalem."

"Then Thrace," Attia whispered.

She understood what Xanthus was saying. It had taken years for the House of Flavius to become a name worth remembering. Vespasian's title had been hard-won. He'd conquered half of the known world to secure his place. As far as Timeus and the ruling houses knew, Attia was the last Thracian—an unremarkable seventeen-year-old girl who was now a slave. Alone, she was hardly dangerous. But if they thought there were more, if there was a possibility that any other Thracian—especially any of the Maedi—had survived, if they knew that Sparro was Attia's father . . .

Xanthus nodded, as though he could read her thoughts on her face. "If Crassus had known who you were, he would never have let you live. They attacked Thrace because your people could have stood in the way of everything they hoped to build. Men like your father were considered grave threats."

"To the Republic?"

"To the empire."

Empire. The word made Attia shudder. She stared sightlessly out the window, the colors of the sky and Pompeii and Vesuvius swimming in front of her. It was so difficult to speak that she thought the wind might have stolen her voice to dance over the Tyrrhenian. She looked back to find Xanthus staring at her intently, his green eyes bright as beacons of Greek fire in the dusk. He was saying so much with that one look. Attia could practically feel the weight of his unspoken words.

"There's something else," she said. "Rory isn't sick. She's not ill or weak at all. And the sunlight—it doesn't hurt her. She's in perfect health."

Xanthus frowned. "So why have Valeria and Timeus been keeping her hidden away all these years?"

"I don't know."

"You can't tell anyone about this. Not even Sabina. They'll kill you, Attia. You can't give them a reason."

"I gave them my father's name."

"You gave that to Ennius," Xanthus said with a shake of his head. "And even that was reckless."

Attia smiled. "I ran to an arena and posed as a gladiator. To say that I was reckless is putting it a bit mildly, don't you think?" The reminder made Xanthus scowl again, and Attia put her hand on his shoulder. "You're not my keeper, Xanthus. Whatever Timeus and the Romans have done, my life is still my own. I am not your responsibility."

"The Roman child isn't *your* responsibility."

"What does Rory have to do with anything?"

"You risked your life to protect her when the camp was attacked."

"It wasn't a risk to do what I've been trained to do."

"You can't save everyone, Attia."

"Who says I'm going to try?"

Xanthus started to speak, but before he could, a slow rumbling crawled through the ground, along the coastline and the road, stretching out from the mountain in the distance.

"What's happening?" Attia's hands gripped the windowsill for purchase as the rumbling became louder.

Xanthus pulled her down to the floor just as a violent tremor shook the walls around them.

Outside, people were shouting, but not with panic. They

calmly called out orders over the sounds of cracking stone and brick.

The chair in the corner of Xanthus's room toppled over, and the little table shuffled along the floor and blocked the doorway. But the walls held, and Xanthus held her. Just as suddenly as they'd started, the tremors stopped.

Attia rose to her knees to look out the window.

Vesuvius was huffing and puffing at the sky. Steam rose up in sharp bursts, displacing cool, low-hanging clouds before drifting down again like rain. The smell of sulfur burned her nostrils and made her eyes water. The mountain settled again, and the people below went about their business as though nothing had happened. Or as though it happened all the time.

Attia sat back on the floor and let Xanthus wrap his arms around her. But the silence slithered between them, dark and thick as the mountain's breath. She could feel words swirling in his chest and threatening to burst from his mouth, a torrent of rebukes and fears and worries. But how could she worry about anything else? After everything that had happened, how could it possibly get any worse for them?

After a while, she took his hand and led him to their bed.

And he followed, hesitant but wanting, and held her again in a tight embrace, as though he was afraid she might try to bolt at any moment. In the curve of his arms, she closed her eyes, and finally, finally found sleep.

Xanthus's eyes snapped open sometime in the night. It was a different kind of waking—abrupt and complete, as though he hadn't been sleeping at all. The height of the moon beyond the window told him that dawn was at least four, maybe five hours away. But he was restless, and he didn't know why.

Attia slept beside him, pressed close from hip to ankle. She'd completely wrapped herself in the blanket, and only her head and the tips of her toes were visible. Xanthus placed a soft kiss on her temple before rising and walking to the window.

The weather was turning cold. He could feel the promise of winter in the air. The snow would already be knee-deep in Britannia—a thick, deceptively soft-looking blanket of white coating everything from the steep crags of the north to the shallow bogs of the south. Winter in Rome was little more than a frost, a season of dead things and indoor plotting. He'd never seen snow in the Republic. He wondered if the council of the Princeps would view it as an omen.

The patricians were remarkably superstitious for supposedly educated noblemen, even more so than the priestesses of the Tor. They believed in the terrible signs of raven and crow, the messages that appeared in bleached bones. Some even subscribed to the portents of tea leaves. *Tea* leaves.

Xanthus was no seer and no druid. But the Romans knew absolutely nothing of the Sight. Not that they needed it. If they just looked ahead with reason and logic, they'd see how unsustainable their greed really was. The best and the worst of them would only turn to ash. Just like everyone else.

Xanthus sighed, ready to go back to bed when he heard the clatter of hooves. The gate squeaked as it swung open. Quiet as a shadow, he opened his door and walked to the archway that separated the training yard from the main courtyard.

Three horsemen had arrived, all clothed in black. Moonlight and torches shone behind them, sending eerie, elongated shadows across the courtyard. They carried swords, but Xanthus could tell they were neither soldiers nor Praetorians. Timeus stood in front of one of the horseman, along with several of his personal guards. One of the riders handed him a tightly rolled scroll, and as his cloak shifted, Xanthus caught sight of the sigil embroidered on his clothing—the silver wolf of the House of Flavius.

Timeus spoke quietly with the rider for several minutes before the man nodded and tugged on the reins of his horse. He and the other horsemen disappeared down the avenue that led back to the city.

As the guards closed the gate again, Timeus looked over his shoulder, his eyes landing directly on Xanthus. He didn't seem angry, just weary. He inclined his head for him to approach. When Xanthus was close enough, Timeus said, "Tycho Flavius is coming."

"When?"

"In a month, more or less. He wants to . . ." Timeus glanced down at the scroll in his hands and read, "'. . . protect those interests that are dear to the House of Flavius.'" He crumpled the letter in his hand and shook his head. "Bloated ass."

Xanthus frowned. "So what does he really want?"

Timeus's blue eyes narrowed, caught between a scowl and an amused smile. "You know, Xanthus, sometimes you're too smart for your own good, and one day, that just might be what kills you."

Xanthus waited.

"He wants to meet Spartacus," Timeus said.

"How did he even hear about the match?"

"The House of Flavius has eyes everywhere," Timeus said. "A better question would be how in the gods' names am I supposed to say that Spartacus isn't here? How am I supposed to tell Tycho Flavius that my champion and my idiot nephew *lost* Spartacus in Ardea?" He threw the crumpled scroll to the ground. "Good thing I've already hired men to track Spartacus down."

"Track him?" Xanthus asked, trying to keep his voice even.

"Lucius told me how the man fought," Timeus said, "and I have no intention of losing someone like that to another ludus. As soon as we left Ardea, I sent out word to hire trackers—mercenaries. They'll be here at sunrise."

Xanthus felt his chest tighten. "How will you find him?"

"The mercenaries' leader, Kanut, claims he has experience with this kind of thing. He sounds confident, and he'd better be. I'm paying a small fortune for this. Then again, I'm not the only one looking for Spartacus. Fido has sent out his own men."

Xanthus's vision reeled. People were looking for Spartacus. For *Attia*. Gods, what had they done?

"What if no one finds him?" Xanthus asked. "What if you can't track him down?"

Timeus stayed quiet for a long minute. His eyes focused on a distant point on the road before drifting upward. The moon washed his face in yellow-tinted light. "I am a patient man," he said.

Xanthus glared at him. *You'll have to be.*

As promised, the mercenary arrived at sunrise.

Xanthus, Lucius, Ennius, and Timeus all wore deep scowls as they waited for him in the study.

"Is this really the best course of action, Uncle?" Lucius asked quietly. "You can't trust a hired sword."

"Spartacus disappeared under your watch, Lucius. Does that mean I can't trust *you*?"

Lucius flushed and said nothing more.

Someone knocked on the door to the study, and two guards escorted the mercenary inside.

Xanthus knew immediately that the man was no Roman. His

dark hair was pulled into a tight knot at the nape of his neck, smoothed back from a tanned face and heavy beard. The wrinkles around his eyes and mouth gave away his age—he was old enough to be Xanthus's father, though his wide shoulders and barreled chest still exuded strength. The way he shifted his weight told Xanthus that the man was a trained fighter, even if he looked more like a random plebeian from the street. He wore no cloak or armor. No insignia or family crest. His plain clothing was the color of sand. Really, he could be anyone. Or no one. A mercenary indeed.

For his part, the man looked at each of them in turn. His dark eyes appraised them in moments and dismissed them just as quickly. He smiled to himself as he stepped more fully into the study. With a flick of his wrist, he produced a small sharp dagger and started cleaning his fingernails.

The guards nearly jumped forward before Timeus called them off.

"I thought you searched him," he said with a glare in the guards' direction.

"We did, Dominus."

The mercenary grinned. "Don't blame your men. They did their best." He turned his gaze to Xanthus. "So, you are the Champion of Rome." He had to crane his neck back to meet Xanthus's eyes. "You know, I thought you'd be bigger."

Lucius, standing by Timeus's desk, raised an eyebrow. "You're the man my uncle hired?"

"The name is Kanut, and I am here to find Spartacus."

"He's come all the way from Sicily," Timeus said.

Kanut chuckled. "Farther."

Now that he was standing so close, Xanthus could see fairly new burns layered around Kanut's wrist. Unlike the razor-sharp lines of Albinus's scars, these were blotchy, uneven, and lumpy.

A patch near the man's palm was still red. The burns couldn't have been more than four or five months old.

Kanut noticed him staring, sheathed his dagger, and held his hands up to Xanthus's face. "Beauty marks," he said with a grin.

Lucius turned his face away with a disgusted sigh.

"When can you be ready?" Timeus asked.

"Everything is already prepared," Kanut said. "My men wait for me at the borders of the city. We can leave right now, if you wish."

"What, today?" Lucius said, frowning with skepticism.

"Why not? We'll need to move quickly. If the rumors are true, Spartacus could be halfway to the underworld by now." Kanut palmed the air in front of his face as though he saw a mirage. "Spartacus, the Shadow of Death!" he said dramatically. He chuckled. "Your man sounds like a demon, Timeus. But if anyone can find him, I can."

We'll see about that, Xanthus thought.

"If you're as good as you say you are, one more evening can't hurt. You'll leave tomorrow morning," Timeus said. "And of course, to keep you honest, you'll also take some of my men with you. Men I can trust."

Kanut laughed again. "I work for money, Timeus, and per our deal, I don't get most of it until I return with your prize. That should be all the *trust* you need."

"It's not," Timeus said.

"I'll go," Lucius said. Skeptical as he was, he sounded eager. Too eager, maybe. Xanthus wondered when Lucius had taken such a keen interest in his uncle's business.

Timeus seemed to be wondering the same thing. He cocked his head. "Really?"

"I saw Spartacus. I asked him questions. I can help identify him," Lucius said.

"There cannot be any . . . *mistakes* this time," Timeus said, the warning in his voice clear.

"I can do it, Uncle."

"How old are you, boy?" Kanut asked.

Lucius crossed his arms in front of his chest. "Eighteen."

"And do you have experience with a sword?"

"Of course."

"Ever been in a fight?"

"Of course."

"Have you ever had your life threatened? Believed you might not see the next day?"

Lucius narrowed his eyes. "Yes."

"Have you ever killed a man?"

A muscle in Lucius's jaw twitched, but he answered clearly. "Yes."

Kanut stepped right up to Lucius, their faces just inches away from each other. An unsettling smile crossed the mercenary's lips. "Have you ever wanted to die?"

Lucius took an involuntary step back. His arms dropped to his sides. "What does that have to do with anything?"

"It has to do with everything," Kanut said. "The best fighters don't just have courage. They have skill, confidence, aggression, pride. And they fight for a reason, be it money or fame or loyalty. Or survival. But from what you say, this Spartacus had something more than that. He appeared out of nowhere, jumped into that arena, and killed more men in one night than you've probably fought in your entire life. Do you understand what it takes to do that, boy—to throw yourself willingly into the pit? To look death in the face and smile?"

Lucius had gone pale.

"It takes someone who doesn't care if he lives or if he dies. And if you've never felt that," Kanut said, almost gently, "how do you think you could ever recognize it in another?"

Lucius's expression lost its tough edge. His eyes were shiny and uncertain.

"I'll take *one* of your men, Timeus. For your peace of mind. But only one," Kanut said.

Xanthus lowered his head. He felt as though the weight of the world had just settled on his shoulders, because he knew what was coming next.

"Xanthus will go with you," Timeus said.

Kanut nodded. "I know."

Xanthus stood at the gate and watched the mercenary ride away.

"What are you going to tell her?" Ennius asked.

"The truth."

"Are you sure about that? If she finds out that Timeus is sending you away for this, she might burn the city down."

A reluctant smile tugged at the corners of Xanthus's mouth. "And wouldn't that be a blessing?"

Once Kanut disappeared around a bend in the road, Xanthus turned to Ennius.

"She deserves the truth now. Besides, I know what I have to do."

Ennius sighed. "Killing the freemen seems harsh, but if you have to . . ." He chuckled when Xanthus gave him a hard look. "Well, that's what I would do."

"No, it's not. You would tell Timeus's hired thugs exactly what you saw in Ardea—that Spartacus was a giant, bigger and taller than me. That he had black eyes and a scar across his cheek."

"That he spoke of his home in the far east," Ennius added. "A wife, and six—no, seven sons."

"And that he planned to journey to . . . Egypt, perhaps?

Maybe old Persia. I haven't decided yet. Or rather, my memory is only just coming back to me."

Ennius nodded. "Almost as good as my plan. Anyway, it's probably more dangerous to lie to Attia than it is to lie to the freemen."

"Mercenaries," Xanthus corrected. He turned in time to see Lucius walking out of the villa. He'd changed his clothing and was headed straight for the training yard.

"He's not happy," Ennius said. "Do you want me to talk to him?"

"I will."

Xanthus had to move quickly to catch up with Lucius before he reached the other gladiators. Even then, Lucius could barely look at him.

"My uncle has always said that softness has no place in the arena."

"Lives are gambled, Master Lucius."

"Yes. And my uncle only gambles on the best. Like you."

"He's not sending me because I'm better. He's sending me because I'm expendable."

Lucius scoffed. "Horseshit."

"You and I both know that the chances of finding Spartacus with such little information are phenomenally low. Do you really think your uncle would risk his only heir on what will probably amount to a fool's errand? Chasing ghosts through the Republic?"

"My uncle will do whatever it takes to win."

"There's another reason he wants you to stay," Xanthus said.

Lucius narrowed his eyes, waiting.

"Tycho Flavius is coming. He wants to meet Spartacus. Your uncle needs you here, at his side, when Flavius comes."

At the mention of the name, Lucius's careful mask slipped

back into place. Neutral. Empty. As though he'd been two completely different people in just the last few seconds.

Xanthus wasn't particularly surprised by the reaction. Tycho Flavius had a less than flattering reputation in Timeus's household. Valeria and Lucius took pains to avoid him whenever possible, and like most of the world, he'd never even seen Rory. All Xanthus knew or cared about was that Tycho owned Decimus. Nothing else really mattered to him.

"Master Lucius?" Xanthus said.

"Let's train," Lucius said, and stalked away before Xanthus could say another word.

Xanthus's brothers were training with wooden swords this time. As soon as they saw Lucius, they changed their pairings. Iduma and Albinus were never willing to partner with Lucius, and Castor kept his distance from everyone but his brothers. It was Lebuin who took position in front of Lucius with a brief nod.

Xanthus hesitated. The last time he'd seen Lucius so upset was at the clearing right after the attack, right after he'd been forced to execute a man in front of the household. He wondered if the coldness in Lucius's eyes had anything to do with Spartacus anymore. The uncertainty made him nervous. But he couldn't stand still forever. He gave the command for the others to begin. Five gladiators and one young Roman slave master moved in unison.

The exercise was intentionally coordinated, meant to enforce muscle memory through repetition. It had been Ennius's way of instilling their bodies with new reflexes, and they used it still. Each man followed the same sequence, blocking and thrusting as one unit. That didn't stop any of them from hitting as hard as they could.

Wood splintered with each impact, cascading down to the

ground in chunks. The sand of the courtyard swept up and around, coating their feet in dust. Over and over. Strike, spin, attack, block.

Lucius was just a little bit slower on the last turn, and Xanthus could see exhaustion beginning to eat away at him. Soon, he was nearly a full second behind the others. His breath was coming fast, and Xanthus noticed a thin trickle of blood running down his wrist. He was gripping his practice sword too tightly, and the wood was cutting into his skin.

Xanthus was about to call an end to the exercise when Lucius raised his sword and slashed.

Lebuin wasn't expecting it—that move wasn't part of the sequence—but his training kicked in, as it was meant to. He blocked easily, moving out of the way as Lucius charged forward again.

The other gladiators immediately cleared out, positioning themselves around Xanthus. They weren't at all interested in getting involved. In fact, Iduma had a wicked grin on his face. He was probably hoping to see Lucius drop to the ground in the next few seconds.

But Lebuin had always had more patience than the rest. He simply continued to block and roll. He never attacked. He just let Lucius push him around and back in wide circles.

A feral look entered Lucius's eyes, making them gleam in the sunlight. Sweat matted down his short hair and made his tunic stick to his back. With each impact, his hands shook. Finally, he lowered his sword, panting hard.

Lebuin took the motion as a concession, and he looked at Xanthus with a raised brow. He wasn't even winded. But while his head was turned, Lucius raised his sword and swung again. The weapon struck Lebuin's temple with a loud crack, knocking him out cold. His body fell like a tree.

Lucius was panting and shaking, standing over Lebuin, look-ing shocked. He swayed slightly as the practice sword fell from his hand. The hilt was coated in blood and sweat. Lucius looked down at his shredded palm for a second, almost unseeing.

No one moved. No one said a single word. The gladiators' faces were still and calm as stone, as though they'd simply been watching the clouds move across the sky. And they stayed that way as Lucius turned and rushed back to the villa. Only when he'd left the training yard did the gladiators walk calmly to Le-buin's side.

Iduma brought a water skin and unceremoniously emptied it onto Lebuin's face. "Wake up, sleeping beauty," he said in a flat tone.

Lebuin's eyes fluttered open. "Well," he said. "Didn't see that coming."

"You should've broken his other arm," Albinus said.

Gallus scoffed but said nothing.

They stood back and let Lebuin get to his feet alone. He picked up his fallen sword and took his old position again. "Ready," he said.

"Idiot," Albinus grumbled. They all knew who he was talk-ing about, and it wasn't Lebuin.

Everyone paired off again, and Castor flung Lucius's bloody sword into a far corner.

CHAPTER 17

A strong wind blew in from the sea, making the night colder and clearer than it had been since they'd arrived. Attia felt it sharply as she sat on the railing of a balcony on the upper floor.

She hadn't seen Lucretia since they'd left Ardea, and she felt guilty for feeling relief. The lifeless look in the woman's eyes was so much harder to stomach than the bruises or the cuts. Sabina said that Lucretia was recuperating somewhere in the villa, and Attia decided it was probably better for Sabina to be with her anyway. Lucretia needed peace to heal, and all Attia had to offer was her rage.

Bracing her hands on the balcony, she leaned forward and looked past her toes to the raging surf below. The salty air filled her senses, and she took a deep, steadying breath.

That was how Ennius found her, dragging his uneven step to stand at her side.

Attia waited for his musical voice, waited to hear the message he was holding in the space between his words. Instead, he simply leaned against the balcony beside her, a small lantern in his hand. The light reflected off of something hanging from his neck, and Attia recognized a braided leather cord similar to the one that Xanthus wore. It too held a silver pendant, but instead of a crescent moon, Ennius wore a sharp inverted triangle with serrated edges.

"What is that?" Attia asked. "A symbol of one of your gods?"

Ennius reached his free hand up to touch the pendant. "No. A tooth."

Attia nearly laughed. "A tooth," she repeated, skepticism coloring her voice. The triangle was nearly as long as her thumb.

"Not a real one, but a decent likeness."

"I've never seen an animal with a tooth like that."

"Off the coast near my village, there were water monsters fifty times bigger than the fish you see here, long and blue-gray with fins that rose up above the surface. They had rows and rows of teeth, and they hunted the seals that came to mate on the beaches."

Attia had never heard of such a creature. "What did you call them?"

Ennius's mouth moved in a series of clicks, whistles, and consonants that she couldn't identify. He laughed at her expression. "And," he said with a grin, "they could fly."

"Now you're teasing me."

Ennius shook his head. "When they hunt, they swim up from the seabed as fast as they can and break through the surface so that their whole bodies sail through the air like birds."

"You've seen this?"

"Many times," he said. "When I was young."

"A fish that can fly," Attia said with wonder.

"What men call impossible are simply the things they haven't seen yet."

Attia smiled. "You should have been a philosopher, Ennius. But I suppose we all should have been many things."

Ennius nodded and turned away, but it was too late. She'd already seen the stricken expression that crossed his face.

"What's happened?" she asked.

His gaze stayed on the dark water below as he answered. "Timeus has hired a group of freemen to search for Spartacus. Xanthus will go with them."

The irony of it might have made Attia laugh if the wretched fear that filled her wasn't so powerful. Her hands gripped the railing until her knuckles turned white. "So Timeus has no idea," she muttered.

"That Spartacus is a slave girl in his own household?" Ennius said. "No, and he probably wouldn't believe it. But you must have realized that word of you would spread. Now that others have seen what Spartacus can do, there is no going back."

"What happens when they don't find what they're looking for?"

"I'm not sure. They have almost no information, but Timeus is as tenacious as they come. I can't tell how far he'll take this. Especially since the match with Decimus is so soon."

"Decimus?"

"Xanthus will fight him at the Festival of Lupa." He glanced at Attia and sighed. "He should be the one to tell you." Ennius put a gentle hand on Attia's shoulder. "He leaves tomorrow. Go to him. For both your sakes."

When he'd gone, Attia swung her legs back over the railing and let her body sink to the floor of the balcony, curling her knees up under her chin the way she'd done as a child. Moonlight flooded the narrow balcony like liquid silver, illuminating even the dark places in the room behind her.

Attia's vision wasn't nearly as clear. A cavalcade of emotions marched through her skull like foreign soldiers on parade. Helplessness blended with resentment and anger, fear of loss but also fear of wanting. Before she came to Rome, she'd lived by very simple truths. All that mattered was family—the people bound to her by blood and by oath. The easiest thing she'd ever done was take up a sword in their defense. Without that—her cause and her purpose—she felt lost. Adrift. She didn't know what to do anymore. If she were the praying kind, she might petition the gods for guidance. But the clarity she sought had little to do with gods or even men. Until now, she'd been blinded by grief and placated by tenderness.

This then was her prayer: remembering.

On the last day of the previous summer, she'd been on a scouting mission with a small unit of soldiers. As daylight waned, she'd sat on a hilltop with the calm expanse of the Aegean spread out before her. Her blood-brother Jezrael was there, too, his dark eyes narrowed against the sunset, emphasizing the crooked angle of his nose—a souvenir from their childhood and the day when he had teased her until she kicked him in the face. He was fiddling mindlessly with a frayed strand of red wool that had come undone from his cloak. For a long time, they said nothing, just stared out into the blue.

"I'm going to ask Mena to marry me," Jezrael finally said into the silence.

Attia took care to keep her face neutral. She'd known the announcement was coming, but it didn't make it any easier to hear.

"I've already spoken to the elders and Mena's parents. King Sparro has given his blessing."

Attia gritted her teeth. Even her father had been told before her.

217

"I'm going to marry her in the spring." He glanced at At-tia. "I'm sorry. I know we always swore that we would never marry. That we would just turn into old, fat, useless warriors together. Like your father and Crius."

A snort of laughter burst out of Attia before she could stop it.

"They've really let themselves go," Jezrael continued.

Attia had to bite her lip to keep from laughing.

"It's sad."

Attia shook her head.

Jezrael's voice lowered, losing that laughing edge. "She's the one, Attia. The one I've been looking for since . . . since before I knew I was looking. It's not enough to say that I love her. I can't *breathe* without her."

Attia turned to look at him. His face was so open and vul-nerable, and he looked so hopeful.

"I know, Jez. Of course I know."

He took a deep breath. "We always said—"

"That doesn't matter now."

"Then why are you upset? Talk to me, Attia."

"It's just . . . if *you* get married . . ."

He watched her face carefully, and Attia knew the instant he understood. He took her hand in his and squeezed. "You think that if I take a wife, your father will make you take a husband."

"Jez, I'm not ready for marriage, and I don't know if I ever will be."

"Maybe this is part of growing up."

Attia pulled her hand from his.

"I just want you to be happy," he said.

"But I *am* happy. What do I need a man for?"

"Family? Love?"

Attia shook her head. "I have that already."

"You might change your mind one day, Attia," he said. "Maybe you'll find someone—someone strong like you—and you won't be able to imagine a life without them. Marriage or no, children or no. You'll find a person who makes you feel whole, and then everything will be different." He smiled earnestly, and the tension between them eased.

Attia subtly dug her hand into the dirt, scooping up a handful of the dark soil. "Will it *really* be different?" She threw the dirt at his face.

He ran after her, laughing and shouting as they raced down the hill and across the shoreline. The soldiers watching them smiled.

It was a beautiful memory. One of her last good ones.

But now there were other people, other memories to add. Sabina combing out her hair with gentle hands. Rory wrapping her arms around Attia's waist with such complete trust. Xanthus holding her with the only comfort she'd found in this damned country. She couldn't separate that anymore. Her path had never been an easy or a straight one, and as she sat there in the cold with her memories and her fury, the whole world seemed so incredibly broken.

Except for one thing.

She didn't even have to knock on his door. Xanthus opened it immediately and pulled her close. He'd been waiting for her.

Attia thought she should probably say something—ask about Decimus or the search—but she didn't want to talk. Instead, she wrapped her arms around him and let her kiss say everything that she couldn't.

Xanthus's lips never left hers as he lifted her into his arms and carried her to the bed. Her hands wandered across the line of his jaw and the cords of his neck while he pulled the pins from her hair, freeing the dark mass to tumble down around her shoulders like a veil.

Attia's heart was beating so loudly that she almost missed it when he whispered something against her lips. It was a different language, rounded and sweet and fluid like a bubbling brook.

"What does that mean?"

He smiled as he buried a hand in her hair. "I'll tell you when you're ready to hear it." Then he pulled her mouth back to his, and the touch became rougher, more demanding.

Something flared to life inside of Attia, a heat she'd never felt before. She lost herself to Xanthus's kiss, hardly caring when he twisted her around to lie flat on the bed, his arms braced on either side to hold his weight. The roughness of his hands flooded her senses as he nudged her knees apart and settled between her legs.

"Attia," he whispered.

At the sound of his voice, awareness came rushing back. For a moment she couldn't control her breathing or her panic. She must have made some small noise, because Xanthus suddenly became still on top of her.

She wasn't frightened, exactly. After all, it was just her body. She'd done worse things with it—she'd used it to kill and to maim. She'd used her knowledge of sword and staff and bow to revel in death. *But maybe,* she thought, *maybe I'm not meant for this. Maybe I am only a warrior, a killer. Maybe I can never truly be a part of a beautiful thing.*

The immensity of such a terrible possibility weighed down on her chest until she thought she might collapse from so many broken promises. What was she that now, with a man she could respect and adore, she seemed so incapable of love?

Xanthus waited for her, patient and undemanding as ever. His thumb rubbed light strokes against her cheek, and he brushed his lips against her temple. "It's all right," he said. She could feel his heart hammering in his chest, but his voice was steady. "Do you want me to stop?"

Attia knew that if she said yes, he would back away immediately. Xanthus was the kind of man who asked rather than took, who begged the gods to forgive his sins with whispered breath. He was the man who'd fallen to his knees before her, who had held her close until the night was over, who would give anything to keep her whole.

So when he started to pull away and the cold rushed back in, Attia wrapped her arms around his neck to keep him against her.

"No," she whispered. "Don't stop."

They stayed tangled up in each other, so close that Xanthus wondered if she was truly a part of him now—a piece of his very soul. He entwined his fingers through hers and whispered in her ear. He knew she didn't understand the words, but in a way, he thought she probably understood them more clearly than anything he'd ever said. He held her close in the dark as their breathing finally slowed.

Outside, a heavy gray cloud of smoke bubbled up from the crest of Vesuvius. White flakes drifted down from the summit to scatter at the base of the mountain. The waves crashed to the east, insistent as a heartbeat.

"Are you asleep?" Attia whispered.

He nuzzled her neck in response. "Are you all right? Did I hurt you?" The possibility pained him.

She laughed. "I'm fine. I just didn't expect it to be like this."

Xanthus smiled. He knew exactly what she meant.

After a while, she said, "Ennius told me about the freemen. The search."

"Mercenaries," Xanthus said. "I don't want to go, but maybe it's a good thing. I can keep you safe this way. I can convince them that Spartacus is lost, or at least paint a particularly unhelpful picture. Ennius said something about a giant man with seven sons."

Attia giggled. "An apt description. I've always considered myself taller than average," she said. She turned in his arms to face him. "There was something else that Ennius said."

Xanthus held his breath.

"He told me that you're going to fight a gladiator named Decimus at the Festival of Lupa." Attia ran her fingers down his cheek. "But he said to ask you about it. Is there something I should know?"

Xanthus turned his head to kiss her hand. He wasn't sure where to start or how much to say. But he realized that his earlier words were still true—Attia deserved honesty. Complete honesty. When he finally found his voice, it was little more than a whisper.

"Decimus was a legionary of low rank, and ten years ago, he showed the Romans a route into the deep hills of Britannia."

Britannia. With that one word, he saw understanding dawn for her.

"You have to understand. Vespasian wanted that island desperately. He wanted to be the first Princeps to venture so far north. So he sent his kinsman, Crassus Flavius."

Attia's hand tightened around his.

"It was a massacre. The old were burned alive. Children were drowned in the lake. And the women . . ." Xanthus shook his head. "I learned later that only a tenth of the people in my village were allowed to live. It's a common practice. The Romans call it *decimatio*. Those of us who survived became slaves."

"Is that why they call him Decimus?"

Xanthus nodded once. "I'm sorry I kept this from you, Attia. I didn't want those memories to taint whatever it was we had. And then I just didn't know how to say the words. But if there's anyone I hate in this world, it's Decimus. I've waited ten years to face him. "

"For vengeance?"

"For justice."

"I understand," she said.

Xanthus put a finger under her chin and held her gaze. "After this," he said. "After I convince the mercenaries that Spartacus can't be found. After I meet Decimus in the arena. After I finish this, we'll run."

Her eyes widened. "You'll escape with me?"

"Yes. It won't be easy. I told you—Timeus will hunt us across the known world."

"Let him try. We'll die somehow, but not as slaves."

Xanthus caressed the side of her face. "I just need a little more time, Attia. I know I have no right to ask it of you, and if you say no, I'll understand. But I just need to finish this."

Instead of answering, she kissed him again.

Xanthus lifted the silver pendant from his neck and looped it around hers. The twisted leather was dark against her golden skin. When she looked up again, her eyes were bright with promise. She wrapped her arms around him and pressed her forehead to his. So close, and yet not close enough.

"I'll come back for you," he said.

"I'll wait."

CHAPTER 18

Leaving was harder than he thought possible. But it was the best way to protect her, and Xanthus forced himself not to look back. Especially with the mercenary riding beside him. Especially with Timeus watching from the gate.

Just before Xanthus mounted his horse, the old man had grabbed his arm. "Find him, Xanthus," he said. "Whatever it takes. Find Spartacus and bring him to me."

"And if he won't come?" Xanthus asked.

Timeus had narrowed his eyes. The chill in them reflected the dead blue of the winter sky. "Just find him."

Kanut whistled after they passed the bend in the road. "That dominus of yours is one uptight ass, you know that? I've never had a patron try to tell me how to do my job," he said with a laugh.

"You're lucky he didn't come himself," Xanthus said.

"I understand why he sent you, gladiator, but I must say that I'm surprised he did."

"And why is that?"

"Champion or no, you're still a slave." He said it so easily, reaching over to tap the brand on Xanthus's arm. "How old is it?"

Xanthus didn't answer.

"I'd guess nine, maybe ten years. Am I right? Of course I'm right." Kanut extended his own arm, pulling the sleeve up to show Xanthus the full extent of his burns. They reached from his palm all the way up past his elbow. Xanthus thought they probably stretched over his shoulder and back but couldn't be sure. "These are much newer," Kanut said with a ghoulish wink.

"How did you get them?"

"Drowning," Kanut said sardonically. Xanthus rolled his eyes, and that made Kanut laugh harder. "Men came and tried to burn my home to the ground with me in it."

"How did you get out?"

"Maybe the gods favor me," Kanut said. "Then again, I hear you're the *son* of a god, and you're a slave. So. To hell with what the gods think, eh?"

"Didn't your mother ever tell you that you shouldn't believe everything you hear?"

"Oh, but I hear such interesting things, gladiator. For instance, I hear that Spartacus was something of a little demon— covered in black from head to toe, leaping about the arena like a shadow." Kanut grinned, watching Xanthus out of the corner of his eye. "Just tell me one thing—was Spartacus as good as they say?"

For the first time since he'd left Attia's side, Xanthus allowed himself a brief smile. "Better."

Attia didn't watch Xanthus leave. She couldn't. Instead, she stood at the window in his room, listening to the clatter of hooves disappear down the road and looking out at the heavy gray clouds that blocked the morning sun. Her fingers caressed the pendant that hung from her neck. Below, the townspeople kept the night-lamps burning on their poles in an effort to cast out the shadows. Xanthus's own short candles—ringed with hemp and feathers—burned steadily by the window.

After a little while, she entered the villa and headed for Rory's room. But before she could get far, she ran into Ennius.

He greeted her with a quirked brow. "What are you doing?"

"Walking."

"Walking?"

"Yes. Placing one foot in front of the other and moving forward. Why, do you need me for something? Will it take long or can it wait?"

"You know, whenever we talk, I have the strangest feeling that you're just a breath away from giving me orders," he said, with a twinkle in his eyes that told her he wasn't actually offended.

"Habit?" she said with a shrug.

He laughed at that but sobered quickly. "You haven't upset the domina recently, have you?"

"Valeria? No. At least, I don't think so."

"She's sent for you."

"Again? Why? I haven't even spoken to her since the match at the Coliseum."

Ennius couldn't answer that question. They walked together through the long, echoing halls of the villa, Attia subtly slowing her pace to accommodate him. She was struck with an immense feeling of guilt over what she'd done to his leg. He walked a bit easier now, but there was still a pronounced limp.

"I'm sorry," she said. She'd refused to apologize before, but everything seemed different now. "Really. It wasn't personal. I know that sounds like an excuse, but . . ."

Ennius looked at her in confusion until he saw her pointedly staring at his leg. He shrugged. "I'll heal."

"Will you?" she asked. "I've used that technique on others, and I don't think they ever walked straight again. Of course, they were enemy soldiers, and I didn't really stick around afterwards to find out."

"Attia. I said that I would heal, and I will. Straight or crooked, I'm still walking."

"You should hate me."

"Hate you?" Ennius said with a soft smile. "How could I? You make me laugh almost every time I see you. You're clever and strong, and I understand why Xanthus loves you."

Attia stopped in her tracks. "What did you say?" she asked. Or, at least she meant to ask that. She couldn't be sure if any sound came out of her mouth.

Ennius paused, too. When he spoke again, his voice was gentle. "Didn't you know?"

Attia couldn't even manage to shake her head. She just stared at him, unblinking, her brain refusing to work again.

"Do *you* . . . ?" His voice drifted off.

Attia still couldn't think straight. In some distant part of her head, she recognized Ennius's question. *Do I love Xanthus?* But her mind was being rather obstinate and refusing to share the information with the rest of her, so she simply continued to stare at Ennius like an idiot.

He sighed. "Come on, Attia." She was so distracted, he had to guide her by the elbow to keep her moving in the right direction.

A few minutes later, they reached Valeria's quarters. It was a part of the house that Attia hadn't seen before, though they hadn't been in Pompeii long enough for her to explore.

Ennius walked her to the door, but before she left his side, he whispered, "Forget about what I've just said, and pull your-self together now. You'll have plenty of time to think about it all later." A house slave opened the door and let her in.

Valeria's room was bedecked in blinding white. The curtains, the couches, the chairs, the walls—everything was the color of ivory and marble. And it wasn't really just one room. Attia could see doorways branching off on either side, probably leading to a bedroom and washrooms and closets and whatever other rooms wealthy Roman women enjoyed.

Attia took a step forward, and her feet touched a white rug made from the pelt of a snow leopard. She grimaced. What a shame the poor animal had to die to decorate *this* place. She found Valeria in her bedroom, sprawled across her bed. Her beauty paint was smeared across her cheek and pillow, and her eyes were partially closed. Wine stained the sheets. She looked drugged. Or dying. Or both.

When Valeria heard her enter, she opened her eyes and propped herself up on her elbow. "It's you. The pretty little Thra-cian."

"You asked for me, Domina?"

"Yes, I did. Though I can't remember why."

Hopefully not to paint her face again. "Would you like me to go?" Attia asked.

"No!" Valeria said quickly. "Don't go. Stay. Keep me com-pany. Tell me about the champion. What's he like behind closed doors?"

"Domina?"

"Does he treat you well?"

"Yes, Domina."

Valeria let herself fall back onto her pillows with a sigh. "You're lucky. It's been so long since a man treated me like any-thing. I knew one once who had the gentlest hands. When he touched my cheek, I . . ." Her voice broke, and her glazed blue eyes filled with tears. Then she blinked and turned away. "But that was a long time ago."

"I have heard a little about Legatus Bassus—that he was a strong, honorable man," Attia said, and it was true. Lucius had told her of his father—the Roman general who believed in Roman decency.

Valeria's eyes focused on Attia. "Oh," she said finally. "Him. Yes. Lucius Bassus was quite strong and . . . *honorable*." The last word was said with a bitterness that surprised Attia. "My son is like him in some ways. He's also like me."

If she's expecting me to say that she is honorable, I'll eat my sandal, Attia thought. But apparently, Valeria didn't expect that at all.

"Do you sing, Thracian?" she asked.

"No, Domina."

"Did your people not have songs?"

"Some."

"Sing for me."

Oh, the woman couldn't be serious. "I can't quite remember any of the words, Domina."

Valeria rolled onto her side. "My children make up their own songs, you know? Meaningless words. No melody at all. I don't know where they learned to do that. Certainly not from me. Old Vespasian once said I sang like the sirens who lured men from their ships."

Attia smiled to herself. Her own father had once told her she sang like a dying seagull. But since she knew nothing of sirens, she couldn't tell if it was a good thing or a bad thing to sound like one. Then Valeria opened her mouth, and chills blossomed across Attia's skin.

She could honestly say that she'd never heard anything so

beautiful. Valeria's voice—shrill and strained when she spoke—suddenly became ethereal and resonant, a sound Attia never would have expected from looking at her. When she closed her eyes, blocking out the sad sight of the woman sprawled on the bed, Attia thought this was probably what the Christians and Jews meant when they spoke of angel voices.

The moment Valeria stopped singing, the air rang hollow and empty. Attia opened her eyes to see a tear slip down Valeria's face.

"Do you believe in the gods, Thracian?" she whispered. "Do you pray?"

"No," Attia answered honestly. "Not anymore."

"Me neither," Valeria said with a sad smile. She blinked several times and craned her neck to look out the window. "It's raining. I think I'll have a bath."

Attia spent the next two hours sitting beside Valeria's gold-plated tub. Neither spoke, though the echo of Valeria's song hung heavy in the air for Attia.

Valeria was far from sober. Every few minutes, her body went slack and she started to dip down beneath the water. Attia had to lean over and pull her up again by her arms. When the water turned cold and Valeria's skin was wrinkled as a prune, Attia wrapped a towel around her—like she'd done so many times for Rory—and helped her back to bed.

"Honor isn't everything, you know," Valeria said as she snuggled under her wine-stained sheets. "For many, it is a cheap word. Easily spoken and easily discarded. There are more important things—love, loyalty. Things men could never understand. I loved once, Thracian. Too much. Now I pay the cost of it. My brother thinks he can barter for power. But you can't trust a Flavian. Not ever." Valeria met her eyes. "Attia," she said, "you care about my daughter. I know you do. Make me a promise: Whatever happens, you must keep her safe."

The twists in their conversation kept throwing Attia into confusion. Valeria's mind jumped from one topic to another with seemingly no connection between them. But her blue eyes were filled with sadness, fear, and regret. She gripped Attia's hand in hers.

"Promise me," she said again. "No matter what. Keep her safe from *them*."

"Of course I'll protect her," Attia answered. "I will always protect her."

Valeria closed her eyes with relief. "Good. Yes. That's good." A minute later, her body relaxed and she was asleep.

Kanut led Xanthus through back streets and alleys, away from the main road, away from soldiers and most of the vigiles. They didn't stop until they reached the Red District, where Xanthus raised a questioning brow.

"Don't judge a man for needing his comforts," Kanut said. But he passed the prostitutes lining the street, turned down another alley, and stopped at the closed door of a crumbling insula. A small, crude image of a bird was drawn in chalk at the base of the door. Kanut barely knocked before stomping inside.

Three men sat or reclined in different parts of the room, and all of them turned to stare at Xanthus. They didn't make any other move—not to stand or grab a weapon or even to show surprise. Either they'd been expecting Kanut and Xanthus at that very minute, or they thought little of strategic vigilance.

Xanthus was unimpressed. "You told Timeus there were nine of you."

Kanut ignored him. "What did the woman say?"

A dark-haired man close to Xanthus's age answered. "Same as the rest." He narrowed his eyes and looked Xanthus up and down, leaning back in his chair. His nose looked like it had been broken a few times.

A big man with graying hair turned in his seat. "He the one?"

"Brothers, meet Xanthus Maximus Colossus," Kanut said. "The Champion of Rome."

The third man was barely a man at all, more a youth who couldn't have been older than fourteen. He had his back to a wall and his legs propped up on a crate. He chewed on a piece of dried meat, walked up to Xanthus, and craned his neck back to meet his eyes. "I thought you'd be bigger," he said.

Xanthus raised an eyebrow. "I thought there would be more of you."

Kanut clicked his teeth. "What about Fido's man?"

The youth looked back at Kanut and grinned in response.

"Good," Kanut said. "Let's go."

The ground began to shake.

"Not again," the older one murmured.

They streamed out of the insula just before the weak roof caved in, littering the ground with debris. A cloud of dust bloomed out into the street. The horses panicked, rearing and neighing wildly. Kanut and Xanthus grabbed their reins to keep them from bolting. Around them, the prostitutes were laughing as men ran from the insulas, hurrying down the street in their layered, disheveled tunics.

As soon as the ground was still again, Kanut mounted his horse. "One hour," he said to the others. "Let's go, gladiator." They left the three men in the street and rode off.

Again, Kanut chose a route through the back alleys of Pompeii. Every so often, he would whistle—a sharp, piercing sound that grated on Xanthus's nerves. Kanut wouldn't say where they were going or why. He just rode and whistled, and Xanthus had no choice but to follow him. They reached the city's borders as another tremor raced through the ground. At least that one only lasted a couple of seconds.

"I'll be glad to be rid of this city," Kanut grumbled.

A mile out from the gates, Kanut turned west and started leading them toward the forest. Xanthus caught subtle movements in the trees around them but heard nothing. Then Kanut started that damn whistling again.

Nine men melted out of the shadows. Xanthus recognized three of them as the men from the Red District. The others were strangers. All nine wore the same dark clothing, and they all watched him with open suspicion.

"Gladiator, meet my men," Kanut said.

So that's what he'd been doing with his irritating whistle—calling to them. "Why hide?" Xanthus asked.

"Not your concern," someone answered.

"You've already met my lieutenant," Kanut said, pointing to the dark-haired one with the slightly crooked nose.

"And the others?"

"Not your concern either," Number Two said.

Xanthus sighed. "Well, this has been a productive meeting."

"We've been gathering our own information for some time," Kanut said. "Now we have questions for *you*—the man who actually fought beside Spartacus."

Here we go.

"What did he look like?" Number Two asked.

"Like a black mask," Xanthus said. "His face was covered. I never saw it."

"Size?"

"At least a foot taller than me, and muscular."

"Tattoos? Marks?"

"None that I saw."

"How did he move?"

That made Xanthus hesitate. "What do you mean?"

"How. Did. He. Move?" Number Two repeated each word slowly and deliberately, as though he were speaking to a child.

Xanthus pictured Attia in the arena, running circles around their opponents as though she walked on air, maneuvering her sword as though it were an extension of her own body. She fought with the merciless precision of a Maedi warrior, yet she was lithe, graceful. Lucius had been right to dub her the Shadow of Death.

"He was heavy," Xanthus said. "Not very light on his feet, but strong. He knocked down his first opponent with one strike." *Well, the last part is true.*

Kanut smiled at Number Two.

"What kind of weapon did he use?" one of the others asked.

"A gladius."

For some reason, everyone nodded.

"Did he say anything?" Kanut asked.

"No. He was mute."

That made Number Two laugh.

"What's so funny?" Xanthus asked.

Number Two cleared his throat. "The prostitute in the Red District—she . . . serviced one of Fido's men, found out a few things. Everyone seems to agree that Spartacus never spoke, and well, I've never met a mute. Seems like a funny sort of affliction to have. Almost unbelievable."

Xanthus stared back at him with a straight face.

Kanut's smile become thoughtful. "You're not a very emotive man, are you, gladiator?" The teasing note was gone from his voice. He sounded more curious than anything.

"No. I'm not," Xanthus said.

"And you don't trust us."

"Of course I don't."

The others smiled before lifting up small packs that Xanthus hadn't noticed before. Without an order, saddled horses came trotting out of the woods.

"That's smart," Kanut said. "You shouldn't trust anyone."

High above, a falcon wheeled and cried.

Attia didn't expect it to be so difficult to sleep without him.

The night after Xanthus left, she bolted upright in their bed, her eyes open and her senses sharp even though it wasn't yet dawn. When she couldn't force herself back to sleep, she opened the door and looked out into the gladiators' training yard.

A low mist hovered above the ground. The yard was empty except for Lucius. His hands were wrapped around a wooden sword, eyes focused on one of the training dummies in the farthest corner. He held the sword in front of him but didn't move. He just stared at the training dummy, unblinking. It seemed Attia wasn't the only who couldn't sleep. She slipped back into Xanthus's room before Lucius noticed her.

On the third day, Lucretia appeared while Attia was preparing Rory's midday meal. Her bruises had started to fade, but she still wore a loose, long-sleeved dress. Her black hair was pulled back in a leather thong, exposing the cuts on her face and the swelling of her jaw. At least she was healing. She said nothing while Attia worked, and Attia found that she didn't mind the quiet company.

In the evenings after the sun had set and Rory had fallen asleep, Attia and Lucretia secreted away to one of the gardens along the western wall. Attia always brought food for the two of them, and Lucretia would stretch out in the grass to stare up at the stars. The garden became their own little sanctuary where words weren't necessary. But it was in the garden that Lucretia finally broke her silence.

"It's quiet out here." Her voice was raspy from disuse.

Attia wondered if these were the first words Lucretia had spoken to anyone since Ardea. The ring of bruises around her neck was still dark against her skin. Attia must have been looking at her with some concern because Lucretia smiled tightly and took her hand.

"Sabina's tonics help."

"I know." Attia stretched out to lie beside Lucretia, their hands still clasped. "They helped me, too. Before."

"I heard about the champion and the freemen." Lucretia turned her head to look at Attia, and their hair tangled together in the grass. "I hope you're not worried. Xanthus is strong. He'll be safe. And . . . and he cares about you. He'll come back." She said the last part with a sad smile. Attia could see the sorrow in her eyes, and it made her cringe. "You're lucky, Thracian."

Again, Attia saw Lucretia on that dark morning in Ardea, covered in bruises and cuts and wounds, some too deep to heal. She turned her eyes back up to the stars, trying to purge the images from her head.

Lucretia was quiet for several long minutes. "How's your mark?" she asked gently.

Attia shrugged. "Sabina used her salves to treat it in the beginning and make sure infection didn't set in. Now I try not to look at it." Attia knew the skin around the brand had healed well, all things considered. It was only slightly wrinkled and a bit shiny. The raised edges of the brand were still tinged with pink, but Attia doubted that would ever fade. Maybe one day, she'd just take a sharp knife and . . .

"It fulfills its purpose," Lucretia said as though she could hear Attia's thoughts. "It forces us to remember."

"I think I would rather forget." Attia bit her lip and frowned. "Were you always called Lucretia?"

Lucretia's eyes focused on the velvet blackness of the sky above, and her pupils dilated just a little, making her look as though she was entranced by something Attia couldn't see. "I can't remember," she finally said. "I know what you mean about wanting to forget, but I've forgotten so much already."

"How do you stand it?"

"I just think of darkness—total nothingness. It's warm and cool, tiny and infinite all at the same time. And you're alone, but you realize that you've never truly been alone. The universe spins on around us and through us. What makes it unfathomable is what makes it so beautiful. Everything just . . . stops."

When she said it like that, with her eyes looking into the distance and her voice drifting on an unseen breeze, it almost sounded beautiful. But Attia knew better. "You speak of death," she said.

Lucretia turned her eyes back to her. "I speak of peace. For some of us, it's the same thing."

Attia remembered dreaming that way, too. But not anymore. She had Xanthus now. What did Lucretia have but her few moments of darkness and silence? Attia gently squeezed her hand, eyes still looking up at the starry sky as Lucretia fell asleep beside her.

Two nights later, Attia and Lucretia were talking quietly in their little garden when someone appeared in the doorway to the villa. The boy's bald head and simple loincloth identified him as a eunuch before he even spoke.

"I've come to collect the dominus's woman." His high-pitched voice grated along every nerve in Attia's body.

Lucretia's face went blank, and she took Attia's hand in hers as they stood.

No. Attia felt as though her blood were freezing in her veins, numbing the tips of her fingers and toes. The bruises were better. The cuts were healing. Lucretia had only just started talking again. How could he call for her now? He couldn't do this. Attia couldn't let him.

"No," she said out loud. "She's ill. Tell Timeus she's not coming."

The eunuch's eyes widened as he shook his head. "But I can't. The dominus . . . he gave orders . . ."

"I said to tell him no!" Attia shouted.

The boy flinched. Lucretia moved to stand between them, her hand gentle on Attia's shoulder.

Attia gritted her teeth together, pain radiating along her cheek. She refused to let go of Lucretia's hand. "I won't let him," she said. "I won't let him take you."

Lucretia put her arms around Attia and held her close. "Don't worry about me," she whispered. "I can always forget, remember?" She kissed her cheek before turning away, walking out of the garden and back into the villa with the eunuch close on her heels.

A second later, she was gone, and it was all Attia could do to stop the scream of outrage welling in her throat.

Xanthus had to admit—Kanut and his mercenaries were experienced.

For two days, they stayed a safe distance from the road. Scouts went on ahead or stayed behind. Never the same riders. They shifted their formation constantly and in random intervals. One minute, Number Two was riding beside Xanthus. The next, he had disappeared to scout through a copse of trees.

The rocky terrain helped conceal their trail, but even then, they rode in circles, retraced their steps, moved on foot through wooded areas, and led the horses through every stream they could find. Only three or four slept at a time, and usually while they were riding. They just looped their reins through their belts to keep from falling over. Then they woke again without a sound, without a single word spoken among them. Xanthus had never seen such discipline.

In fact, none of the mercenaries spoke much at all, to Xanthus or to each other.

Except for Kanut.

Who couldn't shut up.

For even one.

Single.

Minute.

"You see, birds are mercurial creatures," he was saying. "Fiercely loyal. But give a falcon the wrong look, and she'll bite. Hard. Maybe growl a bit while she's at it." He laughed and turned to Number Two. "Do you remember the gray one?"

Number Two, who'd been frowning all day, suddenly grinned. "I still have a scar from that one."

"Exactly my point," Kanut said, turning to Xanthus. "You always remember the bird who gave you your first scar."

"What does that have to do with *anything* that you said before?" Xanthus asked with exasperation. He'd learned on the first day that ignoring Kanut only made him worse, but it was so difficult to take him seriously.

"My point," Kanut said, "is that birds are like people."

"Oh, of course," Xanthus replied. "Except for the feathers, claws, beak, flight—"

"Don't be pedantic, gladiator. I like you much more when you're aloof and cold. Now, wolves are a different matter."

Kanut droned on, and Xanthus found himself remembering

the fight with the wolves in Ardea. He'd thought his heart had stopped when Attia fell and that gray body shuddered on top of her. He remembered knowing—instantly—that if she died, well, there wouldn't really be much point to anything.

That same reasoning was why he now found himself on the road with mercenaries who wouldn't speak and another who couldn't stop: to keep Attia safe. Xanthus thought it might well be that everything he did in the future would be for her sake.

Kanut's grating voice broke through his thoughts. "Tell me again how you defeated the Taurus." He bit into an apple, chewing with noisy, wet smacks of his lips.

"I killed him," Xanthus said.

"Obviously, gladiator. But *how?*" Kanut pressed.

"I sliced his head off."

Kanut slapped his knee and laughed. "Brilliant! Is that how Spartacus killed his men?"

Xanthus rolled his eyes. Kanut wasn't even trying to be coy about it anymore. His incessant questions about Xanthus were peppered with inquiries about Spartacus. He was no doubt trying to catch him off guard, hoping that Xanthus would release more information than he intended.

"No," Xanthus said. "Spartacus beat the first man with his bare hands, remember?"

"Bare hands," Kanut repeated with a nod and barely suppressed smile. "Rather impressive. And was his opponent armed?"

"To the teeth," Xanthus said yet again. He glanced to the side just in time to see Number Two mouthing the words along with him. "At least one of you has been paying attention."

"You've told us the same thing at least a dozen times now, gladiator," Number Two said.

"Maybe that's because you've asked the same question at least a dozen times now. It's not my fault you can't listen."

"There is one question you haven't answered," Number Two said.

"And what is that?"

"How did you learn his name?"

"What?"

Number Two turned in his saddle to look at Xanthus. "Spartacus was mute, you said. Didn't say a single word, correct? So how did you learn his name?"

Xanthus met the man's challenging gaze full on. "You'd have to ask Timeus's nephew. He was the one who introduced him at the arena."

A charged silence passed between them, broken when Kanut laughed forcefully. "Oh, who cares? What is in a name? I've had plenty of names in the past few months alone."

Number Two turned forward.

"I'm more concerned with *what* Spartacus is," Kanut said. "A demon? A monkey? A frog?"

"All viable options," Xanthus muttered.

"Or perhaps she was a giant, as the gladiator says."

She.

Xanthus nearly fell off his horse, his hands involuntarily jerking on the reins for balance. The beast reared up with a loud noise of protest.

But neither the mercenaries nor Kanut nor his Number Two were paying attention to him, because in the distance, two scouts were racing back and waving their arms wildly.

Kanut translated. "Fido's men. Follow me, gladiator!"

The mercenaries dispersed, spreading out in every direction. There was no time for questions.

Xanthus urged his horse into a gallop, following in Kanut's

wake as he scanned the horizon. The others had already disappeared, but dust rose just ahead.

Kanut saw it, too. He forced his horse into a sharp turn. They barely made it fifty yards before they saw the dust rise again. Kanut made another sharp turn, then another. But Fido's men were coming at them from all sides. There was nowhere to go. Their horses trotted nervously as the men rode closer to them.

"Maybe you should lend me a sword," Xanthus said.

"Maybe you should follow my lead."

"Because that worked out so well for me just now?"

Kanut chuckled and raised his hands above his head as Fido's men finally came into view.

"What the hell are you doing?" Xanthus growled.

Kanut smiled. "Surrendering."

CHAPTER 19

Rory ran to the shutters, her small hands struggling with the latch. She and Attia were finally alone, and the child had been whispering about this all day.

"Hurry!" she said urgently, beckoning to Attia to come and help.

Attia reached over with a smile and let the shutters swing open.

Orange-tinted light filled the room, warming the air with the glow of the sunset. Rory's giggle was a sound of pure delight, and she spread her arms wide.

"We almost missed it. Why don't people do this all the time?" she asked, spinning in circles that made her sleeping-tunic swirl around her ankles.

"It's different when you're older."

"I wish I could do this all day, not just at sunset."

"You can't do it for too long, Rory," Attia said. "The sun will toast your skin brown and then what will your mother say?"

"She wouldn't notice," Rory said.

Attia couldn't argue with that. Valeria so rarely made appearances anymore, not even at the evening meal. Attia doubted that she'd even seen her daughter since they left Rome. "What about your brother? He would certainly notice if you start to look like a raisin."

Rory lowered her arms and her voice. "Lucius wouldn't, either. He hasn't come to visit me in so long. He used to tuck me in some nights. But I haven't seen him in days and days. I wish I could tell him. I wish he could see me in the sun."

Attia understood the affection that Rory had for her brother. In many ways, it seemed like he'd raised her more than Valeria had. But then again, Attia was grateful that Lucius hadn't come to see his sister. The young man she'd seen that morning in the training yard with his glazed eyes and trembling hands was so different from the Lucius whose hands she'd bandaged in Rome. The attack on the camp—and what he'd been forced to do because of it—had changed him immensely.

"Attia, look," Rory said. Her little face peered over the marble railing of the balcony. "It's like the mountain is breathing."

Cloudy black exhalations surrounded the entire summit of Vesuvius. The edges of the clouds turned red in the setting sun, as though tinged with fire. A layer of gray-and-white ash coated the roofs of the houses and shops at the base of the mountain.

"We should go back inside, Rory." Attia gently ushered her back into the room and closed the shutters.

Rory didn't argue. It was nearly dark anyway and time for her supper. Ever since Attia had started letting her play in the evenings, Rory had been eating more and more. She'd already gained a few pounds, and her skin no longer looked like it was hanging on bone. Even if her family hadn't yet noticed the new glow to her skin, it was only a matter of time before *someone* saw that Rory was getting stronger. *Let them see,* Attia thought. She wasn't going to starve a child. Not for the Romans, and certainly not to keep their secrets.

Attia left Rory to her little games while she went downstairs to pick up their supper from the kitchens. But her steps slowed on the way back when she found Lucius sitting on the stairs that led to the upper rooms.

His body was stretched across the bottommost step, his left foot tapping a soft beat against the floor. The cup of wine in his hand was nearly empty, but he stared into it as though there was a message to be read there. He looked like he hadn't slept in weeks.

"Have you heard?" he said, still staring into his cup. "Tycho Flavius is coming."

Flavius. The name rang in Attia's ears.

"Two weeks, the messengers say. Maybe my mother has the right idea—maybe we should all just drink ourselves into oblivion so that we can stomach the fool's presence." He chuckled to himself, threw his head back, and drained the cup.

It was obvious that Lucius was less than pleased by this information, but Attia was more concerned about whether or not Tycho would bring his father with him. Just the thought of having both Timeus and the Legatus Crassus in *this* house, close enough for Attia to drive her blade into their chests . . .

"Is he coming alone?" she asked, trying to sound as calm as possible.

Lucius turned to her with a thoughtful frown. "He may bring soldiers with him, if he's cautious. But he doesn't know that *I* know."

It was Attia's turn to frown. She had no idea what Lucius was talking about. She watched him reach into his pocket and hold up a gold coin between his fingers.

"Did you know," he said, eyes intent on the coin, "that after the House of Flavius rose to power, they restandardized the Republic's currency? They didn't want there to be any question that Vespasian was the rightful Princeps. Now all coins are engraved with Vespasian's profile on one side, and an inscription that reads 'Vespasianus Augustus, Noble Father of the Roman People' on the other." Lucius toyed with the gold coin in his fingers before reaching out his hand and offering it to Attia.

She took it hesitantly. The coin was almost solid gold—shinier and heavier than the Republic's currency. It bore no profile, no long inscription. There was only the image of a wolf's head on both sides, along with a single word. "Flavius," she read.

"After I executed that bandit, this coin fell out of his pocket. I hid it before the guards or the soldiers could see. The guards are my uncle's men, and the soldiers are loyal only to the Princeps. I didn't know who I could trust."

"Do you really think a Flavian ordered the attack on the camp?"

Lucius nodded at the coin in Attia's hand. "You can't trust a Flavian." His words were an eerie echo of Valeria's.

Attia handed the coin back to him. "Have you told Timeus?" she asked, even though it was obvious that Lucius hadn't told anyone besides her.

"This coin is the only proof I have. I don't even know what the motive would have been for such an attack. To prevent us from reaching Pompeii? To kill us outright? I can't imagine they were looking for anything." Lucius shook his head. "Besides, my uncle is ambitious. Even if he knew, he's dependent on Titus for political favor. He can't accuse the family of treachery. Then there's that wager he's made with Tycho—my uncle will win a seat on the Senate if Xanthus wins the match against Tycho's new gladiator. So for now, he just wants to keep all the right people happy." His face hardened, and he looked up at Attia. "Especially his champion. You are the prize Xanthus gets for being a skilled murderer. I take a single, miserable life, and now I can barely sleep at night. Xanthus takes dozens, hundreds of lives, and everyone loves him for it. He *must* enjoy it."

"If you believe that," Attia said, "then you don't know him at all."

Lucius scoffed. "You told me once that nothing matters but the present. Not redemption or the afterlife or the gods. Only what we do here and now. Xanthus is what my uncle has made him. We all are. And nothing in this life or the next will ever account for that."

Attia bit her lip to hold back the words that wanted to spring out of her mouth—that there *would* be an accounting. That Rome would pay dearly for its sins. Maybe not tomorrow or the day after, but someday their precious Republic would come to ruin, and it wouldn't be the work of the gods or fate. A living, breathing, suffering soul would make Timeus and his ilk suffer as they'd made so many others suffer. And it would be called justice.

With the cup cradled lightly in his hand, Lucius stood and tucked the coin back into his pocket. "I see it now," he said. "Xanthus is a monster, just like the rest of them. And I am so sorry that you were given to him, Attia. I am so terribly sorry."

Attia's heart tightened at the utter sincerity in Lucius's voice. Gods, he truly believed what he was saying. She gripped the basket of food in her hand and hurried back to Rory's room.

She found the child drawing in the ash by the fireplace. Rory's tiny fingers were wrapped around a long, narrow stylus. Her tongue stuck out from between her lips in concentration. Attia decided she would have to steal some real papyrus from Timeus's study for the girl to draw on.

Rory looked up as Attia put the food on the table. "I'm practicing birds," she said.

"What kind of birds?"

"All of them. But mostly the big ones."

Attia sat beside her and watched as Rory took great care in shaping a wing, then a beak. She had surprising control for a child so young.

"What kind is that?" Attia asked.

"A seagull," Rory said. She pointed at another drawing. "And that's a vulture. It's an ugly one."

Attia laughed and noticed a familiar-looking shape, drawn larger than the rest. "And what is that one?"

"I don't know what it's called, but it's special. Oh, but I forgot the other parts." She leaned forward, and all Attia could see was the end of the stylus wiggling back and forth. When Rory sat back again, there were new details around the bird—wavy lines at its feet and a small circle in its chest. "I think that's water," Rory said, pointing to the lines. "This circle is a stone."

Attia felt like she'd forgotten how to breathe. "Where did you see that, Rory?" Her voice was tight and strained.

The child's eyes lowered, and she nibbled on her lower lip. "It's a secret," she whispered. "I don't want to get in trouble."

"You can tell me," Attia said. "I'm good at keeping secrets, remember?"

Rory's sweet face crumpled in a frown, and she threw the stylus aside. "I didn't like him."

"Who?"

"The man who came to our house. I was supposed to stay in my room. But I was curious. He had so many men and horses. I thought he was someone important, so I snuck down and . . ."

"And?"

"He had this on his cloak. It was silver."

Attia's heart was threatening to burst from her chest. "When, Rory? When did you see the man?"

"Before we went to Uncle's house in the big city. Mother said we needed to get away."

"What else did you see, Rory? Who was the man?"

"I don't know," Rory said. "Someone. I can't remember." Her voice wavered between a whine and a sob.

Attia pulled her into her arms and placed a gentle kiss at her temple. "It's all right, Rory. Don't worry. Why don't you draw me something else?"

"I don't want to draw birds anymore."

"You can draw whatever you want."

"Horses?"

"Yes," Attia said. "Draw me a horse." She picked up the stylus and handed it to Rory.

While the little girl bent over the ash to start her new drawing, Attia tried to control her breathing. She knew what Rory had seen, of course—the pendant that rightfully belonged to her as the crown princess of Thrace. But who'd been wearing it? He couldn't have been a Maedi. There was no way he could be Thracian. Or was there? What if Xanthus had been wrong?

What if—somewhere, somehow—there were other survivors from Thrace?

Fido's men were armed as heavily as they had been in Ardea, though the fat bastard himself was noticeably absent.

Xanthus spat into the dirt for the third time in as many minutes. The ride had lasted nearly a day so far, and he felt like he was choking on sand. He couldn't even wipe his mouth because his hands were bound behind his back. At least the Ardeans had let them keep their mounts.

"Again, *fantastic* plan, Kanut."

The mercenary shrugged. "Thank you."

"We could have fought them."

Kanut glanced around. "All twelve? Do you think so?"

"Easily. If your men hadn't run. I didn't know you employed cowards."

"Only the best," Kanut said with a grin.

"I hope you haven't paid them yet."

Kanut leaned forward and squinted. "Oh, look. We've reached Capua."

Xanthus saw the wall first—brown brick and stone nearly fifty feet high. Men in brown tunics patrolled along the top of it, and beyond the walls, brown insulas rose in uneven intervals. Even the road beyond the wall was brown.

"A whole city made of sand and dirt," Kanut said.

"Enchanting," Xanthus replied.

They dismounted, and the Ardeans smuggled them past the gate using an abandoned tunnel under the southern wall. The air was thick with the stench of sewage and standing water. The Ardeans put hoods over Xanthus's and Kanut's heads and pushed them roughly along. They were obviously trying to confuse them—leading them over rubble and through broken walls, into a maze of alleys and streets. But it was easy for Xanthus to keep up.

When Xanthus turned fourteen, Timeus had forced him to fight a match blindfolded. For weeks, Ennius had trained him, honing his hearing, teaching him to fight by sound and reflex. The ring of a swinging sword still resonated in Xanthus's head. It was one of the reasons he'd been able to defeat the Taurus so easily.

Those same senses guided his path now. They were being led northeast, to the poor district by the sound of it. There would be few people to watch and even fewer to care when the Ardeans killed them.

Xanthus knew they'd finally reached their destination when a distinct smell wafted through the air—the smell of old cheese and dirty feet.

"Hello again, Fido," Xanthus said.

The hoods came off, and there was the leader of Ardea in all his greasy glory.

Fido chuckled, the rounded protrusion of his belly bouncing up and down. "Hello, champion. Miss me?"

In answer, Xanthus spat again, this time aiming at Fido's feet.

"Who's your friend?" Fido asked.

"He's not my friend, and you don't care."

Fido put a hand to his chest in mock indignation. "Why, champion—of course I care about your friends. Especially your old friend, Spartacus, whom I hear the two of you are searching for. It would be a mistake, I think, for you to continue on your little quest."

Kanut quirked his dark brows. "And why is that?"

"Because I'm going to find him first," Fido said. "You see, I was *there*. I know what Spartacus looks like."

"So do we," Kanut said. "It should be easy enough, finding a giant."

Fido laughed loudly. "A giant? Someone has lied to you, freeman. Spartacus was half the size of the champion, small like a boy with short legs and—"

Xanthus sighed. "Since no one can seem to remember the same man, perhaps we should all save ourselves the trouble and simply stop looking."

"We searched the entire city after you left," Fido said. "Every alley, every house, every insula. *Nothing.* Spartacus was already gone. That could mean he left the city alone after the match, as you claim. Or it could mean that Spartacus left *with* you."

"Intriguing," Kanut said. "What else have you heard?"

Fido scowled.

"I only ask because I know the Ardeans still speak of Xanthus and Spartacus," Kanut said. "With fear, too. And no small amount of disgust. But I can see that you are all rather fearful, disgusting men, so I am not at all surprised."

Fido turned red in the face, and the Ardeans reached for their weapons.

Kanut wiggled his brows at Xanthus and grinned. "This is getting fun."

"Gods, please strike me down now," Xanthus muttered.

"Anyway, I think a household caravan would have noticed a stranger amongst them," Kanut continued.

"Unless Spartacus is *one* of them!" Fido said. "A member of the auxilia, perhaps—a soldier turned gladiator."

"A giant who is also a soldier but looks like a young boy? Of course. Why didn't I think of that?" Kanut said.

"It's a miracle, Fido—you've discovered something that Kanut didn't already know," Xanthus said. "You ought to try your luck at walking on water."

Kanut turned to Xanthus with a straight face. "You are very humorous, gladiator, I must say. Unexpectedly so."

"Thank you," Xanthus replied with an equally impassive expression. He turned back to Fido. "You're wasting your time. If Spartacus was a member of the household, why would Timeus bother hiring mercenaries to look for him? I think you're both wasting your time. You can't hunt down a ghost, not with rumors."

Fido scoffed. "You won't shake me off so easily, gladiator. I want Spartacus."

Kanut nodded in agreement. "As do we. Besides, we're all still gathering information. There are rumors and then there are *rumors.*"

Xanthus sighed heavily. "Well, I wish you all luck with your rumors."

"Spartacus would make me a fortune," Fido said. He cocked his head. "But if you expect me to stop looking, you'll have to make it worth my while, champion."

"Not that I care, but how would you expect me to do that, Fido? With all of the land and gold I have at my disposal?"

Fido shrugged. "You could fight for me here, in Capua. Then return with me to Ardea—as a *free* man."

"No," Xanthus said.

"That was fast," Kanut commented.

Fido looked incredulous. "*No?* You wish to remain a slave? Are you really so happy being Timeus's pet? I can give you matches you've never had before. I can give you greater rewards than Timeus has even thought to give you!"

Xanthus straightened his back, using his height and his size to stare down at Fido. He wanted his next words to be very clear. "Fido, there is not a single thing in this whole damn world that you could ever offer me."

Fido seemed genuinely surprised by his response. "I don't understand you," he said, shaking his head.

Kanut turned to Xanthus with a slight smile. "Oh, I think I understand you perfectly, gladiator."

"If you won't leave with me, then you won't leave at all," Fido said. "I certainly won't set you free to keep searching for Spartacus."

"Oh. Now *that* is a pity," Kanut said. Then he whistled.

Xanthus would have sworn the mercenaries melted from the walls. They made quick work of Fido's men. Their movements were sure, silent. Bodies dropped around Xanthus like stones. He realized that their surrender and capture had all been a ruse to get to Fido.

Number Two cut through their bonds, glared at Xanthus, then turned and gutted a man who tried to run past them. The mercenaries turned on Fido as one.

Kanut massaged his wrists before accepting a spear that Number Two held out to him. "Last words?" he asked.

Fido started to scream. Kanut raised the spear and threw it with such power that fat Fido was launched backward and pinned against the brick wall. But even though the man was dead, the scream didn't end. It just came from somewhere else.

Xanthus turned quickly to see a young boy watching from a break in the wall. Before he could run, one of the mercenaries caught him by the collar of his tunic.

"And who the hell are you?" Kanut asked over the boy's shouts of protest. A quickly stuffed piece of linen muffled his cries.

Xanthus guessed the boy couldn't be more than eight or nine. His knees were scraped raw, and dirt covered every inch of his scrawny frame. From the way his skin hung on his bones, it didn't look like he'd eaten a proper meal in weeks. The mercenary who held him pulled a dagger from his belt and poised it at the boy's throat.

"Not happening," Xanthus said. He smashed his fist into the man's face and caught the boy with his free arm. "We're not going to start killing *children* now."

"Who says this is the start?" Kanut asked. "We don't need witnesses, gladiator. He can't live."

"No one touches him," Xanthus said.

The mercenaries watched him with blank expressions. No one moved.

"Bring the boy with us," Number Two finally said. "We'll free him once we're out of Capua."

The echo of men's voices began to drift toward them.

"Vigiles," Kanut said. He turned to Xanthus. "You want to save him? You can carry him."

Xanthus looked at the men lying dead on the ground, at Fido's bleeding body pinned to the wall. The mercenaries were already hurrying away.

Damn it all.

He tossed the boy over his shoulder and ran after them.

CHAPTER 20

If Attia got through the day without murdering someone, she would consider it a good day. Or she might just be sorely disappointed.

She found Lucretia in the early morning, stumbling up the steps to the upper level of the villa and clutching her tattered tunic to her body. Even in the darkness before sunrise, Attia could see the way Lucretia glanced nervously over her shoulder, as though she thought some monster lurked there.

Attia whispered her name, called to her as quietly as she could. But Lucretia either didn't hear her or didn't want to hear her. It wasn't until Attia stood right beside her that Lucretia even lifted her eyes.

She refused to let Attia touch her, shrinking away when Attia reached for her hand. It was like another morning in another city. It was happening all over again, just when Lucretia was beginning to heal. Just as she said it would. She winced with every movement. One eye was completely swollen shut. New bruises covered her wrists. Her neck was ringed with red. Spots of blood on her tunic told Attia that her nose had probably bled at some point, too.

Attia's first instinct was fury. More than ever she wanted to slit Timeus's throat and tear the old man apart. It was only the waning light in Lucretia's eyes that stayed her hand. Lucretia needed Attia's comfort, not her vengeance. She needed solace and warmth. And Attia wasn't good at any of that. So she simply took Lucretia to their little garden, and rested the woman's head in her lap as dawn lightened the sky.

"It's getting worse," Lucretia whispered. "He's been angry before, but ever since Ardea . . ." Tears slipped slowly down her cheeks. A few minutes later, she fell into a fitful sleep, her hand curled around Attia's.

Sabina found them soon after, ready with her basket of salves and ointments. She sent Attia to fetch Rory's morning meal, promising she would tend to Lucretia as she had done so often before.

Attia did what she was told. It seemed she had become a good, domesticated little pet, after all. But her thoughts were still in the garden where Lucretia's battered body curled in the grass, and her blood screamed with anger and guilt.

Lucretia said things had gotten worse since Ardea, and the only explanation for that was the sudden disappearance of Spartacus. Timeus's rage would only escalate the longer he went without finding his prize, and Attia knew that Lucretia couldn't survive his wrath for much longer. The next time Timeus took his anger out on Lucretia, she could very well die.

And it will be my fault.

✦ ✦ ✦

That night, Attia lit Xanthus's candles by the window but curled herself on the corner of the bed, far from the candles' light. She'd never minded the shadows. They'd been her friends long before the Maedi had bowed before her. She was a child of the dark, after all—born on the Winter Solstice, the longest night of the year. Darkness had always nipped at her heels.

Still, it took hours for her to fall into a fitful sleep. It was long past midnight when her eyes snapped open again, and every hair on her body stood on end.

Someone was in the room.

Someone was watching her.

Without moving, she squinted at the figure leaning against the closed door and prepared herself.

"I'm impressed, Thracian. You're a hard one to sneak up on."

Albinus.

"You walk like an elephant," Attia said. "What are you doing here?"

"With Xanthus away, I could ask you the same thing."

"And yet I asked first."

"And yet I don't care," he said.

They stared at each other in the darkness.

"Truce?" he said after a while.

"For now." She sat up on the edge of the bed and hugged Xanthus's pillow to her chest.

Albinus took a seat on the chair by the door. "So what *are* you doing here?"

"This is where I sleep. Didn't you know?"

"Even when Xanthus is absent?"

"I can't stay in that house."

"Because of the concubine." It wasn't a question.

Attia bristled. "What do you know about Lucretia?"

"I know that Timeus likes to hurt her just as much as he likes to bed her. The man has a twisted idea of a good time."

"How long has she been here?"

"I'm not really sure. She might have come before us or after." Albinus shrugged. "I didn't notice much in the early days."

"Timeus deserves to die," Attia said.

"Careful, Thracian. It's one thing to take down Ennius, another to speak of assassinating your master." Despite his words, Attia heard a note of amusement in his voice.

"You never answered my question," Attia said. "What are *you* doing here?"

Albinus chuckled. "Gareth—well, Xanthus—asked me to watch over you."

"I'm surprised you call him that. I'm surprised he lets you. I've wondered if that name is more of a curse than anything."

"Memories often are," Albinus said. "For some of us, at least."

"I once knew a man who said his loved ones' names every night like a prayer, and I knew another who said the names of his enemies. I suppose remembering makes us who we are."

"Hmm. Perhaps." Albinus stood up and nodded to Attia. "Good night, little Thracian. Try to stay out of trouble."

The rain came down in sheets, beating an unforgiving cadence against the walls of the villa. In the past, Attia had found downpours like this soothing. Winters in Thrace were wet, and it had rained like this on the night she was born. But it had also rained like this the morning the Romans invaded.

It was the sound of the rain more than anything else that called her to the upper level of the villa. The sky wept, and she wanted to see it. It was really only by chance that when she looked out of one of the windows, she turned and saw Lucretia.

At the easternmost balcony, Lucretia leaned over a narrow railing, hands braced on either side, black hair dripping heavy around her face. Below, the frothy waves swirled and tumbled, wrestling with each other and the current. Attia could only imagine the sharp rocks and boulders that waited beneath the surface. She called out, but her voice was swallowed by the wind.

One of Lucretia's hands slipped, and she pitched forward suddenly, her torso crushing against the balcony. Her face pinched with pain, but her eyes never strayed from the waves.

Attia ran as fast as she could down the hall, her feet skidding across the marble floor. She burst into the room and shouted Lucretia's name again.

The other woman finally turned around and looked over her shoulder.

"Lucretia, come back," Attia said, trying to sound calm. "You . . . you're too close to the edge."

Lucretia slowly swung one leg over the stone balcony. "Am I?"

"Come back." Attia extended her hand. "Please."

Lucretia smiled painfully. "What for?"

Attia didn't have an answer for her. Really, what did Lucretia have to live for? A household that scorned her? Fellow slaves who resented her? A ruthless, violent master who would inevitably kill her?

Ennius told Attia that Xanthus loved her, but maybe she'd already forgotten what that word meant. She'd loved her mother, her father, her unborn brother, and her people. She'd loved them in a way that meant she would kill or die for any one of them. Was that what love was? The willingness to step before a blade and bleed?

Then what would she call this? What do you call the willingness to step over a ledge and jump?

"Lucretia," she said again, her throat tight and achy. "Please.

Come back." Attia closed the distance between them and gently pulled Lucretia's shivering body into her arms. The other woman felt as cold and brittle as ice.

"Almost," Lucretia said through chattering teeth. "I was almost able to do it."

"Let's get you warm." Attia half carried her to Sabina's small room. This time, she didn't leave her side.

"It was intentional, wasn't it?" Xanthus asked Kanut. "Letting Fido's men take us. That's what you were scouting for, not a clear road. You wanted to find them."

"Yes," Kanut said. "And now we know what he knows. Well. *Knew.*"

"You could have told me."

"It was more amusing this way. Besides, you're not a particularly convincing liar."

Xanthus knelt down in the middle of the road. It had rained earlier that morning, softening the dirt and showing telltale signs of a caravan—horses, men, wagons.

"A group of fifty, at least," Kanut said. He looked up and down the road, squinting his eyes. "They couldn't have passed more than a few hours ago."

"They're going south," Xanthus said.

"To Pompeii."

"Do you have any idea who they are?"

"Well, they could be men, women, children, old, young, sick, healthy, soldiers, merchants—"

"Thank you, Kanut," Xanthus said. "Your insights are illuminating as ever."

"It's a caravan, gladiator. Probably one of the patricians moving to a warm villa for the winter. Why does it matter?"

"We should know who's on the road with us."

"Ah, but we are not on the road," Kanut said with a chuckle. "We're over there in the trees, remember?"

"Do you know who the patrician might be?" Xanthus asked.

"From the size of the caravan, perhaps a magistrate or a senator. Perhaps it is Tycho Flavius."

Xanthus turned sharply. "Timeus said he wasn't expected for another two weeks, at least."

"Oh, of course," Kanut said. "Silly of me to think that the House of Flavius would *ever* show disrespect for the schedules of others."

Xanthus stood. At his full height, he towered over Kanut so that the other man was forced to crane his neck and look up. "What do you know?"

Kanut shielded his deep gray eyes from the sun and smiled. "I know that Naples is less than a day's ride away. We should continue our mission, gladiator. Unless, of course, you don't think Spartacus is actually in Naples. Are you ready to share your secrets?"

"I said that I don't know anything about the man. Not everyone has secrets, Kanut."

"Then you won't mind going on to Naples. Just to be sure." Kanut turned and vaulted up onto his horse. "Shall we?"

Xanthus glanced back down the road, looking in the direction of the caravan, in the direction of Pompeii and Attia. He wanted to go back. If Kanut was right and that caravan carried Tycho Flavius, then Xanthus wanted to be there to protect Attia. And to make sure she didn't do something reckless. But he worried that if he insisted on going back to Pompeii, Kanut—and inevitably Timeus—would have quite a few questions. Questions that Xanthus knew he could never answer.

However much Xanthus disliked it, he realized that he stood

the best chance of protecting Attia by making sure her identity was kept secret, even if he had to do it from afar. So he climbed onto his horse and nodded to Kanut.

"Naples," he said.

CHAPTER 21

The household went into a massive panic just after dawn.

Attia watched them from her vantage point on the second-floor balcony. Slaves and servants and guards and Valeria—all running around the courtyard of the villa like ants. All frantically trying to put the house in order before the guests arrived.

Tycho Flavius was two weeks early. He would be at the villa by nightfall.

The whole charade of welcoming a person who was obviously not welcomed tired Attia. She was witnessing firsthand the Romans' greatest skills: the fake smiles, the cold, open arms. The dagger in the back. It was exactly what Timeus deserved.

"Why are you sad, Attia?" Rory asked her later that morning.

"I'm not sad," Attia said.

"Yes, you are. I can see it on your face. Is it because the visitors haven't come yet? Who are they? Will I get to see them?"

Attia's heart clenched. She clearly remembered Valeria's plea to keep Rory hidden, but even if she didn't, she had no intention of exposing Rory to the likes of a Flavian. *Any* Flavian. Especially not after what Lucius had shared with her.

She tried to keep her voice light when she answered. "They're your uncle's guests, silly bird. But you absolutely cannot see them."

"Please?" Rory begged, putting her little hands together. "I never get to see anyone!"

Attia knelt down to meet the child's height. "Rory, you have to promise me that you'll stay in your room and keep the shutters closed while the visitors are here."

"Even in the evenings? But the sunlight—"

"It's not because of the sunlight."

"Then why?"

Attia tilted Rory's chin up and looked into her wide blue eyes. "It's because a monster is coming," she said.

The little girl gasped and her entire body froze. Her immediate fear sent guilt lancing through Attia, but she tried to calm herself with reason. It was worth frightening the child if it meant she was also protecting her. She pulled Rory into her arms.

"I won't let him come anywhere near you, Rory. But that's why you have to be brave for me and promise not to go downstairs. No matter what you hear, you *must* stay in your room. Do you promise?"

"I promise," Rory whispered.

"Promise again."

"I promise."

"Again."

"I promise, I promise, I promise," Rory said, her voice muffled against Attia's shoulder.

"That's three promises," Attia said. "And I promise, promise, promise I'll keep you safe, no matter what."

There was a knock on the door before Sabina poked her head into the room. "Attia, come. I need you."

Attia planted a kiss on Rory's cheek and followed Sabina out into the hall.

"Are you all right?" Attia asked as they hurried down the stairs to the first floor.

Sabina looked more than a little flustered. The fine silver hairs around her temples had started to pull free of her braid. There was a light layer of perspiration on her forehead, and she was frowning. "It's never a pleasant experience when Tycho Flavius comes to visit."

With Lucius's disturbing theory rolling around in her head, Attia didn't doubt the statement. "Does he visit often?"

"No, not often. He sometimes brings his father, but I hope Crassus won't be with him this time."

And I hope he will be, Attia thought.

"Relations between Crassus and Timeus have always been . . . well, tense. You know, Crassus and Lucius Bassus—Valeria's late husband—conspired together during the Batavian Rebellion. Vespasian became Princeps because of his generals."

"Rome's politics tire me," Attia said.

"They shouldn't. As the heir to Thrace, you should know—"

"Sabina!" Attia said, glancing around to make sure no one heard.

"Well, it's true!" Sabina responded in a harsh whisper.

"Do you *want* them to find out about me?"

Sabina stopped abruptly, and her face softened. "Gods, no. I . . . of course not, Attia. I'm sorry. So much is happening. I'm not thinking straight. Just . . . go to the kitchens and help them." At Attia's alarmed expression, she sighed. "Please?"

"They'll just throw me out. Don't you remember what happened the *last* time you sent me to the kitchens?"

"Please just go, stay out of the way, and try not to set any fires."

Attia folded her arms over her chest as she watched Sabina hurry away. Then, for lack of anything better to do, she actually went to the kitchens and offered to help. The slaves there eyed her up and down and shook their heads. Attia couldn't blame them after her performance in Rome. But in the end, they needed the assistance, so they tasked her with washing plates and cups while the ones with gentler hands laid out the food.

Then they waited.

The house became unnervingly still. Timeus stood at the steps leading from the courtyard to the villa. Beside him, Valeria looked like a statue, unmoving, barely blinking, pale and detached. Lucius tried to keep just as still, but he had a deep scowl on his face, and his fingers fluttered behind his back in agitation. Time passed in a blur of color—black and gray and red at the edges, like a mountain waiting to erupt.

Soon, the sound of thundering hooves and creaking wagons echoed down the road. Most of the household had gathered in the main courtyard, and Attia watched the proceedings from the shadow of a pillar.

She'd thought that Timeus's caravan from Rome had been an elaborate production. It was nothing compared to the entourage of Tycho Flavius. Carts bearing people, food, chests, wine, and a few exotic pets streamed into the courtyard. There were dozens of horses, and even more slaves—all ornamented in tunics and bridles of silver and black. And there were soldiers. At least a hundred members of the auxilia accompanied Tycho's caravan. They streamed through the courtyard and into the villa, guarding every door, window, and crack in Timeus's house.

Attia scanned the crowd, searching out their master. She burned with curiosity to see the infamous Tycho Flavius. But after just a few minutes, she knew that he wasn't there. He hadn't arrived with his caravan.

When the soldiers had taken their places, everyone looked west to the sloping cliff that bordered the villa and the sea. Three long ships appeared on the horizon. Their hulls and sails were dyed black, the canvas fluttering in the wind like demon wings. As they came closer, Attia could see that even the men at the oars wore black tunics. The sail of the center ship bore the image of a silver, snarling wolf's head.

Tycho Flavius had arrived.

The ships eventually disappeared by the edge of the cliff. There must have been some unseen pass there, because soon men emerged into the courtyard through a passage that Attia hadn't even known existed. She was so anxious to see if Crassus had come with them that every muscle in her body was as tight as the strings on a lyre.

The courtyard was nearly full and yet almost completely still. There were people everywhere who'd simply stopped moving, an unsettling juxtaposition to the frenetic activity of the day. Only a few men walked through the gathering. Attia strained her neck to see over the crowd, and her eyes met those of the gladiators, who stood in place with blank faces. Lucius's eyes, which had been so dull and lifeless these past weeks, now seemed to blaze with frightening intensity.

Attia could hear Timeus greet someone. Slowly, the small group of men approached the villa. Her eyes scanned the group, searching out the face that had haunted her dreams for months now. But it seemed that Crassus hadn't come, and disappointment sank deep to fuse with old anger. Then another face caught her attention, and she found herself staring at another member of the House of Flavius.

Tycho stood nearly a head shorter than Timeus. His skin was

pasty white, and a cap of short, curly auburn hair framed rounded features. When he turned his head to look up at the villa, Attia noticed how small his nose looked compared to the rest of his face. Coupled with thick, round lips, it gave him a disjointed appearance, as though he was caught between the façades of two men. Only his clothing seemed to complement the Flavian name. His tunic was the color of new cream and partially obscured by the heavy drape of purple fabric that hung off of one shoulder. Attia wondered how silly he must feel—dressing for deep winter in a place that only knew the occasional rainfall. As he moved, the dying sunlight reflected off a gold torque around his neck, and something silver peeked out from under his purple sash.

Attia frowned. Was that it, then? Was this short, pasty frog of a man *the* Tycho Flavius? The man who supposedly ordered the attack on their camp? The one who seemed to inspire fear and anxiety in hundreds of people? The son of Crassus Flavius, the infamous legatus who defeated the greatest warrior kingdom in the world?

"Mind your expression, little Thracian. You look disgusted," Albinus said behind her.

Attia glanced back to see that Albinus and the gladiators towered around her like mighty sentinels, all exposed muscle and hard expressions.

"I'm unimpressed," she said.

"What were you expecting?" Gallus asked.

"A man."

Iduma faked a cough to hide his laughter.

The small group paused at the entryway to the villa, and Timeus snapped his fingers. Lucretia appeared at his side dressed in her black gown. The thin material barely managed to disguise the bruises that still lingered on her hips and legs. The swelling

269

in her jaw was hidden by the way she'd styled her hair to curl about her neck.

Attia couldn't hear what was being said, but Lucretia bowed gracefully before Tycho. Her dark eyes lifted slowly to meet Attia's.

Again, that little smile appeared, but her eyes were cold. Then she lowered her head, turned, and followed Timeus into the villa.

By the time they arrived in Naples, Xanthus decided that he had finally atoned for his sins and now deserved the highest reward in the afterlife.

Not for his prayers.

Not for protecting Attia.

Not even for saving the boy, Balius.

But just for having enough self-control to keep from pushing Kanut off his damn horse.

Most of the others—including Number Two—had branched off to scout through the night. Xanthus was left to deal with Kanut's excessive conversation alone. He took a deep breath as he pinched the bridge of his nose.

"I simply wish to state—for the record—that this is a stupid, foolish, asinine idea, if ever I've heard one," Kanut said.

"I find that surprising," Xanthus said.

"Who the hell taught you to be so damn spineless? We could have killed the boy and been done with it."

"Well, we didn't kill him, and we're not going to," Xanthus said. "Consider Timeus's bounty money adequate payment. You know, you are surprisingly ungrateful for a man who will soon be a good deal richer."

"Yes, well, we'll have to find Spartacus first, won't we? And this sniveling infant certainly won't help."

"The Shadow of Death?" a small voice asked.

Xanthus and Kanut both turned in their saddles to look at the young boy who rode with them.

"What was the rule, Balius?" Xanthus asked.

The boy pouted. "To keep quiet or you'd sell me to a ludus in Naples."

"Exactly," Xanthus said. He and Kanut turned around.

"The gods only know why you spared him. Or why you *brought* him!" Kanut said.

"It is one thing to kill animals in the arena. But he is a child, not a gladiator. Or an Ardean."

"I'm no child! I'm almost nine years old," Balius said with conviction. "I'm very nearly a man."

Kanut glared at him until Balius turned bright red and fell silent again.

"Besides, he's an orphan," Xanthus said. "We can find a decent family to take him in, and that will be that. No cost. No blood."

Kanut scoffed. "He may have been free, but he was still too expensive, if you ask me. I don't like children. They're irritating. Obstinate. Loud."

Xanthus couldn't help but smile at the irony of hearing *Kanut* say that.

"I knew a feisty one years back. The little monster broke two of my ribs."

"I am very sorry that you let a child beat you," Xanthus said with mock solemnity.

Kanut surprised him by grinning. His eyes lost focus, as though he was seeing something far away. "You've never met a child like that before, gladiator—stubborn as a bull, but brave. So very brave."

"Your child?"

271

"Near enough," Kanut said.

Xanthus waited to hear more, but now that he was marginally interested in what the man had to say, Kanut decided to drop the subject.

"Hold on tight, young Balius," he said. "If you fall, I won't turn back to catch you."

It was a good dream.

Attia was in Thrace again, sleeping with her head on her horse's flank while Jez and the others snored around her. The tide pulled at the shoreline some thirty yards away, and overhead, the moonless sky twinkled with the first sprinkling of stars.

Then a voice called out her name.

"Attia. Attia! Wake *up*!"

Eyes still closed, Attia sighed.

It was a good dream.

"By the gods," Sabina was saying, tugging at Attia's blanket, "I never realized how lazy you are. Wake up!"

"Is it morning?"

"Yes, and you need to help me prepare for the feast tomorrow night."

Attia let her limbs go slack. "Oh, I think I'm falling asleep again," she mumbled.

Sabina finally pulled the blanket right off, leaving Attia shivering in Sabina's cool room. She wrapped her arms around her legs, curling up and trying to conserve her last bit of warmth.

"You're enjoying this too much," Attia groaned. She opened her eyes and looked up to see Lucretia standing just behind Sabina, her eyes already glazing over with the cold and the numbness. She suddenly felt like a profound ass.

"I'm sorry," she said. "I'm awake."

And so she spent the day trying to help Sabina and Lucretia prepare to entertain Tycho Flavius.

Trying.

Attia ruined another bouquet of flowers while she watched Lucretia practice a dance in the middle of the great room. Sabina clucked her tongue and shoved Attia's hands away to fix the arrangement.

Lucretia finished her performance with her hands extended upward and her still-bruised face expressionless.

Attia shook her head. "It's too pretty. Try extending your fingers like this and then bringing your hand down near his neck," she said, flattening her palm and making a striking motion through the air.

Lucretia sighed. "It's a dance, Attia. Not a fight."

"We can fix that," Attia said earnestly.

"You're not being helpful at all," Sabina scolded.

"I can help by painting Lucretia's face for the banquet."

At that, Lucretia actually smiled, her hands falling to her side. "Oh, gods help me if I ever let you *anywhere* near my face."

A deep, melodic voice called from the doorway. "Having fun?" Ennius asked.

"Have you come to rescue me?" Attia said as Lucretia started the first steps of the dance again.

"Do you need rescuing?"

"From Sabina and her wretched flowers? Absolutely."

Ennius inclined his head toward the hallway.

Attia followed him out, suddenly wary. "What is it?" she asked.

"The freemen have sent word—Fido is dead."

Attia raised a brow. "Good. But how?"

"I don't know. By the time the message came, the freemen

were already on their way to Naples, which isn't far from here. I suppose we'll just have to wait and see."

"Attia, come back in here and make yourself useful!" Sabina called from the room.

"She's a harder taskmaster than I was," Ennius said.

"Harder than you and all the furies combined," Attia said, loud enough for Sabina to hear.

"If it means you'll actually come in here and help a little, I'll take that as a compliment!" Sabina shouted back.

Attia went back into the great room, pretending to help Sabina while she watched Lucretia practice. Her eyes drifted over the wounds that covered Lucretia's body. She could already imagine the sounds of drunken festivities wafting down the hallways of the villa. She could see Sabina and other slaves helping Lucretia dress for the evening. She could feel the familiar anger simmering just below her skin.

"What else is going to happen tomorrow night?" Attia asked. "You dance, they celebrate for no reason, and then what?"

"Why do you ask?" Lucretia said over her shoulder.

"I've never been to one of Timeus's parties. I'm curious."

Sabina and Lucretia shared a brief glance.

"Attia, if you can help it, just stay away tomorrow," Lucretia said. "I'm sure you'll find it all rather tedious." The words were spoken lightly, but Lucretia's face had tightened. The mask was back.

"She's right, Attia," Sabina said, ushering them both out of the great room. "Stay with the child tomorrow night."

Attia frowned with suspicion but followed Sabina and Lucretia back to their sleeping quarters.

"Ah. It's finished," Sabina said as they entered the room.

A long gold gown hung from two hooks on the wall. It was more translucent than any of the stolas Attia had seen Lucretia wear before. The sleeves were long, but the back was completely open down to the waist. Lucretia lifted the thing from the hooks and held it to her shoulders.

Attia stared in shock. "*That's* what you're wearing? You'll practically be naked. Why bother wearing anything at all?"

"I won't be wearing it for long," Lucretia said, holding the gown so that Sabina could examine the hem. "I'll take it off as I dance."

Attia had to fight the sudden urge to gag.

"It's a common enough performance," Lucretia said. "I've done it plenty of times. What did you expect, Thracian?"

Attia felt so sick she could barely speak, but through clenched teeth, she managed to say, "I hate him."

"Stay with the child," Sabina said again.

Attia knew she was talking about the night of the party, but she couldn't stand to see Lucretia "practice" any longer.

She turned on her heel and left the room. Neither Lucretia nor Sabina tried to stop her.

They found shelter in Naples's Red District.

Naturally, Xanthus thought.

It seemed the mercenaries enjoyed surrounding themselves with women of the night, even if they didn't partake in what those women offered.

"They keep better secrets than most," Number Two explained.

"Wasn't it one of those women who told you about Fido's men?"

Number Two shrugged. "She liked my face."

They all bedded down on the third floor of an abandoned insula. The poorer districts had lost numerous tenants in recent months, due in part to the massive taxes Titus had levied to pay for the construction of the Coliseum. Xanthus didn't understand the point of eviction; no one paid rent on empty insulas anyway. He settled into a corner of the room while Kanut's men perched themselves at the windows and the doorway. Always watching.

Xanthus looked around. "Why don't the rest of you talk?"

"Maybe we're like Spartacus," one said. "Mute."

The one Xanthus had punched in Capua said, "Or maybe we just don't like you."

Xanthus shrugged. "I suppose your leader talks enough for all of you."

"Capua was a dead end," Number Two said, ignoring the banter. "And I have a feeling we won't find much more here."

"Are you ready to amend your previous statements, gladiator?" Kanut asked.

"About?"

"About the giant with seven wives and a home in the far east."

"Seven *sons*," Xanthus corrected.

"And that's why we don't like you," said the mercenary with the smashed nose.

"The feeling is mutual," Xanthus said.

Number Two smiled. "That hurts our feelings, gladiator."

But they stopped asking questions.

Xanthus lay on his pallet, though he was too wary to sleep just yet. Kanut and Number Two had taken first watch, and he still didn't trust either of them. Especially not with the boy. Balius slept at his side. Small as he was, his snores racked his body, making his shoulders tremble with each breath. The sound reminded Xanthus of Albinus when they were younger. His old master used to hit him in the face with a piece of wood when he wasn't cutting into his skin. The damage to Albinus's nose had resulted in a particularly resonant snore, especially on cold nights.

Xanthus turned to look at Balius. It was a good thing he'd found him, probably. He wouldn't have survived another winter on his own. Number Two was willing to spare him, but Kanut still wanted to *simplify* matters, as he saw it. So Xanthus couldn't sleep. Not until they'd let the boy go. He was still awake several hours later when he heard the whispers start.

"He's Timeus's champion," Number Two said. "He wants to stay that way and . . ."

Balius's snores drowned out the rest.

". . . something else," Kanut replied. It was the softest that Xanthus had ever heard the man speak. "He's not just lying . . . hiding something."

". . . he'll never tell us . . . damn statue."

". . . statues break."

". . . need more information," Number Two whispered. "Fido said . . . and the Ardeans . . ."

"Small and light . . . possible?"

They stopped talking, and Xanthus thought they were done.

Then Kanut said, "His horse . . . before Fido's men came."

Number Two's silhouette stiffened. ". . . caught him off guard . . . You think . . ."

Oh, hell.

". . . we were right," Kanut whispered. Xanthus's heart plummeted. "Spartacus is a girl."

CHAPTER 22

I have to kill them, Xanthus thought.

All of them. There was no other choice. Ennius had made the suggestion in jest. But the farce had gone on long enough, and now that they knew the secret of Spartacus, they had to die.

Kanut must have been planning something, too. From the moment the sun began to rise, his eyes were on Xanthus's face. In that first look, Xanthus understood. Whatever happened would be between them. He'd have to kill Kanut before he could get to the others.

As if to confirm Xanthus's unspoken thoughts, Kanut gave his orders to the mercenaries—spread out, search the city's ludi. Information only.

Most of the men nodded their heads, though Number Two hesitated. His eyes shifted back and forth between Xanthus and Kanut. He probably knew what was about to happen, and maybe he wasn't sure if he should let it. But he was a good boy, and in the end, he did what he was told.

The mercenaries disappeared out the door, and Xanthus put his hand on Balius's shoulder. "Run," he said.

The boy took one look at Kanut's face and fled.

A stillness began to settle over Xanthus, the same dark quiet he'd felt in the clearing when the bandits had attacked. There wouldn't be any prayers today. No guilt. No remorse. Kanut and his men deserved exactly what was coming to them.

"Consider the boy's life a gift," Kanut said. He already held a throwing dagger in his hand.

"How magnanimous of you." Xanthus had no weapons, but when had that ever been a problem for him?

"Before I kill you, tell me what you heard."

"Everything," Xanthus said.

Kanut scoffed. "I said before that you're a bad liar. Still, this will be a shame. I have come to think that, in spite of everything you are, you are also good."

"You overestimate me," Xanthus said.

"No," Kanut said, tossing the dagger and catching the tip of the blade between two fingers. "I think not." Before the last word was out, Kanut's dagger was flying.

Xanthus dodged it by less than an inch and caught the handle before it hit the wall. The first dagger was quickly followed by a second dagger and then a third. The last one sliced Xanthus's arm before tumbling out the window.

When Kanut saw the blood, he charged at Xanthus and punched him in the gut. All of his body weight was behind the hit. A sharp kick followed, colliding with Xanthus's shoulder.

Gods, he's strong.

He was twice Xanthus's age, but Kanut's body seemed made of iron. A ringing pain shot up Xanthus's arm when he hit

Kanut's ribs. He knew he'd broken at least two of them, but the man didn't stop. Not for a second.

More daggers came out. Xanthus still had the first two that Kanut had thrown at him. Their movements quickly became a flurry of rushing blades. They stabbed at the same time, each cutting edge deflected by the other. Each time getting closer and closer to the other's throat.

Kanut never pulled back, never tempered his aim or his blows. They weren't in the training yard. This wasn't practice. Kanut wanted to kill Xanthus just as badly as Xanthus needed to kill him. And for the first time in Xanthus's long years as a gladiator, he thought he'd finally met his match. Kanut was easily the best he'd ever fought.

They broke everything around them, smashing into tables, shattering chairs against the wall. No matter how hard Xanthus hit, Kanut wouldn't go down. And no matter how Kanut attacked, Xanthus wouldn't stop.

"Having fun yet, gladiator?" Kanut asked.

"Most definitely."

"I won't let you leave here," he said.

Xanthus shook his head. "You'll never find Spartacus."

Fury burned in Kanut's dark eyes, and that actually surprised Xanthus almost as much as when he suddenly dropped his daggers. "You know," Kanut said, "I think I'd like to kill you with my bare hands."

Xanthus tossed his own blades aside. "You're welcome to try."

Kanut rushed at him again, this time with an angry shout as he raised his leg to kick at the joint of Xanthus's knee. For some reason, the image of Ennius and his broken leg flashed through Xanthus's mind. He leapt forward just in time, catching Kanut beneath the jaw with his skull. Pain blossomed through his head, obscuring his vision. Xanthus heard Kanut smash against the wall. The man blinked his eyes up at the ceiling, and it was just enough time for Xanthus to launch himself at him.

He caught Kanut's neck in a chokehold and started to squeeze. But before he could actually kill him, something sharp stabbed him in the back. Xanthus stumbled away, hands flying up to protect his face from a flurry of feathers and a sharp beak.

The falcon didn't stop attacking until Xanthus was several feet away from Kanut. Then it swooped down to land on Kanut's shoulder. Xanthus was too stunned to speak, and Kanut was still too dazed to move from the wall. He raised his hand to gently pet the falcon's back, and the bird squawked loudly. When the echo of it died down, the only sound left was the men's fast breathing.

"Your reputation is well deserved, champion," Kanut said.

"Go to hell."

Kanut grinned. One of his teeth had chipped. Blood ran from his nose and dripped onto his tunic. "If you'd been smarter, you would have helped us. You could have traded information for your freedom. Why do you want to go back so badly? Do you enjoy the arena that much?"

"I don't *want* to go back," Xanthus said. "But I have to."

"Why? Because you're the champion? Because Timeus claims ownership over you?"

Xanthus started to shake his head, then thought better of it. His vision was shaky enough. "You wouldn't understand."

"You're wrong," Kanut said. "I know all about Decimus, and I know you see him as your enemy. But that match has nothing to do with you. It's about Timeus's wager, not your sense of justice. Do you know what your dominus stands to win? A place in the gentes maiores and a seat in the Senate. Timeus will get everything he wants, and yes, you may kill Decimus. But you'll still be a slave."

"And you think you're any better? You're a hired sword. You kill and betray for the highest bidder. You have no right to speak of honor or justice."

"Just admit that when you crawl back to Timeus, it will be to feed your pride. That's the reason you'll go back to chains, to a lifetime of slavery."

"As opposed to working with a bastard like you? One who would murder a child if it was convenient? No. I go back for *her*."

"A woman?" Kanut laughed bitterly. "Let me guess—she was given to you as a prize. Is that right? What makes you think that she isn't just Timeus's little pet? Now I truly understand you, gladiator, and I must say, I'm disappointed. Your master gives you a whore, and now he's got you by the—"

Xanthus grabbed Kanut's tunic and practically lifted the man off the ground. The dizziness, the pain, that damn falcon—all of it faded from his mind. "Attia is no whore, and if you suggest it again, I'll send you to the underworld with fewer limbs than you started with."

Kanut's face changed instantly, the exhaustion melting to fury then to disbelief, and then—hope. "Attia of Thrace?"

Xanthus felt the world tilt on its axis. He dropped Kanut as though the man's tunic were on fire.

"Answer me, gladiator!" Kanut shouted, grabbing Xanthus by the collar and twisting the fabric in his scarred hands. "Is Attia of Thrace alive?"

"How do you—?"

"Is she in Pompeii?"

"What do you know about her?" Xanthus demanded. "And what have you told Timeus?"

"He knows nothing," Kanut said. "He certainly doesn't realize that he has Thracian royalty living under his roof." He was smiling, but tears were slowly filling his eyes. "I knew it. I knew

282

it had to be her. Who else but a Maedi could be the Shadow of Death? Who else but the heir of Spartan kings would take a name like Spartacus?"

Xanthus felt unsteady again, and not from the fight. Kanut loosened his hold on him.

"The Romans tried to burn me alive. I watched as my people were crucified and left to die in the hills. I thought I'd lost everything—my king, my princess, my brothers. I thought all memory of Thrace would die with me."

Xanthus couldn't blink. He could barely breathe. "Who *are* you?" he whispered.

"I am Crius, first captain of King Sparro of Thrace. I am a Maedi." He reached around Xanthus and pushed open the remains of the shattered door. "And so are they."

The mercenaries were waiting outside. It seemed they'd been waiting the whole time, waiting to see who won. They'd caught Balius, too—Number Two gripped his neck as though he was a puppy rather than a boy.

And now that Xanthus looked—really looked—he could see that all of the mercenaries wore a bloodred length of fabric tied around their necks, mostly hidden by their dark, plain clothing. He was surprised that his knees didn't give out right then. He barely heard the next words of the man he'd known as Kanut.

"We never wanted Spartacus," he said. "We only wanted our princess. And now that search is over. You're getting your wish, Xanthus: We're going back to Pompeii."

CHAPTER 23

It was all quite ornate. Brightly colored silk drapes hung in loops from the ceiling and caressed the pillars. There were couches, chairs, and pillows spread all over the tiled floor. If Lucretia fell during her dance, she'd probably just bounce right back up again.

From where she hid in a shadowed doorway, Attia could smell the vast assortment of food—roasted and cold meats, warm breads, sliced cheeses, exotic fruits. There was just so much, and all of it for Tycho Flavius. Attia found it nauseating.

The man himself sat on a dais near the back of the room with thin drapes hanging all around him and partially obscuring his face. Attia was glad. He hadn't been pleasant to look at the first time. She was, however, surprised to notice that he was sitting in Timeus's chair. The old man was left to stand at Tycho's shoulder like a servant. From the scowl on Timeus's face, he wasn't pleased with the arrangement at all.

Sabina had told her to stay in Rory's room, but Attia felt like she would be abandoning Lucretia again if she did that. Moving silently through the crowd, she took a place near the front and watched as Lucretia moved to the very center of the room.

The sheer gown she wore shimmered like spun gold, and Attia was surprised to see that the color and the candlelight actually did a fair job of obscuring Lucretia's bruises, even if you could see nearly everything else. She moved as gracefully as ever, despite her injuries. Attia was probably the only one to notice the hesitation in her step, or the way she only extended her arms a little because she wasn't quite healed yet.

Attia's own body strained with violence, and it took everything in her to keep still while Lucretia danced ever closer to Tycho's chair, her body twisting in ways that must have hurt every bruised muscle she had. When her hands subtly touched her shoulders, Attia knew she was preparing to peel her dress away. The crowd sensed it, too, and began to call out with loud cheers and obnoxious whistles.

Attia swallowed hard. Her hands clenched into fists, and she took an involuntary step forward, accidently knocking into the arm of a nobleman and sending his cup of wine shattering to the floor.

The music stopped instantly, and suddenly, everyone was silent and staring at her. Timeus's face hardened as her eyes met his.

"Who," Tycho said with a slight slur, "is *that*? Bring her here."

Lucretia had gone pale, and she shook her head slightly. Attia was nearly overwhelmed by the look of pity on her face. Her dark eyes practically screamed "*I'm sorry*," as though she could have shielded Attia from this. And there Attia was trying to protect *her*. The irony struck her hard, and she had to concentrate to walk toward the dais where Tycho and Timeus waited.

As she walked, she felt a strange trembling beneath her

feet, and she had to change her stance to stay balanced. But no one else noticed it, and it left her wondering if it was only in her head. The Romans were so loud that sometimes it seemed like their cheers could rattle her teeth loose.

"Wherever did you find her, Timeus?" Tycho asked as Attia approached.

"The gods guide them all to my door, Tycho. But I suppose I have your father to thank for this one."

"Is that so? How fascinating. Something he brought back from the savage lands, no doubt." Attia was trying to keep her focus, but a movement near the door in the far corner caught her eye—a shock of red hair and pale skin.

". . . from Thrace," Timeus was saying.

"Oh, savage indeed. Though undoubtedly beautiful. Bring her closer."

Attia didn't have another second to think about it before she stepped forward. But she refused to bow her head. She refused to give a Flavian the satisfaction of her deference.

"Closer," Tycho said.

She took another single step, her eyes raised and scanning the far end of the room.

"*Closer*," he said again, his voice becoming hard.

Attia complied, but her thoughts were on someone else entirely. She'd seen Rory. She knew she had. That red hair and pale skin—it had to be the child. And the girl had *promised*. Attia clenched her teeth in frustration.

Behind her, the guests watched with interest, waiting to see what Tycho would do next.

"What is your name?" Tycho asked.

Attia seriously considered the possibility of not answering at all. But she heard Timeus clear his throat loudly.

"Attia," she said.

"What? I can't hear you."

Attia sighed before raising her voice. "My name is Attia," she said, her words ringing clearly through the room.

"Attia," Tycho repeated with a sigh of his own that set her teeth on edge. There was an audible intake of breath around her as Tycho stood from his seat. "Look at me," he said from just a few inches away.

Attia clenched her fists.

"*Look at me,*" he nearly shouted.

With a deep, steadying breath, Attia shifted her eyes from the back wall to look into his.

Yes. He looked just as he had when he arrived—short, pale, soft. And now drunk. She felt a split second of amusement when she realized that she was actually slightly taller than him.

"Oh, she is lovely," Tycho said in a husky whisper. "Thracian, you say?"

Timeus nodded. "The last Thracian."

"Of course. So *you* were the one my father spared." A sour smile spread across his mouth. "He said you tried to save old Sparro—ran to his side like a little soldier with a sword of your own. But you were too late. My father had already cut him down. Did you hear Sparro beg for his life? Funny that a weak girl like you would have more courage than that old fool. No wonder his heir wasn't worth knowing about. A man like that probably spawned a pitiful son."

Attia could feel her lips twitching, as though she wanted to snarl at the bastard. She clenched her hands at her sides to keep still.

Tycho cocked his head at her while his fingers reached up to his chest to toy with something pinned to the fabric there. Attia's eyes inadvertently followed the movement, flitting down past the luster of the gold torque around his neck and the purple sash across his shoulder. Past the gold threads on the neckline of his tunic, and down to a pendant fastened to his clothing.

In that one moment, the entire universe—from the particles of dust in the air to the very breath of the gods—stopped. All Attia could comprehend was the distinct silverwork of the pendant, the falcon in flight, the sparkling fire of the clear stone in the center.

This was what Rory had seen. Tycho had had it all this time. *Her* pendant.

Something inside of Attia shifted then. She'd heard men call it a trance, a bloodlust, a berserker fury that overwhelmed warriors with the need to kill. But there was nothing numb about this feeling. It was hot and cold and fast and slow, all at the same time. It was like lightning in the middle of the sea, an inferno in the heart of a storm. And before she could think another thought, she had her hands wrapped tight around Tycho Flavius's neck.

The soldiers and guards rushed into action. They put a knife to Attia's throat to try to stop her. Like Xanthus, she had no fear of the blade. She didn't care if they cut her or bled her dry, but they got in her way, loosening her grip for a fraction of an instant.

Tycho crumpled to the floor, gasping for breath. As he tried to crawl away toward the back wall, his eyes went wide with shock, trained on a spot in the back of the room—on a terrified little girl curling up in the corner. His face twisted.

"Titus . . . ," he whispered, just as a thunderous boom echoed through the villa.

Attia took the chance to fight off the guards and reach for Tycho again. But another roar shook the walls, and chunks of marble began to fall all around them.

Everyone ran.

They screamed and pushed and clawed their way to the doors as the air vibrated with sound. Marble and dust rained down, and Attia struggled to her feet, pushed along by the stampeding Romans as they rushed into the courtyard. Almost immediately, people doubled over, gasping and choking.

Smoke and sulfur filled the air. Small flakes of white stuff floated gently to the ground. It looked like snow, but it was warm rather than cold, and it turned to dust at the slightest touch.

Ash.

"Gods, help us!" someone screamed, and Attia followed the man's terrified gaze to the northeast.

It was only then, as they all stood beneath the ink-black sky, that she saw it: Mount Vesuvius, alive and furious, spitting fire onto the city of Pompeii.

CHAPTER 24

The blackened crest of the mountain spewed flame into the sky. The ground shook violently as a river of molten rock spilled out from Vesuvius and began to snake its way through the streets like a fiery serpent. It consumed the houses and people in its path, slowly but steadily.

The air was still cool around Timeus's villa by the sea, as though it hadn't quite realized that the world around it was burning. Attia couldn't move. She stared around the courtyard in a daze, the sounds of the Romans' terror muted and dull. All she could comprehend was their mouths opening wide in silent screams. She saw the tears streaming down their faces and watched as they ran over each other like frantic animals.

A red-hot rock fell into the courtyard, making the ground around it steam and sink. Attia was knocked down onto her hands and knees by a woman running past her. Less than a second later, another rock fell right on top of the woman with a terrible thud, breaking her back and melting her skin like wax. The sight jarred Attia out of her paralysis, and suddenly the sounds were magnified. The woman screamed. Gods, how she screamed.

Attia tore her eyes away from the woman's burning body to focus on the main gate, where dozens of people were fighting to get out. Then she saw that a handful of men were trying to get *in*.

And Xanthus was leading them. He and a group of men dressed in black pushed through the gate, every one of them armed. She kept her eyes on Xanthus as they ran to each other. She didn't stop until she could wrap her arms around him, holding tightly so she knew he was real.

"You're alive," he whispered into her hair. "Thank the goddess, you're alive."

"I told you I'd wait," Attia said, but her voice was cracked and dry from the smoke.

"My brothers!" Xanthus shouted, pointing toward the training courtyard. One of the men in black ran to free the gladiators from their quarters while the others focused on ushering slaves and servants to the gates. None of them paid any mind to the patricians screaming for help.

The gladiators appeared and headed straight for the outer storeroom, filling their arms with skins of water and sacks of grain. Sabina was helping corral the kitchen slaves out of the villa, and Lucretia tugged a long tunic over her sheer dress as she led the house slaves into the courtyard. Albinus and Ennius accepted swords from the men in black.

Attia knew she should be doing more than simply standing there. But there was someone else who'd appeared with the group—someone she'd thought she would never see again. Someone she'd thought had died in the hills along the Aegean.

"Crius?" she gasped.

Her father's captain kissed her hand before pulling her roughly into his arms.

"How are you alive? How—?"

"Later, Attia. We need to get out of here."

"But . . ." She turned to stare at the other men, the strangers in black with the bloodred strips of cloth banded around their necks. And she realized they weren't strangers at all. They were Maedi.

How? How were they alive? How had they survived the war and avoided capture? And where? Where had they been while she'd lived as a slave in Timeus's house? *And why?* Why hadn't they come for her? Why had they abandoned her to the Romans?

The questions practically choked her as they fought each other to her lips. But in the next second, all coherent thought flew out of her head anyway.

A new sound cut through the night, shattering the unnatural silence of her shock. A sound clearer than anything else—a child's scream coming from inside the villa. "Attia!"

Rory was still inside, alone and terrified because Attia had left her behind when she'd been pushed out to the courtyard. She'd promised to keep her safe, and now the child called for her. That was all Attia needed to know.

She ignored the protests of Crius and Sabina and Xanthus, sprinting straight back into the collapsing villa just as another volley of burning rock landed in the courtyard and blocked the doorway behind her.

Inside, the opulence of Timeus's house had been reduced to ruins—a grotesque husk of marble and stone. Huge chunks of the walls and pillars had crashed to the floor. Food, linens, and dead bodies were strewn everywhere. Dust and ash hung heavy in the great welcoming room, already coating the floor.

Attia ran past all of it, calling for Rory. She finally found her near the back of the room where Tycho's dais had stood. The child was curled into a tight ball and weeping, but otherwise unharmed. Attia pulled her into her arms.

"It's okay. You're okay. I'm going to get you out of here."

The northern entrance was blocked. The eastern door—a massive bronze thing that Timeus had imported from Greece—was so hot that Attia couldn't even stand near it. There seemed to be only one way out, and that was up.

Attia pulled Rory up the stairs to the second floor, searching for a room with a window that looked out over the courtyard. Just as her feet hit the top step, the whole house shook, causing a wall to collapse behind her. She pushed Rory out of the way just before a piece of marble the size of her head slammed right against her left arm. She fell to the side with a pained cry.

When the house was still again, she swatted at the dust that coated her face and tried to inspect her arm. A long, jagged gash stretched from her wrist to her elbow, dripping blood onto her lap. At least it didn't look like the bone had been broken. The falling columns had completely sealed off the staircase now.

Rory was still sobbing quietly, and she wrapped her arms around Attia's neck.

"It's all right," Attia said. Her voice was steady despite the pain. "I'm fine." And she had to be. She couldn't die yet. Rory needed her too much.

With a determined grunt, Attia ripped the hem of her tunic and wrapped the fabric around her arm, pulling it tight to stem the slow, deep flow of blood. When she was done, she took Rory's hand. "Hurry now! Run!"

The wall along the top floor had buckled, exposing wide gaps between it and the ceiling and weighing down the doors. Attia tried to push into one of the rooms, but it was like shoving her shoulder into a mountain. The doors wouldn't budge. She repositioned herself, focusing instead on the cracks in the wall. If she could find a weak spot, she thought she could make a portion of the wall break completely.

A few feet down, the wall had splintered with a long, deep crack. Attia took a running start from the other side of the hallway and threw all her weight against the wall. It caved, and she tumbled into the room with a spray of stone.

But the impact had dislocated her shoulder with a loud pop. Attia rested her forehead against the floor and tried to hold back a scream. When she could see straight again, she got to her feet and staggered to the door. She took a deep breath, clenched her jaw, and jammed her shoulder into the door, forcing her arm back into its socket. Her vision nearly went black from the pain, but she fought off the darkness. She reached blindly for Rory and took several more deep breaths. The child's pale face was wet with tears.

Attia staggered to the window and saw Xanthus in the courtyard below, his eyes desperately scanning the upper floor.

He shouted an expletive as soon as he saw her. "It's blocked off—we can't get in! You'll have to jump!"

Bodies littered the courtyard. Attia knew that some people had already been killed by the rocks and the stampede. But she also saw dead soldiers and guards with gaping sword wounds. The gladiators and Maedi must have struck them down.

Attia snatched the linen from the bed and threw one end around Rory's waist, looping it several times before pulling the knot as tight as she could. She tied the other end around the post of the bed. Her wounded arm throbbed and bled onto the floor. "Rory, look at me," she said softly, kneeling in front of the child, who had her hands over her eyes.

Attia knew that in another few minutes, the fires would reach the villa. If they didn't escape soon, they'd be left to burn.

Attia hardened her voice. "Rory! Look at me!"

The child reluctantly lowered her hands.

"I need you to be brave now. We can't stay here. I have to lower you down, okay?"

"I can't," Rory sobbed. They were the first words she'd spoken since Attia had found her.

"Don't be afraid. Just hold on to this sheet as tightly as you can and keep your eyes on me." Attia lifted her onto the windowsill. "Be brave, Rory. Xanthus will catch you."

"What about you?"

"I'll be right behind you. I promise." Attia looked out the window. Xanthus was standing ready below, his arms outstretched. "Don't be afraid," Attia said again and kissed Rory's cheek. "Everything is going to be okay."

Rory clung to the linen rope as Attia lowered her to the ground in jagged, uneven intervals. She could only use one arm, and small as the child was, her weight was pulling Attia down. Soon, she was low enough for Xanthus to reach, and Attia felt the relief in the tension of the sheet. Rory looked so small, so frail in Xanthus's arms. Sabina quickly untied her and carried her away, leaving the sheet hanging free from the window.

Xanthus looked up at her. "Your turn!"

Attia was more than ready. She swung one leg over the windowsill, but before she could get a firm grip on the roped up linen, the earth rumbled again and knocked her back into the room. Her head hit the floor with a loud thud.

Everything became fuzzy. The walls, the ceiling, and the sky all blurred together. Even the sounds of shouting were dull, as though she was listening to everything underwater. She knew she had to move. She knew she had to get out. "I'm coming," she mumbled. "I'm coming." But it took so much effort to even lift her head up off the floor.

All she could see out the window were flames. Pompeii glowed red. Vesuvius roared at the sky, and a piece of the mountain broke away, letting loose another torrent of liquid fire. Everything burned. People stood huddled together and screaming on their rooftops, praying for help that would never come.

But *he* came for *her*.

Attia should have known that he would.

Before she realized what was happening, Xanthus had climbed the knotted sheet and was right beside her, cradling her close. He slung her across his shoulders, one hand holding her arm while he used the other to climb back down to the ground.

Crius waited for them along with Albinus, Lebuin, and two of the Maedi warriors. They'd taken some of Timeus's prized horses and were ready to mount.

"I sent the others ahead," Crius said. "We'll have to move fast. Here—I can carry her."

Xanthus said nothing, but a moment later, Attia felt him toss her onto a horse and then vault up behind her. His arms held her tight against him, warming her against the abrupt coolness of the breeze coming off of the Tyrrhenian. In the distance, three black ships sailed away.

"Hold on," Xanthus said. "Just a little farther."

"Too far," Attia said. The fires were getting close. Extreme heat made the air around the villa shimmer like a mirage.

Xanthus's face hardened with determination. "Bullshit." He kicked his horse's flanks, and they broke into a gallop, clearing the crumbled remains of the estate's outer wall with a single leap. The jarring movement made Attia's injured arm throb from shoulder to fingertip.

As they rode away, Attia looked back over Xanthus's shoulder. Behind them, the flames had reached the gate to the villa. The river of fire completely consumed the courtyard in a matter of minutes. A great rumble reverberated through the ground. Attia watched in horror as a whole piece of the cliffside broke away and the western section of the house fell into the sea. The heat of it singed the ends of her hair and made sweat bead all along her face.

The horses proved a tribute to their breed—their little group was actually managing to outrun the flames. Attia vaguely heard Ennius shout out to them from some point ahead.

Then the earth began to shake, and this time, it didn't stop.

A few of the horses stumbled, and the next thing Attia felt was rough grass under her cheek. Her arm dangled over empty space, and she was dizzy. So dizzy.

Everyone was shouting as the ground beneath them fractured, chafing and grinding against itself. Lebuin clung to the turf with one hand. With his other, he tried to hold on to one of the Maedi warriors who lay unconscious beside him. But the man was too heavy. Lebuin groaned as his grip failed and the Maedi fell.

Farther away, Xanthus sprawled on a piece of rock that was starting to separate from the cliff. His eyes were closed, and blood pooled beneath his temple. Attia struggled to reach his hand.

The other gladiators and the Maedi rushed back to help. Ennius limped along behind them as fast as he could. Albinus and Crius grabbed branches and vines—anything they could reach.

Xanthus's eyes fluttered open. He turned his head and looked straight at Attia. "Breaking," he whispered. "It's breaking." He blinked rapidly as though trying to clear his vision.

"Just hold on!" Attia cried.

Lebuin managed to lift himself a little higher, reaching out for the vines, but they snapped as soon as he tried to pull on them. He lunged for a branch hanging nearby and missed. Then he fell, his body slicing through the air and down to the sea. He didn't make a sound.

Attia's voice became sharp with panic as she called Xanthus's name. It took so much of her strength to fight off the darkness that loomed at the corners of her eyes, but she had to.

He'd come back for her. He'd kept his promise, despite the danger. He was willing to die for her, and she didn't think she'd ever loved anyone more than she loved Xanthus in that moment.

With everything she had left, she reached across the divide and finally grabbed his hand. The rock beneath him was crumbling faster, slipping out from under him.

"I've got you," she said. "Just hold on."

Xanthus met her eyes before placing a soft kiss on the back of her hand. The rock beneath him cracked in half. *"Run."*

Then he let go.

Attia screamed and screamed as Xanthus tumbled over the edge, her cries following him down into the depths of the Tyrrhenian.

CHAPTER 25

It took all of the gladiators to keep Attia from following Xanthus into the sea.

Crius pressed his fingers against her neck in a series of movements that forced her into unconsciousness. The silence that followed made their ears ring.

They ran as fast as they could, heavy with so many burdens. Pompeii burned in their wake.

By the time Attia opened her eyes again, dawn was only a few hours away. They'd stopped to rest at the base of a grassy hillside. Their backs were turned so that they didn't have to look at the devastation they'd left behind.

Attia scrambled to her feet, looking frantically around. Forgetting. Just for a second. "Xanthus!"

Crius stood and shook his head, reaching for her. "He's gone, Attia."

"No!" She pushed him away with a violent lurch, her eyes

skittering desperately over the landscape. "No! We have to go back!"

"He fell. No one could have survived that."

"But—"

Crius gripped her shoulders, forcing her to meet his eyes. "He's dead. Xanthus is dead."

Attia pulled away with a wordless cry. The others gave her a wide berth as she staggered past. Then all at once, the world she'd known came crashing down around her. She fell to her knees, dug her fingers into the earth, and wept.

So much had been taken. So many had been lost. And so often, she'd failed the ones she loved. She could all but see their blood on her hands. Maybe Lucius was right. Maybe no amount of penance would ever wipe her clean, and she would carry the memory of her failures to the bitter end. The shame was more profound than any she'd ever known. And she wasn't sure if it was worth fighting anymore.

With quiet deliberation, tears still streaming down her face, Attia stood and walked to the edge of the cliff. A harsh wind whipped at her hair and tunic, as though it knew the agony that coursed through her.

Lucretia was the only one who moved—the only one who could even begin to understand the urge to stand at the edge and fall. She stood shoulder to shoulder with Attia and whispered, "Come back."

Why? Attia couldn't even say the word.

But Lucretia must have heard it in her own way. She reached out and put something hard and cool in Attia's hand. "Please come back."

Attia looked down to see the warped remains of her pendant. The iron ring had broken away in jagged intervals, and much of the silver had melted, distorting the edges and giving the once finely carved falcon a hideous tail. Deep black burns scarred the wings so that they looked more like scales, and the waves in its claws looked like deadly blades. Only the stone in its chest remained whole and clear, mocking the emptiness inside of her.

Lucretia left her then, and Attia stared out at the sea, waiting for her thoughts to clear.

"I'm sorry," Rory whispered behind her.

Attia hadn't even heard her come close. She turned to look at her.

"I think . . . I think it was my fault." Tears tracked down Rory's face, and her blue eyes were red and swollen.

Attia shook her head. "No," she said firmly. "None of this was your fault."

"But you came back for *me*," Rory said.

A few feet away, Sabina put her face into her hands and began to sob. Ennius stared at the ground with a glazed look on his face.

"Of course I did." Attia reached out her arm and Rory hurried into her embrace. "I couldn't leave you."

"What happens now?" Rory asked. "Where's Lucius?"

Attia closed her eyes. How could she tell the child that her family had abandoned her to the fire and smoke? How could she tell her that life would go on, that it would somehow be good again?

How would she ever be able to forget what she'd lost?

"I don't know," Attia said. Her voice broke on the last word. It was the only honest thing she could think to say, and yet it was so inadequate. "I don't know."

Rory lifted her small face and looked at her. "Don't worry," she whispered. "I won't leave you either."

While the others slept—or tried—Attia watched the smoke from Mount Vesuvius unfurl slowly throughout the night. It made her think of the mists that Xanthus said covered his home in Britannia.

He would never again see those rocky hills, just like she would never again see Thrace. But the yearning she'd held on to, the regret and heartsickness, had all transferred onto something else. She'd wanted to go home. She'd wanted to be free. But now she would trade all the minutes left in her life for just one last chance to see Xanthus.

She couldn't help herself from replaying those final seconds as she watched him fall. But slowly, the better memories came— the first time she saw him truly smile, laughing beside him in the middle of the night, feeling his lips brush against hers and knowing that when she woke up, he would be beside her.

She would never have any of that again. One morning very soon, she would wake up alone. And she feared that more than any weapon she'd ever faced.

So as the long, black night of the Winter Solstice crept on, she kept a new vigil. Not for the gods or her sins or the spirits that waited for her in the underworld. But for Xanthus, for her father, for her people.

For them, she faced the darkness and waited for the dawn.

CHAPTER 26

Albinus woke first. He sat up in the gray light of morning, and his eyes immediately focused on the low-hanging cloud that spread across the horizon. "What is that?" he asked. "Is that smoke?"

"And ash," Attia said. "Wake the others. It's time to leave."

"Have you slept at all?"

"Hurry."

Sabina and Lucretia stirred a minute later, and Crius barked a threat that Albinus wasn't to touch him if he wanted to keep his fingers. The others woke to Albinus's foot in their backsides, and soon they were all mounted and ready to leave.

Attia carefully picked up Rory, who'd fallen asleep in the grass beside her, before handing her to Sabina. The little girl opened her eyes before dropping her head onto Sabina's shoulder and falling asleep again.

"There's nowhere for us to go," Gallus said. His usually smiling face was drawn with grief.

"I can't even remember what my life was like before this," Iduma said in a quieter voice than he'd ever used. "I couldn't get home if I tried."

"We could keep going north to the mountains," Ennius suggested. "No one would follow us there in the middle of winter."

"They wouldn't follow because they wouldn't want to freeze along with us," Crius said. "We should go south to Egypt. The weather will be fair this time of year."

Albinus shook his head. "Egypt is just another province. We won't be safe there. The western islands are better. Sicily, perhaps."

As they argued, Attia tugged on the reins of her horse and turned away.

"And where the hell are *you* going?" Crius called.

"Rome," Attia said over her shoulder.

Albinus spurred his horse forward to block her way, forcing her to stop. "I think you may have missed the part where we decided it was in our best interests to *avoid* the Romans," he said.

"I am going to Rome," Attia said again, her voice firm and even. "I am going to find Crassus Flavius, and I am going to kill him and every member of his family."

The others all stared at her in shock.

"You want to kill the *Flavians?*" Crius said as he pulled his horse up alongside hers. "Are you mad?"

Ennius frowned. "Attia, I don't think . . ."

"You're a fool if you think you can reach Crassus or that you can assassinate the Princeps of Rome!" Crius shouted.

"It's suicide, even for you," Iduma said.

She silenced them all with a look she'd learned from her father. "If the Flavians hadn't invaded Thrace and Gaul and

Britannia, none of us would be here. Our homes would still be standing. Our families would be whole."

My father and Xanthus would still be alive.

There was fear in Sabina's warm, weathered face and a wary scowl on Ennius's dark one. Castor was quiet as ever. The Maedi simply looked at her, all of them warriors she'd known since she was young—gentle Dacian, the twins Rhesus and Teres, sturdy Haemus.

And Jezrael.

She looked at her old friend, her blood-brother, and steeled her voice. "The House of Flavius will fall to my sword. You can either help me or get out of my way."

Crius sighed heavily. "You are your father's daughter," he said with a sad, lopsided smile. "But are you sure you're ready for this, Attia? Revenge is a dirty business."

Attia calmly met his gaze. "This isn't revenge, Crius. This is war."

AUTHOR'S NOTE

Many of the events and individuals in *Blood and Sand* are based on true events, including the eruption of Vesuvius, the destruction of Pompeii, the completion of the Coliseum (also known as the Flavian Amphitheater), and the political undercurrents surrounding the Flavian dynasty. But to say that I took liberties with historical facts here would be like saying that the earth has a slight curve to it. Nearly everything—while rooted in truth—has been altered to fit the narrative, especially when it comes to dates.

It is true that in A.D. 79, Mount Vesuvius erupted over Pompeii, killing thousands and burying the city under layers of volcanic ash and rock nearly ten feet deep. Over the past three centuries, archeological excavations have revealed the surprisingly well-preserved remains of homes, buildings, forums, roads, and even people. Historians have since used the artifacts discovered in Pompeii to provide context for the city's cultural and architectural facets. According to historical documentation, the eruption lasted approximately six hours, and the few people who escaped the destruction did so by boarding naval ships that had been docked along the coast. The eruption of Vesuvius was so massive that it caused the fall of neighboring cities, including Herculaneum and Oplontis. Wind currents carried surges of heat and ash southward nearly thirty miles to the Gulf of Salerno. It is still considered one of the most devastating natural disasters of the ancient world.

That same year, Titus Flavius became emperor of Rome—not Princeps—succeeding his father, Vespasian. Here, then, is the beginning of the numerous divergences between history and this story. The transition from free Republic to empire is a major plot element in *Blood and Sand,* but in truth, Rome had already entered its imperial period as early as 27 B.C. Emperor Vespasian—not the fictional Crassus Flavius—was the legatus responsible for invading Britain in A.D. 43. His son Titus earned a reputation during that time as a competent military commander, though he became best known for completing the construction of the famous Coliseum in Rome. He married several times before dying without an heir and was succeeded by his younger brother, Domitian.

The quote at the beginning of *Blood and Sand* was written by an actual historian who lived in the early Roman Empire, one of many well-regarded men who based their records largely on eyewitness accounts, anecdotal evidence, and word of mouth. Primary documents recording history in ancient times are rather like the culmination of a particularly long game of telephone. That is really how stories were passed along in the ancient world—from person to person, over miles and decades, until they were written down and became canon. And now we come to the crux of this alternative historical fiction: the identity of the rebel slave known as Spartacus. By most accounts,

Spartacus lived sometime around 70 B.C., nearly one hundred and forty years before this story takes place. After escaping from slavery with a group of gladiators, Spartacus went on to lead what was called the Third Servile War, in which some seventy thousand freed slaves fought against Roman legions and nearly brought the empire to its knees. Historians agree upon that much, at least. But the details of Spartacus's identity and early life not only differ but are often wildly contradictory. No one knows who Spartacus was before the war, or if "Spartacus" was a real name or one chosen by the Romans. No one knows where Spartacus was born, what language he spoke, whether he was a soldier or a gladiator, or whether he ever married. And no one can agree on why Spartacus fought the war to begin with, or whether he even survived it.

It may seem odd that a historical figure whose name has inspired songs, films, poems, and novels can be such an enigma. But if there was one major theme that I learned as a history major, it is that history is imperfect because we are imperfect. History is nothing but a collection of stories, colored and twisted and shaped by time and bias and language. It shifts depending upon the lens through which you look at it, and you may find it slowly grow or shrink or change altogether as the years pass and your experiences accumulate. As Napoleon Bonaparte once infamously said, "What is history but a fable agreed upon?" And so my dear, curious, clever reader, I implore you to ask questions and challenge narratives. Facts may be indisputable, but truth is a wily thing. Discover it for yourself, and maybe somewhere along the line, you'll see the world—and its possibilities—in an entirely new light.

ACKNOWLEDGMENTS

Telling a story and sharing a story are two very different things. The first can be a solitary, often isolating experience, whether by necessity or circumstance. But the second—well, that's a horse of a different color. Sharing a story with the world, giving it a name and a cover, finding it a home on shelves and in hands takes the passion, faith, and dedication of every person who comes in contact with it. Those people deserve to be named and thanked, as well as I can. So here they are, the glorious folks who've stuck around, supported me and this story, told me when I was royally screwing things up and then giggled with sheer joy when I finally got something right. Thank you, thank you, thank you, *thank you*.

To my parents, for their constant love and willingness to buy me all the books I asked for, even when those books started to take up more space in my room than clothing or furniture.

My teachers and mentors from middle school to college,

especially Mrs. Tisdale, Deborah Hoffman, Francille Bergquist, Helmut Smith, Vereen Bell, and Katherine Crawford.

The people who cheered for this book before even reading it and kept me going with virtual cookies and very real words of love: Tiffany Flecha, Kelsey Tricoli, Katilyn Walker, Jessica Scales, and Anna Priemaza.

One of my oldest friends, Ben Quigley, who's been willing to read my words—the good, the bad, and the oh so damn ugly—since we were eighteen.

My lovely, bright-eyed agent, Sandy Lu of L. Perkins Agency, who has advocated and fought for me, and who may or may not have missed a subway stop or two while working on this book.

My editor, the tireless Susan Chang, who devoted tears and sweat and probably years off her lifespan to this story, as well as the entire team at Tor, from artists to copy editors, who have helped me make this debut as good as it could possibly be.

To my literary sister, Dot Hutchison, who wove her own stories with equal parts magic and possibility, who shared her knowledge and passion for fiction, and who ultimately made me believe that I could write this book at all. It exists because of you.

To my adopted sister, Katrina Cuddy, who found me when I was lost, who is bound to me by love rather than blood, and whose unwavering loyalty has given me more strength than any creed I have ever known. I've survived because of you.

And to Karl, who has made me the kind of vows you make in the soul. Who knows me down to my bones and loves me anyway. Who has kept so very many vigils with me in the dark, and who has helped me turn to face the light. I *am* because of you.

Turn the page for a preview of

FIRE AND ASH,

coming soon from Tor Teen.

CHAPTER 1

They called for her in the darkness. In the quiet. The voices of the dead reached through the ether with words like blades. A cacophony of whispers and cries and furious epithets.

Disgrace. Coward. False queen.

And when Attia closed her eyes, she saw them: the faces of all the ones she couldn't save.

It had been three days.

Pompeii was gone, buried under a mountain of fire and ash. A strong western wind blew in from the Tyrrhenian sending slate-gray smoke billowing out for miles in a suffocating fog, its edges sharp with the screams of the dying.

Attia and her people could barely outrun it. Their horses began to stumble with the burden of their retreat. They didn't have the luxury of stealth. Crius and the other Maedi knew a dozen different routes between Pompeii and Rome. But the paved main road was the most direct, and as the third day passed into

313

the fourth, whatever apprehension they had about being caught by the auxilia or vigiles was burned away by the relentless flames spreading inland.

Herculaneum fell. Then Oplontis. And suddenly, they weren't the only ones running.

The other cities must have had some warning because there were survivors—thousands of them. An exodus of displaced Romans venturing north and east, fleeing the wrath of the gods. The flood of bodies—plebeian and patrician, slave and free— swept over the countryside like a wave.

Among them, Attia and her people could be anyone and no one. Still, they kept to themselves, forcing their tired limbs to move until the sun set on the fifth day and they could finally stop. It was the first time they'd been able to rest since the sky started burning.

Attia's eyes were red and heavy with exhaustion. She collapsed onto the grass with the others, and her lids began to fall shut. But all at once, the faces and the voices rushed in, crowding out every other thought in her head. She jerked awake, gasping for breath. There would be no sleep for her. The souls of the departed haunted her, and she found she could not face them.

She'd once thought it was Xanthus's curse to remember and hers to forget. But as she sat there with her demons and her ghosts, she wished for oblivion. She wanted to forget the faces and the voices. She wanted the void. She wanted the darkness.

But not death. Not yet.

Attia glanced over her shoulder at the others. Sabina and Lucretia sat curled together around Rory and the little boy, Balius. The gladiators and the Maedi had formed a loose circle around them, some resting, others keeping watch. In a shallow valley just to the north, Linus slept with the horses.

What a strange, broken family they made. Attia wondered again why they'd chosen to follow her. They were no longer slaves. They'd survived, and they were *free*. And Attia was no general. Certainly not a queen. Was she even a Thracian anymore? She didn't know. She didn't know anything, except that Rome would burn—and that she would be the one to light the flame.

She looked up at the smoke-dimmed stars overhead. *Five days*. It had been five days, and she could still hear his voice. Xanthus. He'd come back for her. He'd kept his promise, and died. For her.

She remembered the rock breaking away from the cliff, crumbling out from under him.

"I've got you," she said. *"Just hold on."*

He'd met her eyes before placing a soft kiss on the back of her hand. *"Run."* Then he let go.

"Ashes to ashes, dust to dust." Lucretia approached as silently as a ghost, her hair a wild tangle around her face. Purple and blue shadows ringed her tired eyes. "Isn't that what the Christians say?"

"I wouldn't know," Attia said. "I've yet to meet a Christian." Her gaze focused briefly on the mass of refugees huddled together in the valley below. Then she unsheathed the gladius she'd taken from one of the soldiers in Pompeii, took a whetstone from her pack, and began to sharpen the blade with slow, deliberate arcs. The iron whispered softly in the silence.

"Who are you?" Lucretia said. "For reasons beyond my comprehension, the others have agreed to follow you. But you are not the only one who will suffer and die in this crusade of yours."

"Tell me how you truly feel, Lucretia," Attia murmured. She tried not to flinch when Lucretia put a firm hand on her arm.

"They obey your orders without question, without hesitation. You have the loyalty of gladiators and warriors. You have *my* loyalty." Lucretia almost frowned at those last words, as though she'd surprised herself by speaking them out loud. "We've always been honest with each other, Attia, so be honest now. *Who are you?*"

Attia sighed. "It's a long story and difficult to explain."

Lucretia's face creased. She cocked her head. "I think we've got the time."

"All right. I'll make you a trade," Attia said. "*Quid pro quo,* as the Romans say. I'll tell you who I am, if you agree to tell me your true name."

Lucretia's jaw clenched. Her dark eyes shifted. After a brief moment, she nodded.

So Attia told her. In a low voice that only Lucretia could hear, Attia told her who she was, who her father had been. She told her about Crius and the Maedi and the genocide of the Thracians. She told her about the night in Ardea when she'd fought beside Xanthus. She told her about Spartacus.

Lucretia said nothing as she listened. Her face a mask, and Attia was grateful for it. She had too many of her own emotions to deal with. And even when she was finally done, Lucretia stayed silent for a long time.

Attia followed her gaze back to the valley, barely visible now through the descending ash and smoke. The refugees murmured among themselves in subdued conversation. The stink of burned cloth and flesh hung heavy in the air.

On the road, the Maedi and the surviving gladiators from Timeus's ludus had spread through the crowd, listening and watching for any information that could be of value. Ennius had hobbled along on his damaged knee, refusing to ride while the gladiators and Maedi walked. Rory had stared at the sea of refugees with wide eyes. It was the first time she'd been around so many people, and the only thing that stopped her from going wild with excitement was Sabina's firm hand. The little boy, Balius, had been another story. He'd walked by Sabina's side, seemingly afraid to be separated from her for even a moment. Attia wondered where he'd come from, where his family was. The same thing she wondered about the dark-eyed woman sitting beside her.

"Your turn," Attia said.

"My name is Lucretia."

"You're breaking our deal."

Lucretia shook her head. "No, you don't understand. It's the only name I can remember now. It's been too long. In my dreams, there's a face and a voice—I think they belong to my mother. But between that time and the summer that Timeus claimed me, there's . . . a gap."

"How long of a gap?"

Lucretia tilted her head in thought. "Two years, I think."

"You have no memory of your first two years in Timeus's house?"

"All I know is that for as long as I've been in Rome, I have been called Lucretia. So that is my name."

"But it's not," Attia said.

Lucretia smiled. "Would you rename me, Thracian? A third name for a broken woman?"

"No," Attia said, shaking her head firmly. "But you could do it yourself. If you can't remember your first name, you could pick a new one."

"No man—or woman—chooses their own name. You didn't choose to be called Attia. You didn't choose Spartacus."

Attia thought back to that night in Ardea, fighting beside Xanthus and waiting for the dawn.

"Didn't I?" she whispered. "You're right about one thing: This is my war, not yours, and I don't want anyone else to die because of me. Once we get everyone to safety, I'll go my own way. You needn't have any part in this. None of you do. You can live new lives, start over. You can be free."

Lucretia laughed, a faint, breathy sound. "*Free*," she said, as though the word tasted bitter in her mouth. "I don't even know what that means anymore."

Attia reached into her pocket and pulled out her father's pendant. The fires had done a grand job mutilating the once proud symbol of the Maedi swordlord. The fine details of the Thracian falcon were disfigured now, all slashes and scars, scales and claws. Lucretia had burned her hand snatching the thing from the fires.

"Albinus calls you the 'little falcon.' Did you know that? Maybe he ought to think of something else. That pendant certainly doesn't look much like a bird anymore."

"Why did you save it?" Attia asked.

This time, Lucretia's laugh glittered with delight. "You tried to kill Tycho Flavius for that thing," she said. "I guessed it must be important. And what can I say? Perhaps I'm sentimental at heart."

"Spartacus, the Lizard of Death," Attia said dryly.

Lucretia snorted. "That is truly awful. We'll have to come up with something better if this is going to work."

"*We?*"

"A war needs soldiers. Soldiers need a general. And a general needs a name—one that inspires. You already have gladiators and Maedi warriors willing to fight with you. Others will come. They'll have their own reasons, but you can't afford to be picky."

"I'm not being picky."

"No, you're trying to be noble. But it's not your place to decide others' fates for them."

Attia sat quietly, mulling over Lucretia's words.

"Accept help when it is given, Attia. Even if it is given by a broken concubine."

"Lucretia . . ." Attia's voice faltered as she considered the implications of what her friend was saying, of what they would be *doing*. "This is going to be dangerous."

"Wars generally are."

"But it won't be like any war that any of us have ever fought. There are no rules for what we're about to do. There are only risks."

"What is life without a little risk?"

"Some of us may die."

Lucretia smiled grimly. "We're all going to die. But we can make certain that our lives—and our deaths—mean something. Whatever happens, whatever comes, we'll face it together."

ABOUT THE AUTHOR

C. V. WYK graduated from Vanderbilt University with a B.A. in English literature and European history. *Blood and Sand* is her first novel. Born in Los Angeles, California, she now lives in Maryland. Look for her online at twitter.com/icvwyk and cvwyk.tumblr.com.